WRITTEN AND DIRECTED
BY **BOBBY HALL**

Simon & Schuster Paperbacks

SUPERMARKET

New York   London   Toronto   Sydney   New Delhi

Simon & Schuster Paperbacks
1230 Avenue of the Americas
New York, NY 10020

First Simon & Schuster trade paperback edition March 2019

SIMON & SCHUSTER and colophon are registered trademarks
of Simon & Schuster, Inc.

For information about special discounts for bulk purchases,
please contact Simon & Schuster Special Sales at 1-866-506-1949
or business@simonandschuster.com.

The Simon & Schuster Speakers Bureau can bring authors to
your live event. For more information or to book an event,
contact the Simon & Schuster Speakers Bureau at 1-866-248-3049
or visit our website at www.simonspeakers.com.

Interior design by Carly Loman

Manufactured in the United States of America

10 9 8 7 6 5 4 3 2 1

Library of Congress Cataloging-in-Publication Data

Names: Hall, Bobby, author.
Title: Supermarket / written and directed by Bobby Hall.
Description: First Simon & Schuster trade paperback edition. | New York :
    Simon & Schuster, 2019.
Identifiers: LCCN 2018060849 | ISBN 9781982127138 (paperback) |
    ISBN 9781982127152 (ebook) | ISBN 9781508294757 (eaudio)
Subjects: LCSH: Suspense fiction. | CYAC: Psychological fiction. | BISAC:
    FICTION / Psychological. | FICTION / General.
Classification: LCC PS3608.A54679 S87 2019 | DDC 813/.6—dc23
    LC record available at https://lccn.loc.gov/2018060849.

ISBN 978-1-9821-2713-8
ISBN 978-1-9821-2715-2 (ebook)

To Mike

CONTENTS

PART ONE

PART TWO

PART ONE

CHAPTER 1

THE BEGINNING OF THE END

So this is how it feels to take a man's life. Forced to kill for one's own survival.

I looked down at the puddle of blood by my feet, locking eyes with my own reflection. Fluorescent lights flickered overhead. How'd I get here? I was just a dude who worked at the grocery store.

Now here I was, standing over a man I murdered.

I guess in that moment it was attempted murder. He was still desperately gasping for air. Sucking in his last breaths. But there was no doubt about it—he was dying a violent death and experiencing every moment of it.

In the mornings when I left my apartment for work, sometimes I would hold the elevator door for Mrs. Huffle. She was a sweet woman in her seventies. Say the elevator stopped and some sick game began where only one of us could leave the box alive. Would she kill me to survive?

Would she have it in her to pull the trigger and meet her friend Dolores in time for brunch? Man, I think about shit like that all the time, too much, I suppose. The funny part is I always thought of myself as such a good guy, you know? Someone who would do anything to avoid confrontation.

What the fuck happened? This wasn't me. But none of this was what it seemed to be, quite honestly.

The blood on my hands smelled metallic. It reminded me of when my uncle would work on his truck. I must have been three years old. You know when you smell something and it takes you back in an instant—back to a memory as vivid as the page you're reading this very moment, even though you haven't thought about it since your brain shelved it decades ago? I was brought back to reality by the feeling of blood crawling down my forearms.

It dripped onto the floor from my fingertips, like a faucet when a child doesn't shut it off after brushing their teeth. It was thick like maple syrup but not sticky, more like red coffee creamer.

Planting my knee on the ground, I reached into the pocket of the dying man's button-down. I took out his pack of cigarettes and silver Zippo. I forced a few cigs from the pack with an upward jolt, snatching one with my lips so I didn't stain the butt with blood. The man was wheezing now. Inhaling in intervals, like someone heaving during a nightmare. Maybe that's what this was, just a nightmare. I mean, to be honest, none of it felt real, except for the blinding pain from the open wound on my head.

And that's when he spoke.

"Flynn, you were doing so well."

Bubbles popped from his blood-covered lips.

Flicking the lid of the Zippo, I tried to light my cigarette to no avail.

"Mmmm-hmmm," I muttered as I struck it again, this time igniting the cigarette. I noticed the words *Vanilla Sky* engraved on the top of the lighter.

I brought my cigarette to the man's lips.

"There you go," I said. "Now puff."

I could hear sirens and fire trucks in the distance.

His lips stained the butt of the cigarette, like the lipstick of a single mom driving an Astro van in the 90s to pick up her fifth-grade son from soccer practice. Poufy hair and shoulder pads, you know the one.

"This is all Lola's fault, you know," he said.

"I know," I said.

He laughed, until the pain in his chest forced out a groan, reminding us both of the whole dying thing happening.

"Flynn, what's—what's my—my . . . last na—"

"I don't know," I said. "I told you that already."

"Flynn, did we have fun?" he asked.

"You ruined my life."

CHAPTER 2

DAYDREAM

I guess the story starts three years ago in a small town in Oregon. I suppose every goddamn town in Oregon is small as far as towns go. Baker City. White as fuck, surprise, surprise. Not far from Idaho. Barely fifty kids in my graduating class. You know what that means. Everyone knew everyone else's business. Dated the same people, went to the same lame parties, ate at the same broke diner. We had a bank, a post office, a library, a supermarket, and a dirty old movie theater that screened Marvel flicks. No mall, no good restaurants, no hospital. No shit to do, really. The most fun you could have was floating down the river with some whiskey and beers. Most people wouldn't want to spend more than a day there. I don't blame them. But it was all right—I didn't have much of a choice now did I, being born there and everything.

I didn't exactly excel at school. I was more interested

in chasing girls and listening to music. The only class I paid any attention in was English. Reading and writing came naturally. I actually enjoyed it. The rest was a struggle or of zero interest. Most kids were into sports but that wasn't really my scene. After high school I dicked around, really. I did a year at community college because my mom forced me to do something, but that was a nonstarter. I spent most of my time drinking and smoking. A lotta my friends got out of town, but me, I was stuck.

The days turned into weeks, the weeks into months, the months into years. I don't know how it happened, but it happened. Time flew. Now here I was, twenty-four, unemployed, depressed from a recent breakup, and living in my childhood room. I know what you're thinking. Pathetic, right? I don't disagree. Trust me, it wasn't where I wanted to be in life.

In a series of fortunate events, I had come across some money. I was about to be fresh out my mother's house for the first time in my life. My mom never had money, so this was a welcome windfall, however small. It was a nice little amount, enough to help me get my own apartment, but not enough to last me long.

That's why I was on my way to apply for a job at the supermarket. I needed a gig. Something. Anything. And Baker City wasn't exactly the land of opportunity. Twenty-four years old and bagging groceries isn't the most ideal situation, but it was real life, and that's what I was looking for at that point . . . *real life.*

It was a beautiful day in April—the time was 12:36 p.m. exactly. I know because I wrote it down in my Moleskine notebook. That thing was beat to hell, but it had become

7

my best friend. Everywhere I went, the Moleskine came with. It had real character. It had lived a life. Black, pocket-size, roughed-up edges, dog-eared pages, with scraps of paper and photos stuffed inside. I wrote everything down in that notebook, recording my thoughts and the world around me. The fir trees swayed that day as the wind caressed each branch, molding their bodies in movement.

I'll never forget crossing the road in front of the grocery store. I saw this guy in black Nike Air Maxes, blue Levi's, and a white T-shirt. He seemed to be forcibly talking at people who walked by. And not in a welcoming way. As I got closer, I realized he was kind of weird looking. A little twisted, contorted. Like he was out of an Egon Schiele drawing. Midtwenties. On the tall side, maybe 6'1", slim. He had a long, bent nose, dark eyes, expressive eyebrows, and wrinkles in his forehead like Hugh Laurie. You know, that guy who plays House. I don't mean like a grown man sitting in front of a plastic tea set talking to a lifeless teddy bear—pretending to be a husband, droning on to his wife about the report his boss demanded be on his desk by Monday, even though when his boss first mentioned it the deadline was Tuesday, and now he would have to work through the weekend. I mean the actor who plays a doctor named House on a television show.

No? You don't know what I'm talking about? I can't tell if you don't know what I'm talking about or if you're just taken aback by my breaking the fourth wall on this page you're reading. Well damn, hold on a second, maybe I shouldn't bring up the fact that you're reading a book. If you realize what you're literally doing this moment, you won't actually be living in the world I'm painting for you.

SUPERMARKET

It's kind of like when you catch yourself blinking while reading and then start to focus on your blinking rather than the words your brain is trying to process, you know?

Oh shit, I've distracted myself . . . wait, what was I talking about? And why the hell am I writing my internal thoughts on this page? Doesn't matter, this won't make the final version of the book anyway. But what the hell was I talking about? Shit . . .

Oh yeah, sorry—the weirdo in front of the supermarket.

As I got closer and closer I tried to avoid him, but he spotted me immediately—kind of like when you catch your own reflection in the tinted windows of the automatic sliding doors. He was definitely a reflection. He seemed to mirror my movements a bit creepily. With every step I took, he took one too, until we met.

"Spare a dollar?" he said.

"Sorry man, I don't have it on me," I said, patting my chest and pockets.

"Help a brother out!" he said, extending his hand.

What the hell, I thought. They need to get rid of the beggars and loiterers. I walked past him, bringing my hands to my backpack straps as I entered the store.

I absolutely loved my backpack; it came everywhere with me and became my trademark. It was a gray Herschel pack with a brown leather bottom. It was covered in pins—*Rick and Morty*, Mac DeMarco, Atari, Pac-Man. An old key chain I'd had since I was a kid dangled from the outside zipper. One of those ones with your name on it that you buy at a gas station. I know, I'm a little old for all that, but my grandma got it for me and it's become my good-luck charm.

Inside this place looked like your typical grocery store. Tiled floors, jammed-up carts, aisles and aisles of neatly stacked food, buzzing fluorescent lights. It was a little run-down, but clean enough for the families in town. I immediately noticed the volume of beautiful girls who worked at this place. Damn! Definitely college girls trying to make an extra buck during the semester, I thought. Walking through the front checkout area, I made my way to the customer service desk, where I asked a middle-aged black woman for an application. Her name tag said *Ronda*. She was kind of like the slightly overweight black woman in every movie. Sassy attitude, lowered eyelids, and judgmental aura. But basing a first impression on her physical appearance really wasn't a fair thing to do. I mean, how can you judge someone simply by—

"You applying for a job dressed in blue jeans and a white shirt, child?"

When she said this, I was actually glad my gut was right, and I wasn't some prejudiced asshole. Not completely, anyway.

"Well, Ronda, I only came in like this to fill out the application. I didn't plan on sitting down for an interview the same day."

She stared at me and let out a single chuckle—one of those *I'm annoyed but this is my job* chuckles—and said, "You know how often I hear that, baby? How many times I've had this conversation? Those pretty brown eyes of yours aren't going to take you that far."

Wow, I could only imagine how many idiots came in just like me, dressed like they didn't care, to apply for a job they didn't give two shits about. But I needed this job.

If I didn't get this job that would be it—my ex would be right, just as she'd always been. I was destined to be a loser who couldn't finish anything.

"Hey there, friend!" a man said. I turned around to a grinning man in his early thirties. He extended his hand to be shaken as if he wasn't going to take no for an answer. "I'm Ted Daniels, assistant manager here." He looked like a corny white dude. Pale skin with a dash of acne held over from his teenage years, buzz-cut flattop, short-sleeved button-down, red tie, and black pleated slacks—the ultimate nerd.

"Hello there," I said, mimicking his attitude as best I could, trying not to think about how he looked like a Mormon who joined the Los Angeles Bloods after two years of mission work down in South Central, throughout Crenshaw and Compton, and was now sporting a bright red tie to prove just how gangster he really was.

"I'm Flynn," I added.

"And are we applying for employment today?" he said. His smile never seemed to go away, even when he spoke.

"Uh, yeah, I mean, I saw that you guys were hiring and wanted to fill out an application."

"Well, golly, aren't we in luck?!" he said. It really annoyed me how happy he was. His whole vibe bothered me. I have no idea what overcame me, but I snapped and punched him in the face. My fist connected with his nose, and blood spewed from the slit created by the explosive blow.

"Oh lawd Jesus, these white people done did it!" Ronda screamed. Ted hit the floor screaming in agony.

"Why???" he bellowed.

I stood there, frozen. I couldn't believe what I had

11

done. Something just came over me. How the hell could I have done such a thing?

"Are you listening to me?!" he screamed. "Why?! Why, Flynn?!"

Seconds later, I was sitting in an old wooden chair in Ted's office. Ted sat behind his desk. His nose was perfectly fine.

"Flynn, are you listening to me?" Ted said.

"I'm sorry, sir . . . what was that last part?"

I had imagined the whole thing, caught in a daydream so vivid I didn't even remember making my way to his office.

"I said *why*, Flynn," he said, annoyed but still smiling bigger than ever.

"I'm sorry, sir, why *what* now?" I replied.

"Why are you here, Flynn? Do you even know why you're here? Everyone is family at this establishment. We have a code, a code of ethics, you could say. We want to help everyone under this roof acquire whatever skills their individual needs may be. So what truly brings you, Flynn? What skills do *you* need?"

A second ago I was surely headed to jail for assault, and now I found myself in the middle of a job interview.

"A job," I said.

"Well, aren't we a wise one?" Ted said with a laugh. "You're in luck. A bunch of the seniors here are graduating and we will need some extra hands come summer. You seem like a nice kid, so I'd love to hire you."

"Seriously?" I said. I hadn't done shit to deserve this offer. Maybe it was my pretty face?

"The job is yours," Ted said as he reached under his desk.

"That is, if you can sell me this bottle of Windex." I couldn't see his lips through his smile.

I looked at the bottle of Windex then looked back at Ted.

"So you're telling me if I sell you this thing I have the job?" I asked.

"Precisely," Ted said.

Without a moment's hesitation I grabbed my backpack, which was resting against the leg of my chair. I opened the pouch, grabbed my wallet, and took out a twenty-dollar bill. I then licked Andrew Jackson's face and slapped the federal note against the bottle, sticking it to its surface.

"Buy this bottle of cleaner as is for five dollars," I said to Ted.

He looked at me, puzzled. "Wait a minute, you're losing money here, Flynn."

"Look, Ted. Would you buy this product from me or not?" I said with a smirk.

"Well of course, but why would you throw away fifteen dollars like tha—"

"The way I see it," I interrupted, "I just spent fifteen dollars to secure a steady income for the duration of my time as an employee at this establishment . . . Boss."

Ted was baffled. He wasn't sure if I had pulled a fast one on him, or if I'd given him exactly what he wanted. But judging by his next words he was definitely intrigued.

"You're hired!" he said, offering his hand for me to shake.

"Seriously?" I said, not believing it.

"Oh, of course, Flynn. I really believe in energy, and I have a good feeling about you."

"Well, thanks, Ted. That means a lot," I said, unsure why this guy was so eager to give me a position. "Wait a second," I said. "What would I be doing and how much money would I be making?"

"Oh, ten dollars an hour. You'll be our floater."

"I'll be a what?"

"I'll explain everything on Monday! See you at nine a.m.," he said, pointing to the calendar on his desk.

With that I was out of his office and walking past customer service, gainfully employed. "See you later, Ronda," I said.

"Mmmmmm-hmmmmmm," Ronda replied with that fierce, strong, black-woman attitude. I loved Ronda's attitude—she gave no fucks, quite honestly, and I absolutely adored her for it.

On my way out, just beside the customer service desk, I spotted a soda machine by the automatic doors. A few employees were loitering. They seemed to be doing everything but their jobs. I pulled out my wallet, searching for a bill to insert in the machine. A picture fell out—a picture of me sitting in the park on a summer day, my arms around a beautiful blond girl, a girl who broke my heart, a girl I was still in love with. She sat in my lap, looking into my eyes. We were in a field of grass. The shutter had caught us midlaugh. It was some Hallmark shit, and she looked stunning. I picked up the photo and put it in the pocket of my jacket.

"Fuckin' bitch," I said.

I pulled out my dollar and inserted it into the machine. A can of Coke dropped. As I stood back up I heard a voice behind me.

"So, I'm guessing you just magically found that dollar you didn't have fifteen minutes ago when I asked for one, huh?"

It was the weirdo from outside. He stared at me nonchalantly, with brown eyes set back by dark circles. He looked like he needed a good night's sleep. He was chewing a toothpick and bouncing a red rubber ball. The kind people play handball with.

"Uh, well, I . . . ," I stammered.

"UUHHHH, WEEELLLLLL, you make me sick, dude. You dick. What if I were homeless, you don't know," he said, pulling an apron over his head. It revealed a name tag that said *Frank*.

"Wait a minute—"

"You're a fucked-up person, man!" he interrupted.

"But I . . ."

"Hey you!" said Ted Daniels, looking in Frank's direction. "Back to work, please! We're on the clock." The group of employees behind Frank walked off to whatever it was they should have been doing. "And none of that from you on Monday," he said, looking at me with a smile. Then he did an abrupt about-face and scooted off.

"You work here?" I asked.

"Hahaha, yeah, dude . . . I'm just fuckin' with you, man," said Frank.

"Wait a second," I said, staring at Frank, puzzled. "You work here and you stand outside asking people for money?"

"Well, I don't know how much 'work' I do," he said with a wry smile, making air quotation marks with his hands. "And plus, when I stand outside, people walk right

15

by me. You were the only one who even said something and didn't just stare right through me. So thanks for being the only person who acknowledges my existence in this place."

"I'll see you on Monday, Frank," I said.

"Oh shit, did Ted just hire you?" he asked.

"Yeah, I guess he did."

"Cool. Well, I'm out. Gonna go try to fuck one of these girls," Frank said, walking in the direction of the college chicks working the cash registers. "Catch you later, Flynn!"

He tossed me his rubber ball as I waved. I nearly dropped it trying to catch it, then began to walk out of the store. I stopped in my tracks.

"Wait a sec," I said, turning around to ask him how he knew my name . . . but before I could, he was gone.

"See you Monday, Ronda," I said on my way out.

"Not if Jesus answers my prayers and takes me in my sleep this weekend, baby!" I wasn't sure if she was playing or serious. Either way, Ronda was pretty dark!

Oh, shit, wait . . . *does that sound racist?* I didn't mean *dark* like her skin tone, because I think all women are beautiful, you know? Like, I mean, I have my preference, sure—I like blond girls with big tits, you know? I'm a guy in his midtwenties from the, like, whitest town in existence. I mean, I'm not saying whites stick together or anything, but . . . fuck! When I said Ronda was dark I meant her sense of humor, okay? Not her skin color.

Shit, man . . . can we just skip to Monday already?

CHAPTER 3

MONDAY ALREADY

It felt as if all I did was blink and there Monday was. There I was. Standing in front of the supermarket, bouncing my red rubber ball. I wasn't sure what to expect from my first day. I was just happy to have the job. I wasn't feeling particularly worried about it. Nor was I feeling overly excited. Just ready to get going. I needed the experience and I needed the money. Heading in, I grabbed a few stray carts, trying to make a good first impression.

"Hey kid!" said an old black man. He was sitting outside of the store playing chess.

"Uh, excuse me?" I replied.

"Where are you today?" he asked with a wise smile.

"What are you talking about, old man?"

He picked up a red knight and moved it up and to the right.

"Where are you?" he demanded. "Where are we? Right now."

"Uuuhhhh . . . clearly at a supermarket." *This guy is crazy*, I thought.

"Oh, that's unfortunate. Well, let's talk when you're actually back." He turned back to his game, moving his bishop.

"Okay man . . . ," I said, a little creeped out. I'd never seen someone play chess against himself. Guess this guy had a lot going on upstairs.

I stared into the store from the outside. I spotted a few customers. One man stood clutching a cup of coffee, holding it to his nose, inhaling, muttering something to himself. Every time a customer would activate the sliding doors, I could faintly hear him. "Coffee, coffee, coffee, coffee!!!!" Dude was into his joe.

Looking around I saw other people, including Ted Daniels, the assistant manager, greeting customers.

"Hello there, friend, welcome!" he said with that unsettling smile.

I'm not sure why he annoyed me the way he did—his smile was so constant that the front row of his teeth had become a permanent substitute for his lips. No one could be that happy all the time. There had to be something dark lurking behind that grin. The only time I caught him without it was when he was eating. Then he would only smile in intervals between swallowing and reeling in his next bite. Something was off about him. He was a little too into his gig.

You know when you work a job in your teens and really give it your all? You really go above and beyond, take pride in what you're doing . . . until about four weeks in. Then you realize your job is completely demeaning. That your sole purpose is to blindly serve people who don't give two shits about your own happiness or future. Then your work ethic starts to slide. You walk into the break room asking yourself who the fuck aspires to be the best grocery bagger or cashier? Who the hell cares how fast you can change the oil at the local Jiffy Lube? Who's impressed that you can memorize the entire menu at the Crab Emporium seafood restaurant? I don't want to be a professional busboy, you think to yourself. Fuck this job.

Then there's Ted.

Ted is the guy who has been working fifteen years not only at the same chain, but at the same goddamn location, and he's still only assistant manager. I mean, for fuck's sake, he's *not even the manager*! Let alone the regional manager.

Just think about that for a second.

You spend fifteen years at a company and you don't own the fucking place? Man, I've met some guys in my day who started working at McDonald's wiping the floors, then went on to fries, then burgers, then cashier, then shift manager, then store management, and before you knew it, they were sitting down with the bank being accepted for a loan to become a franchiser. Not long after that they got a seat at the board table. Real CEO shit, you know?

But not Ted.

Ted was the guy who wanted you to go nowhere and hate every second of it, because that's what he had done. Like most drones in our society, Ted never did what he really loved. He always made an excuse about how he *would* do it, *but* he had other obligations, *but* money was tight, *but* this, or *but* that, or *but you know how it is*. People always say things like *Well I would, but* . . . and that's where they fuck up. As soon as they give a reason for why they can't do something, they're already defeated.

I mean, think about it. If you ask a bunch of people what they would do if money was no object, if they were sitting on five hundred million dollars in an account, the conversation typically goes like this:

"Well, I would definitely invest the money into a tech company or some kind of—"

This is where I would interrupt.

"No," I'd say. "You're missing the point. The point is what would you do if you *had* five hundred million, not what you would do *with* the five hundred million." I would stare at them, waiting for the proper answer—the proper answer being *whatever their fucking heart desired!*

"Oh, uh, I, uh, well, I guess . . . ," they would stammer.

Here it comes, I would think to myself. *Almost there. I guess, uummm 'almost'* . . .

"Well, I guess I would probably travel, you know? See the world."

"Then go do that!" I would reply.

That's when they hit me with the money issues or their dying family member or needing to finish college or a million and one goddamn excuses we as a society give ourselves to rationalize our fears without having to face the unbearable inevitable outcome of life.

And that outcome is?

"What is death is imminent, Alex?" *Ding ding ding!*

Now this is where I'd explain that if they want to see

the world: travel to India, wave to the queen's palace in London, cross the Swiss Alps, ride elephants in Thailand, surf in Nicaragua . . . they could do it. Without question. And without asking how, they always seemed to retort with some variation of "Yeah, okay, buddy."

It kills me every time.

"Are you serious?" I would say.

"How the hell am I supposed to do all that?" they'd reply.

"By using your head!" I'd tell them. "I mean, why not become a critic?" They'd stare at me, puzzled, then say something ignorant. "What the hell do movies have to do with traveling?" they'd say, just like a drone with no mind of its own would.

I mean, this is some real break-free-from-the-Matrix shit we're talking about here.

"I didn't say a film critic; I said *a critic*. Why not review hotels across the globe?"

Once again, they'd stare, confused.

"Haven't you ever heard of a five-star hotel?" I'd ask.

"Well, of course," they'd reply.

"How do you think they got those stars in the first place?"

Their eyes would widen enough for me to get through, and if their minds would open long enough, I could reach them.

"Think about it. You can do anything you want in life. It just takes persistence, determination, realism, and wanting success more than your next breath. Whatever you want in life you can attain. As long as you believe it. As long as you say you're going to do it!"

Now some of them, while still open-minded, would

21

give some smart-ass response like "Well . . . what if I want to be an astronaut?"

I've had this conversation with kids under ten as well as adults in their sixties. The only ones who have ever asked me dismissive questions like this are the adults. It was the children who were perceptive. It was the children who took my words as affirmation of the limitless realities they already believed to be possible. They believed in spite of the grown-ups around them, tainting their innocence and imagination while ripping them from their dreams. Dreams of walking on Mars or building jet packs and teleportation machines.

So to that smart-ass with the question, I would say yes.

"Yes, you *can* completely become an astronaut!" I'd say. By then I know they really mean a space traveler. "I said persistence, determination, and *realism* earlier in my speech," I'd explain. "If you look at your dream realistically, then becoming an astronaut is merely a million-dollar Space X ticket—if you live long enough to see it. So all you really need to do is come up with the money to purchase such a golden ticket."

This is where they would roll their eyes and lose interest.

"My point is that you asked *how* and I am giving you the examples, the possibilities, because when I want something, truly want something that my life depends on—which is *purpose* and *happiness*—I will stop at nothing to attain it. It's like breathing. So you must ask yourself: What is your air? What is the thing you literally will fight for to survive?"

I would hear "Wait a second . . . I was asking you what aisle the cereal was on, so, uh, how did we get here?"

Then they would walk away and I'd be reminded that

all the shit I just philosophized goes down the drain when I'm surrounded by the reality of working in this goddamn supermarket. Wait, why was I talking about all that in the first place?

Oh, yes! That's right. I was outside the supermarket, looking at Ted, thinking about my hatred for his smile. Then, the next thing I knew . . .

I was back. Standing here, stocking a shelf with boxes of pasta. Penne, ziti, spaghetti. Pasta for days.

A staticky voice sounded overhead, "Floater to break room, flooaatteerrrrr to the break room, please." The voice reminded me of the show *M*A*S*H*, about surgeons during the Korean War. There was always someone speaking over the intercom.

I was a floater. As a floater, I didn't exactly have a job, but I didn't exactly not have one. I was the guy they told what to do and when to do it. Honestly, I didn't mind. It gave me more ground to cover and kept things varied and interesting. One minute I'd be mopping up spilled cranberry juice, the other I'd be facing cans, the other I'd be walking old ladies' groceries to their cars.

On my way to the break room a woman from the store's pharmacy stopped me.

"Well hello there, Flynn."

"Um, hey?"

"I'm Ann, silly. Don't forget to take your vitamins," she said, handing me three different types of supplements. "It's important for your internal balance," she continued. I pretended to take them, so as to not offend her. Into my right jacket pocket they went. I always rocked my brown suede bomber jacket; it was one of my prized possessions.

"Alrighty then, sweetheart!" she said. "See you tomorrow."

And she was off.

"Bye," I said, waving. This was an odd encounter, but I realized she was just a lady who was looking out for me, I guess. Maybe I reminded her of her son, or the son she never had. I never asked.

Ann was in her late sixties. Not fat but not skinny. Short, white curly hair, with a nurturing maternal vibe about her. That's why I didn't mind her giving me the vitamins, even if I wasn't gonna take 'em.

Truth is, I hated pills. Always had. Just trying to swallow them would make me throw up.

I finally made it to the break room. Inside two girls sat across from each other drinking coffee—one wore a name tag that said *Rebecca*, but the other girl called her Becca. Her counterpart's name tag said *Rachel*.

I got out my Moleskine and took notes. When I looked back up, they were staring at me blankly as I stood motionless in the doorway.

"New guy's a weirdo, huh?" Rachel said out loud, not holding back her rudeness. Staring directly at me, saying it like one of those college girls: *I'm hot and cool and don't give a fuck but was probably molested at some point in my teenage years so I'm always in defense mode and attack others before they can attack me first.* That kinda chick, you know the type. She looked oddly like Kat Dennings with her pale skin, big lips, bright red lipstick, bulging eyes, and dark brown hair that flowed over her shoulders onto her chest—she had a bit of a 1970s feel.

Becca, on the other hand, seemed sweeter, a bit reserved and shy. She had an Emma Watson vibe going on, minus the hot accent.

"Are you lost, new guy?" Rachel said. It reminded me of my first day in junior high. All the big kids already perfectly knowing the school layout, making fun of me while I'm reading off a sheet of paper, looking for classroom A23 and hoping I won't be late for English.

"They said they needed a floater to the break room?" I said, looking away from Rachel. She didn't break eye contact, like a witch casting a spell. Quite honestly, it made me a little uncomfortable. But maybe I liked it. I couldn't tell.

"Must be in your head," she said, the girls snickering like they were at a grade school lunch table.

A shadowy figure entered the room behind me. It was Frank. "'Sup, Flynn," he said in a whisper.

"Hey . . . how do you know my name?" I said.

"I don't know your name, new guy," Rachel said in a smart-aleck tone. She and Becca stood up and started to leave. On her way out, Rachel stopped and flicked my name tag with her acrylic nail. "See ya later, Flynn," she said, her tongue pressed against her cheek in a flirtatious manner.

The two left the room.

Frank nudged my elbow.

"I'm gonna fuck that girl," he said. "And her friend."

He pulled a banana out of his apron and peeled it.

Standing there confused and unanswered, I opened my mouth to ask again, but was cut off before the first syllable.

"Your name tag, dude," he said.

"Oh, yeah . . . duh!" I said. "So how long have you worked here?"

"Long enough to have fucked every chick that's clocked in this motherfucker!" he said, hoisting himself onto the countertop. He peeled a banana, then spit into the sink.

"What the fuck?" I said, a little stunned.

"Well, not *every* chick. They come and go so often it's actually pretty hard to keep up," he continued, his mouth full of banana. "You know . . . ," he said, swallowing. "Most of these fucking girls are Daddy's little princesses, off to college to become a grown-up."

He took another bite.

"And then," he continued, mouth so full I could barely make out what he was saying. "*Mmph*, theth girls gettah jawhb here." He chewed fiercely, swallowed, and continued, his words clearing up perfectly. "And they think, Oh look at me, I'm a working girl," he explained, mimicking with his hands. "Until they see that minimum wage check and realize Daddy's credit card is king."

The room was awkwardly quiet. Light music from the store intercom bled in. It sounded like classic elevator music. Soothing and unsettling at the same time.

"So bananas are your thing, huh?" I said.

"Bananas are your *thing*?" he repeated with a disrespected look on his face. "What the fuck does that mean?" he said. "What are you, a fucking racist? Huh? You saying bananas are my thing because I'm black?"

Frank was clearly white.

"Huh?" he demanded. "You fucking with me, Flynn?"

The faint sound of a Chuck Mangione flugelhorn solo filled the space between us.

"Hahahaha, I'm just messing with you, man!" he said, lifting his arms in the air.

SUPERMARKET

I exhaled, feeling my chest deflate like a balloon at a birthday party. How long had I been holding my breath in suspense?

"I wouldn't say bananas are *my thing*, but—" he said, taking one final bite and raising the peel in the air like a basketball. "Kobe," he said, taking his shot for the wastebasket. Air ball. "Aaahhh . . . *Shaq*." He looked at me. "Not *my thing*, but they are a great source of nutrition for the brain, and the brain is super important, man," he said, motioning at me to come with him. He got up to exit the room. I hesitantly joined him, walking to the back loading dock by the dumpsters.

Standing by the dumpster was a guy I hadn't met. There were so many people who worked here. Too many for the size of the store. He looked to be in his late twenties, white, and full of piercings. He had gauges, a nose ring, a bad Celtic tattoo peeking out of his sleeve, a leather wristband, a big-ass watch, and spiked green hair. Yikes. Not a good look. He stood, arms crossed, leaning against the top rail of a dumpster, smoking a cigarette.

"What's up, I'm Flynn," I said.

"Kurtis," he said as he put out a fist.

Pausing, I reluctantly met his fist with mine.

"I work in the deli," he said. Not exactly the most sanitary looking of fellows.

"Nice watch, where'd you get it?" I asked him, trying to make small talk.

"Can I get a smoke?" blurted Frank, interrupting.

"Get your own."

Kurtis put his pack of smokes in his tan button-down shirt pocket. A silver Zippo followed. The sunlight flashed

27

across the surface of the lighter, revealing the words *Vanilla Sky* engraved on the top.

He walked past me, flicking his cigarette. On his way by, he aggressively bumped into my shoulder, forcing me to drop the picture I'd been clutching in my pocket. It fell to the ground, right next to Kurtis's still-burning cigarette.

"Fuck that guy," Frank said as he shamelessly picked up the butt to smoke. "Whoa, who's the babe?" he asked, grabbing the picture of me and my ex laughing in the park, madly in love on a summer day.

"Oh, that's just this girl," I said, pulling the red ball out of my pocket. I began to nervously bounce it.

"*Just this girl?* This don't look like *just this girl* to me. This looks like a girl you put a baby in and lock down immediately!" He chuckled. "Trap her!"

"Yeah, well, that ship has unfortunately sailed, man. Let's just change the subject." I pulled out my pack of toothpicks and threw one in my mouth. Frank raised his eyebrows, as if to say *ookkaaayyyy*, but let it go.

"So, as I was saying, the brain is very important!" Frank said, motioning with the two fingers gripping the cigarette. He pointed the tips of his index and middle fingers to his temple with his thumb cocked like a pistol.

"And the lungs aren't?" I asked, motioning to the cancer stick he was holding.

"That's different, man. This is addiction . . . you wouldn't know," he said, pointing to me.

"Yes, I would," I said. "I started smoking when I was fourteen. Finally quit six months ago."

Frank burst into laughter. "Six months? Hahaha. Six

months? You high and mighty motherfucker. Talk to me in a year, minimum, bro," he said, inhaling deeply on what was left of the hand-me-down device of death. "Six months," he said, chuckling.

"Yeah, whatever," I said. "Go on, what were you saying?"

Frank paused.

"Wait," he said. "What the fuck *was* I saying?"

We both paused for a moment—you know how it is. One of those moments when you and someone else are discussing something, but one of you gets off track and, for the life of you, you just can't remem—

"THE BRAIN!" howled Frank, completely satisfied with his discovery. "It's a powerful thing. From my research, bananas are some of the best brain food. They are packed with nutrients that help the mind function. You see, there are a lot of foods that are great for the brain—walnuts, flax seeds, and avocado because of their omega acids and nutrients—but bananas have been digested by us since we were swinging in the fucking trees, man!" He was absurdly passionate about this banana.

"Damn, man, you really know your shit," I said with a smile.

"Well, one of us has to take care of your brain," he said as he grabbed another banana from the pouch in his black apron, the one he wore over his tan company-issued button-down. He threw the banana to me. "And you can take care of the lungs," he said, waving a finger at me, mimicking a nagging old woman. "You see, bananas can also help with your mood in addition to your brain. Eating them can help you remember things."

By now we were inside walking through the store. "I mean, without memory, who are we, you know?" he asked. "Just a shell of who we once were . . . with no memory, there's no self, there's no 'I'. Is there consciousness without memory? Is there language? Experience? Without memory are we just living in a loop? Is memory the only thing keeping us sane? Without memory we're just walking around like that guy in *Memento*, scribbling shit on our arms, trying to figure out what the fuck is going on."

"Ummm," I said. "You're giving that banana a lot of weight, man."

"Think about it, Flynn! The mind is a powerful thing!" Frank said, walking us around the store.

We turned down the cereal aisle, where I saw a man wearing a white doctor's coat. He seemed to be a physician, but why he was shopping in his full getup, I had no idea.

"Did you know one standard-size banana provides approximately .4 milligrams of B_6, 450 milligrams of potassium, 30 milligrams of magnesium, 30 grams of carbs, and 3 grams of fiber?" Frank continued as we walked. I looked over my shoulder and noticed the doctor wasn't wearing his jacket anymore—he looked just like a regular customer now. I figured he must have placed his jacked inside his basket and carried on his merry way.

"The facts on bananas are damn near endless," said Frank.

"Who the fuck would remember all that?"

"Somebody who eats a lot of bananas, somebody who cares a lot about their mind," he said. That's when I realized Frank was *perfect*. I mean, he was the ideal candidate.

SUPERMARKET

It was as if fate had brought us together in this supermarket. I pulled out my Moleskine and went down the list.

On the left side of the page it said:

Store/Layout — *medium size, checkout and customer service in front, produce section on the left, bakery, coffee shop, and pharmacy in the back*
Company Uniform — *black pants, black shoes, light brown button-down T-shirt, black apron, and name tag.*
Possible Characters — *Becca, Rachel, Ronda, Ted, Ann, Kurtis*

I added another name.

Frank

Types of Customers — *man who always drinks coffee; let's call him Joe. Wacko out front playing chess by himself, mystery doctor, moms, grandmas*
Different Kinds of Food — *canned goods, juice, pasta, cereal*
Store Gossip —
Love Interest —

On the right side of the page, another list. I went down it, checking items off, as Frank incessantly spoke in the background.

Protagonist

Kind of funny — ✓
Good with women — ✓
Smart-ass — ✓

31

Prick — ✓
Talker — ✓
Normal dude in twenties — ✓

He is perfect! I thought, biting into a banana as I strolled down aisle nine with Frank by my side. Frank finally stopped talking, looking pleased about his deep knowledge of fruit.

The crazy part about this list is that these things were all expected to come from different people, and I could use other people's attributes to create a composite person! One person who was funny, another who was a smart-ass, another who was a bit of a womanizer, but hell . . . all these characteristics within one guy was a dream come true. It was all I could hope for when using a real-life person as the foundation for a fictional character!

Oh, wait, damn, I'm sorry . . . you must be confused. I'm a writer. I know my methods are unconventional, but that's what I was currently doing . . . finishing a book. A book, which I planned to base entirely on Frank. And I wasn't afraid to get weird with it.

Actually, this seems even more confusing now. I think we should take a moment. Step out of aisle nine and take you back to the inception of all this.

Give you a proper beginning.

CHAPTER 4

A PROPER BEGINNING

"It's over, Flynn."

My girlfriend Lola looked at me, her eyes welling up with tears.

"I love you, but I can't do this to myself anymore. It's sickening."

Lola sat across from me inside our favorite booth at our favorite diner. She was the most beautiful I had ever seen her. Her blond hair was pulled back into a bun. The afternoon sunlight crossed her face. The table was clear except for two coffees, napkins, sugar, and silverware. In case you aren't understanding how small this town is, it's so small that the sign over the diner we were sitting in literally just read *DINER.*

"Are you listening to me, Flynn?!" She was not quite yelling, but was extremely frustrated.

In the kitchen, a cook placed two plates on the service counter separating the kitchen from the bar.

"Where's Francis, Amy, and Leslie?" he shouted as the food started to die in the window. "We've got customers waiting!" The waitresses were about to reply when the missing waiter showed up.

"Sorry, Dave! I was out back on an important call," he said.

He hurried over to our table, apologizing for the wait. He seemed so docile. Your average white college kid. He had on black shoes, blue jeans, and a plain white shirt. I watched him tie his apron as fast as he could. He must have sensed that now wasn't the time to chat, so he just topped off our coffees. As he did, I examined his name tag, his facial features, his skin palette, his mannerisms, and the way he walked. He had wrinkles on his forehead, a long nose and high cheekbones, dark choppy hair, a sharp voice, and reserved body language.

You know when you experience an intense moment and every mundane detail becomes extraordinarily vivid? And it turns into an unforgettable memory? This was like that. I never forgot this guy. Maybe it was because of what was going on. The love of my life was breaking up with me. This was emotionally traumatic. The entire scene was seared into my brain.

Our mugs were red. Rings of coffee from her cup spotted the table. If you were staring at us from the side of our table, she was on the left and I was on the right. Our booth was next to a giant window. A little jukebox was fixed to the table—it took quarters. "Ruby Tuesday" by the Rolling Stones played on the speakers.

"Fuck, Flynn, I'm spilling my heart out to you in my final good-bye and even now you can't give me anything?!" She picked up a napkin from the table and dabbed her eyes. I hated to see her cry. It was the worst thing to me. But for whatever reason, I could never console her. I felt damaged in this way. Maybe it was from growing up without a father and never seeing a man treat my mother the way she should have been treated.

"I mean, you're twenty-four, for fuck's sake, and you live with your mother! You don't have a job, Flynn!"

"I write."

"You write? Ha, is that some sick joke?! Flynn, stop it. You aren't an author. You've never even finished a book. You send half-baked, unfinished ideas to publishers, expecting book deals. What's wrong with you? It doesn't work that way! I mean, why do you think every company you send your ideas to replies with the same letter? Every time reiterating what I have been saying for years—'great promise but finish the damn thing!' You can't even keep a literary agent. They all drop you because you never deliver. You put your work ahead of me. You put your writing first in this relationship. You get so caught up in it that you lose touch with reality. I want to be with someone who is achieving their goals. I spent years by your side, Flynn, trying to help you, support you, encourage you, and grow with you . . . but no, you haven't changed one bit, you start amazing idea after amazing idea, but you never finish anything, and . . . and that's why I . . . why *I'm finishing this.*"

She grabbed her purse and exited the booth as fast as she could.

"I don't want to ever see you again, Flynn."

My breath stopped. My chest tightened. The blood left my face. I vacantly stared downward, clasping my hands between my knees. Even though I appeared to be made out of stone, tears began to roll down my face. It was an emotionless, hollow cry.

Seconds felt like hours. I tried to get up from the table, but my legs gave out and I collapsed back into the booth. I tried again, slowly rising from my table. I put on my coat and walked out of the diner. I jumped in my car and sped off. I looked in my rearview mirror. My face was tangled with emotion. Tears poured out. As I drove, I couldn't get an image out of my head: my car hydroplaning on the tears that fell from my face and flooded the streets, veering across lanes, and crashing into the back of a garbage truck. Not wearing a seat belt, I smashed through the windshield, shattering glass and landing twisted in the back of the empty truck. Then the compactor turned on, easily crushing my body into red paste.

As the macabre daydream ended, my car sputtered out. I pushed the accelerator, but nothing happened. Out of gas on the edge of town. I pulled over to the side of the road just under a bridge. This was truly nowhere. I opened the door, left the keys in the ignition, and ran.

I ran and ran, not knowing why. I sprinted with what felt like an empty body, head tilted toward the blue sky. My throat burned. Then my lungs. Then my legs. My whole body felt as if it were on fire. I suppose I ran because I wanted to feel something, anything. The blocks turned into miles, and the minutes into hours. My sprint turned to a wobbly jog. I stumbled off the street, collapsing into someone's front yard. I had no idea where I was. I lay there, my face pillowed by blades of grass, staring into the dirt. My mind empty. My lips salty from snot and dried tears. I pushed myself up and knocked on the stranger's front door.

"Hello, I'm sorry; may I use your phone?"

I called my mother to pick me up.

"What the fuck, Flynn? What happened?" my mom said when she arrived.

I sat quietly in her car, motionless, my head erupting with a fever.

"See, Flynn, this is what happens when you go running in the winter! Who the hell does something like this?" she said in a judgmental yet loving way. She continued to lecture, but the words began to fade, like hearing music from the outside of a nightclub, muffled and dark.

"Lola broke up with me," I said.

"Oh, Flynn, no, I'm so sorry," she replied.

My mind snapped back to reality and I finally thought about what had just happened.

That's when it hit me.

Everything Lola had said was true.

She'd always told me I worked too much, that all I cared about was work, but since I never finished my work it was in vain. She even tried to justify my actions, saying that if I had ignored her for a *cause*, if I had *put our love aside for something greater than myself*, it would be one thing—but I was living in a loop. My creative pursuits were all I had that brought me any joy, and I became fanatically devoted to my craft. It was my way of feeling complete. I would hole myself up for days on end. Wake up, coffee, cereal, write, lunch, write, dinner, write, sleep. Manuscripts piled up, littering my room. I would write, stream of consciousness, uninterrupted for hours, ignoring the world outside. It was a kind of mania. If I wasn't writing I was lost and depressed. I would talk out loud to my fictional characters, figuring out dialogue. She believed that I was detaching myself from the real world through my stories. That I was spending more time with my characters than with her. She'd go on to say that the stories I wrote never ended, and because of this it would never stop. She said every story needs an end, and that if there is no *The End*, then you cannot begin the next chapter.

That's why I'm so determined to finish my novel this time. That's why it's going to be my best work. That's why I'm so damn happy to have met Frank, the perfect candidate to base my protagonist on. If I can't finish this, it's game over. I'm finally feeling ready. Inspired. Ambitious. Focused.

Before we get to that, let me explain the dark months that followed the breakup.

The night of the breakup, after my mom brought me home, I lay in bed burning up, experiencing fever dreams and bizarre hallucinations: phantom visions of Lola next to me, caressing my hair, then evaporating.

My mother would periodically check in to make sure my fever wasn't what she would call "ER worthy." Two days later, the fever had passed, but my depression hadn't.

You know in the movies how they do that cool time lapse where hours on a clock spin by like seconds? Yeah, well, I want you to imagine that . . . but imagine each day feels like a second.

I was disgusting. I barely left my bed. The lights never came on. I would hardly move, maybe to go to the bathroom, but even that felt like an impossible task. I showered once a week if my mother managed to make me. I would sleep for sixteen hours a day. Then I wouldn't sleep for three days. I couldn't tell you if it was day or night, let alone the day of the week. I felt hopeless. Not even sad. Just nothing. I couldn't even cry. The thought of writing was an unimaginable feat. It was a depression so low and flat that I couldn't even envision suicide as a solution.

I felt like a fucking cartoon character because every time I saw myself I was wearing the same goddamn outfit: boxers, a white undershirt, and a burgundy robe. Plates of half-eaten sandwiches lingered on the floor, encircling my bed, piling high, and finally being taken away in the blink of an eye, just like those time-lapse montages in movies.

Along with the sandwiches, the mail piled up. I had more mail than I had ever cared to receive. Every once in a while, my mother would barge in to express that I had received another letter from a publishing company. She would tell me to open it, but quite honestly, I didn't care. I knew what it was and I could hear Lola taunting me in my head—*another rejection letter.*

She was so sweet when we were together. Was I truly the failure she depicted me as?

The clock spun, the montage continued. Winter turned into spring. Then one day, it came to a halt.

"Flynn!" my mom yelled. "Today is the day you are going to shower, shave, put on some clothes, read this letter, and rejoin society or, I'm sorry to say, I'll have to throw out your things."

My mother had never spoken to me this way.

I couldn't tell if she despised me or loved me so much she felt compelled to make such grave threats—threats

39

she was prepared to act on, given her tone. I don't know why I got up, but I did. I went into the bathroom and shut the door. I pissed and turned on the sink and shower. I opened the door and emerged a fresh, clean-shaven man.

I looked in the mirror and didn't recognize what I saw—a handsome, functioning member of society. But I wiped my eyes because I felt quite the opposite.

"Eggs are getting cold!" Mom yelled.

I clunked down the stairs and took a seat in the kitchen, my eyes squinting from the bright sun shining through the window.

"There's my boy!" my mom said. "I can see your face, Flynn. I love that face." She had a big smile. I grabbed one of the many identical letters from our little mail area next to the rotary phone by my mom's recliner.

Another rejection letter. "We regret to inform you . . ." I opened another letter. "We have considered your manuscript, and while there are elements of promise, it is not right for us at this time . . ." I felt the weight of my body returning to its depressed state. I slid my hand across the table, grabbing one last envelope.

On the front, it had my name.

Flynnagin E. Montgomery
465 Cedar Ridge Lane
Baker City, OR 34652

I opened the letter.

TO: Flynnagin E. Montgomery
FROM: Ed Nortan III

SUPERMARKET

Dear Mr. Montgomery,

As you have not supplied a contact number or email, I have been forced to send this the old-fashioned way, via postal service. This is one of several attempts at communication, and I remain hopeful it will be received.

The concept for a realist novel set in a suburban supermarket, and its execution in your initial sample pages, are enough to validate what I first saw in you: great promise. The plotlessness of the work is part of its allure. Anyone can write about mythical worlds, murders, heists, and far-fetched romances. But this—this mimics how life is lived, in all its boring and profound uneventfulness. I think it will resonate with readers in a special way. The timing is perfect as well—the market has undergone a transformation, and contemporary, edgy, authentic young voices are in high demand. Your work, I believe, has the potential to bring in a large, fresh audience.

I believe you are capable of actualizing this story. I have faith in your ability to deliver a dynamic, fully satisfying manuscript. Along those lines, I believe the time has come to meet you in person. Let's talk. I will have my assistant contact you to set up a time for you to come to New York. I look forward to discussing the future of this book and your writing career.

Best,
Ed Nortan III
President, Darjeeling Publishing

I raised my eyes from the letter and stared at the wall in shock. I didn't even remember submitting to this company. Quite honestly, I had never heard of this company.

I guess I had nothing to lose.

I told my mother about it and she cried with joy. I wanted to turn this opportunity into a life-changing moment.

I called the company to set up the meeting. Days later I was at the airport on my way to New York City. I had never been more than a few hundred miles from home, except the time my mom won a trip to Hawaii, but I was so young I don't really remember much of it.

This was the craziest experience of my life. It's insane how someone's fortune can reverse overnight. I'm glad I persevered and kept going through the months of despair.

I gave my mom a hug and kiss when she dropped me off at Departures. I was flying JetBlue. Going through security was intense—I had to take off my shoes, belt, and jacket. I had to damn near strip down. There was a woman in front of me with a little rat dog in her purse with a bejeweled collar and name tag that said *Coco*. She was what you would imagine Paris Hilton would look like in her late forties. Pseudorich, fake Louis Vuitton bag, pink velour pants, spray tan, leather skin, plastic nails, and makeup that was caked on. She was acting all crazy, causing a scene. Yelling, saying how she was about to miss her flight and had to get to her plane. You know the type; she was the kind of person who felt she was more important than everyone else.

As I waited to board I sat down and pulled out my Moleskine. I started writing about the woman, just in case I wanted to base a future character off her. I must have been writing intensely because the guy next to me spoke up.

"Damn, dude, you're really into whatever the hell you're writing, huh?"

"Oh, ha, yeah, man. I feel like when I have an idea I've got to write as quickly as possible because multiple ideas tend to come—"

"At once and you don't want to forget that idea or miss out on the others coming at you!" he said.

"Yeah, dude. Totally."

He extended his hand. "My name's Brian. I'm also a writer."

"Oh, dope, man. I'm Flynn." I shook his hand. "What kind of writing do you do?"

"Actually, I write for television," he said.

"Like drama?"

"Nah, man, I write comedy. I love it 'cause I just draw inspiration from everyday shit, you know?" He took a sip of his coffee.

"Totally. I feel the same way. Worked on any shows I've seen?" I asked.

"Oh, sure, I've written for *Rick and Morty* and *Arrested Development*, and I'm working on a hilarious show right now called *Mixed Feelings*. It's basically *Curb Your Enthusiasm*, but about a rapper and all the crazy, hilarious shit that goes on behind the scenes in the music industry. The stuff nobody knows about."

"Sounds like fun, man."

"What about you?" Brian asked.

"Oh, um, I'm actually working on my first novel. I'm heading to NYC now to meet with a publishing company."

"No shit, dude. I'm on that same flight!" he said.

"Oh, cool, man," I replied.

"What seat are you?" He took his ticket out.

"23A."

"No way, what are the odds? I'm 23C. I pity the poor bastard who has to sit between us." He laughed.

I had made a buddy in the airport. Maybe this wouldn't be such a bad experience after all.

A few minutes later we boarded the plane. Brian and I made it to our seats, only to find 23B was sitting in my seat.

Of course, it was Paris Hilton's skeleton from security.

"Uh, excuse me," I said. The woman ignored me and fed her dog a treat.

"Who's Mommy's little prince?" she cooed. "You are! You are!" The dog began to lick her on the lips as she kissed the dog back. It was disgusting. Any literary description I could give would never be able to do justice to the horrendous sight.

"Hey, lady!" Brian said. "You're sitting in my friend's seat. Get the hell up!"

She turned to us, shocked.

"First of all, I'm supposed to be in first class, but my assistant waited to book the ticket until the last minute. And if I'm going to sit in . . . *coach*, well, I'll be doing it in a window seat, thank you very much!"

Ding! The soothing airplane sound blanketed the cabin before a flight attendant made her announcement.

"Hello, ladies and gentlemen," she said. "JetBlue would like to welcome you to this nonstop flight to New York City."

The announcements continued, and so did the conversation with *The Walking Dead*'s Paris Hilton.

"Are you fuckin' kidding me, lady?" I said. "That's my seat. My buddy Brian here has the aisle. I hate to tell you, but, wait, no, actually, I can tell you *with great satisfaction* . . . you're in the middle. Now move."

"No," she said, staring out the window.

"Dude, this lady is crazy!" Brian whispered to me.

"Listen," I said to her. "You can't just—"

"I CAN DO WHATEVER I WANT!" she yelled, her eyes growing wide like a villainess. "I deserve this seat!"

At this point, half the plane was staring at us. I wanted to choke the woman out, but I obviously wasn't going to do that. Brian, on the other hand, looked like he was going to pop.

"Excuse me, what seems to be the problem here?" asked a flight attendant.

"Well, this lady—"

"Nothing is the problem, thank you," the lady in my seat said.

"Okay," said the flight attendant, then looked at me. "Well, sir, you're going to have to take your seat."

"This lady is in my seat," I said, then explained the situation.

"Oh," said the flight attendant, understanding. She turned to the woman and her dog. "Ma'am, you're going to have to move."

"No, I was supposed to be in first class!"

The flight attendant was taken aback. "What a bitch," she said under her breath as she walked toward the front of the plane. A minute later, the captain came back and told the woman she needed to leave or she would be escorted off the plane.

That didn't go well.

Two officers and a U.S. air marshal burst onto the scene, dragging her down the aisle with her little dog, the entire plane clapping and hollering.

"I will sue this entire airline!" she screamed.

That's when Brian shouted, "YOU JET BLEW IT!"

The entire plane erupted in laughter. Needless to say, it was a flight I'll never forget.

I had a tough time sleeping, my mind racing with anxiety about the upcoming meeting. But I focused on my characters, and I eventually slid into a slumber. Brian and I never exchanged info. I kinda wish we had—he was a cool-ass dude, one of those people you remember till the day you die. I peered out the window, overlooking a rapidly approaching metropolis. Butterflies bounced in my stomach.

Outside the airport, I jumped in a yellow cab and went straight to Midtown Manhattan. The cabbie dropped me off at Forty-Second Street and Fifth Avenue, not far from the publishing company. I'd never been to New York City, and damn, let me tell you, this shit was wild. I had a bum ask me for change and a *Real Housewives*–looking lady shoulder check me all in a matter of minutes. Pigeons were flapping past my head. Cars were honking at me to get the fuck out of the way. This was about as far from my town as you could get in this country.

For those of you who have yet to experience New York City, for a first-timer it is extremely claustrophobic and insanely dirty—and I mean big black trash bags just sitting on the side of the street—and everything is loud, fast, and relentless. Half the cab drivers don't know their way around the city and insist you pull up directions on your phone to guide them, but all this aside, I must say it is a beautiful thing to experience. It's electric. I was happy I had made it!

A few blocks of a walk and I was in front of Darjeeling Publishing's offices. I checked in, and the next thing I knew, I was being shot up to the thirty-sixth floor in an elevator. Mr. Nortan's assistant greeted me and ushered me to his office. I sat there nervously, waiting for his arrival.

His office kind of reminded me of what you see in those Wall Street movies, you know? I gazed over the desk in front of me, peering through the windows into the grand abyss of New York City. I'd never been so high up in a building in my life. On the desk there were piles of manuscripts stacked high. Books lined the walls, floor to ceiling. At the center of his desk lay a smaller packet—my twenty-page proposal that had landed me a ticket to the Big Apple. It had red marks all over the page.

"There he is!" Mr. Nortan said with a big smile as he entered the room behind me.

"Hello, Mr. Nortan," I said, standing to shake his hand.

"Mr. Nortan was my father. Please call me Ed!" he insisted.

"Okay, Ed, sure thing," I responded.

Ed was a burly man from the South—the accent was clear as day—about fifty years old. He had salt-and-pepper hair that leaned more toward the salt end, and he wore white jeans, cowboy boots, a white blazer, a turquoise undershirt, a bolo tie, and, of course, a white cowboy hat to match. To be honest, he looked like he belonged in Houston, Texas, in the beef business rather than in the publishing industry.

"Now, son, let's just get down to it, shall we?" he said in his raspy trucker voice. "To me this is an open-and-shut case. I absolutely love your idea, and if you can deliver, I'm prepared to cut you an advance check of forty thousand right now with a back end of sixty thousand upon completion of the novel. Of course, in the meantime, you get yourself a new agent to oversee the contracts, but I guarantee you the royalties and splits will be more than satisfactory. Let me make it clear though, son. To make this thing real I need you to deliver this manuscript in six months' time. And that's not long. I need this book out next year." This was when it hit me: Ed definitely was in the right business.

"So what do you say?" he said.

I couldn't believe it; it almost didn't seem real. Two days ago I was depressed, sleeping all damn day in my mother's house, unshaven, smelling, and counting sheep next to stacking plates of rotting sandwiches. Today I was being offered a book deal.

Without hesitation, I shook Ed's hand.

He gave me some guidance on my proposal, and sent me on my way with some books to read and a few encouraging words. "I know you can do this, son, and do it well. I'm very much looking forward to working together to make this a success. Talk soon."

In a rush of inspired determination I hurried home without even an afternoon's worth of sightseeing. The next morning I was on a plane, heading back home to deposit a forty-thousand-dollar check and get to work. After I hit the bank, I signed a lease on my own apartment. I even went down to the shelter and adopted myself a dog to keep me company. At this juncture I was single and without too many friends. I was going to need some companionship. He was a little mutt by the name of Bennett, about three years old, mainly black with bits of light brown on his face and paws. Sweetest dog you'd ever meet.

The day I rescued Bennett I got him a fresh red collar and took him for a long walk. On our stroll, I asked this random guy to take a picture of Bennett and me on the first day of our new life together. The guy looked at me like I was insane and stared down at the end of the leash, looking bewildered and scared like the dog was gonna kill him. He took the picture anyway and then sped off. Really didn't like dogs, I guess.

We went home so I could get to business laying the groundwork for my novel. My writing style was like method acting. I got fully immersed in my characters. In an act of radical creativity, I would try to become my characters to make my writing come alive. To pull this novel off I needed to get inside the supermarket. I needed real-life inspiration. What better way to discover the ins and outs of such a place than to work there?

I checked the classifieds for any openings. I saw some help was wanted at the movie theater. That wasn't going to work. I saw an ad for a personal aide to an old man. That wasn't going to work either, and I had no interest in wiping some old guy's ass for him. I was getting desperate. I took a deep breath and looked up.

I scoped out the apartment, which was empty: just a

bed, a desk, and stacks of books across my floor. My record player sat next to my bed, spinning with no needle scratching the surface. An old rotary phone with no cord attached to the wall was on my desk. It was more for show, more for the feel. Much like my Bluetooth typewriter, which sat on a wobbly old IKEA desk in the corner. I stared at the writing machine. It seemed to have its own personality, an aura, even. I was overcome with fear.

Fear. That once again I would not be able to finish what I'd started. That I was a shit writer. That I was a born failure. A loser. A pathetic bum. Fear. That Lola was right. That I couldn't deliver for Ed Nortan. That I'd have to move back in with my mom. That'd I be thirty with nothing to show for myself. Fear. That I would turn out like my absentee father—who wound up a penniless schizophrenic who committed suicide in a psychiatric hospital.

I had already lost the only love of my life. If I couldn't do this, if I couldn't give myself that The End with this book, then my life would never truly be my own.

I gripped the newspaper, stood up, and walked to the bathroom. I set the paper down next to the sink and splashed my face with water. Just then, the lights flared. I rubbed my eyes, and looked in the mirror. There were two of me. My mind felt cloudy. I felt like someone was talking at me. As the other me dissipated, I stared at myself.

"No matter what happens, finish the book! No matter what happens, finish the book! Stay inspired, do anything to finish this book! Finish the book! Your life depends on it."

I repeated this to myself over and over as the lights flickered.

"Just finish the book! No matter what happens, finish the book!"

Repeating my mantra, I began to feel like I was being split in two. Like the old me was out of my body and this new me was here—present and yet not. I couldn't control my thoughts or my body. My head felt as if it were underwater. Flashes of numbness shot down my fingers. The lights flared again and it felt like I could literally see this other me by my side, if for only an instant.

I felt terror but also comfort. I rinsed my face once more and looked down at the newspaper next to the sink. *Muldoon's Grocery* was circled in red.

I'd head there in the morning to fill out an application and hopefully get a job that would inspire me to finish this book once and for all.

But by now you know I got that job.

Now that you're all caught up, we can finish that eureka moment I was having walking with Frank through aisle nine.

CHAPTER 5

AISLE NINE

"Are you listening to me?" Frank said. "You look pretty zoned out right now, and I'm trying to school you with this knowledge!"

The weird part? Everything he was saying, all the information he was blurting out, I felt like I knew it subconsciously. You see, Frank seemed to always have bits of information, like a walking Snapple cap. Imagine all the shit you learn throughout your life, the things your brain keeps locked—spelling, family faces, pattern recognition, first hand job under the bleachers freshman year, visual and spatial processing—all stuff for your survival.

Then there's the shit you "learn" but don't retain—factoring and linear equations, what you had for breakfast three days ago, nutritional information about bananas . . .

Now, Frank, his brain was like *entirely* subconscious.

The shit a normal brain is supposed to throw away, it's like Frank's kept it, replacing the main things you need with the clutter of his own subconscious. And that was another unique reason he was perfect for my novel.

"Flynn!" he yelled.

"Oh, sorry, man, I was just thinking about—"

Oh no, I thought, stopping myself midsentence. I couldn't tell him what I was doing. Why I was really here.

"Thinking about what?" asked Frank.

If I said more, I would blow my cover as an undercover author, potentially ruining my chances of finishing this book. So, I said the first thing that came to mind that was sure to distract him.

"Ever fuck that girl?" I asked, pointing to a girl who had apparently been hired the month before.

"Who, Cara? Oh, yeah, man. Two days in, I polished that off."

Cara worked in the coffee shop at the end of the store, the one by aisle twelve. Cara was maybe twenty-three, blond, and short, and seemed very sweet. She had piercing eyes, full lips, and hair in a tight ponytail, and she wore brown knee-high boots. Kind of dumb-looking, maybe, like a bimbo who gets by on her looks—but she was intelligent. Just naive-seeming.

"One of the tightest I've slayed in my time here," Frank continued. Truthfully, I hadn't expected this. I thought he'd drone on about how he would do her, or had planned to, but the fact that he already had? That was crazy to me.

Either way, my question distracted him from what had been on my mind—writing this novel. As we walked to the front of the store, he elaborated on their sexcapades, ex-

plaining how they went in the back storage area one evening after closing when no one was around. He went on
about this little cupcake tattoo just under her left breast,
right above her rib cage. I asked him to describe the tattoo, gripping my pen. It was a pink cupcake tattoo with
blue sprinkles, he explained, with two cartoon eyes and a
smile to match the little arms and legs. By the time I finished writing this down, we'd reached the front customer
service area.

"How you finding your first day, child?" Ronda said.

"It's going pretty all right, I suppose," I replied. "Just
kinda getting to know the pla—"

At that moment, a door opened behind her.

The customer service area was a ten-by-ten-foot room.
There was an eight-foot-long counter built into the wall
that separated Ronda from the customers who came to
her for help. At the end of the counter, where she sat, was
a latch that allowed the table to lift up—it was attached to
the wall like a drawbridge that could be retracted over a
moat leading to the king's castle.

In the corner of the room, behind Ronda, a man
walked through, mumbling in Spanish—Hector. Hector
was a thirty-four-year-old first-generation Mexican American security guard at Muldoon's. He was overweight and
wore a white short-sleeved button-down, a black tie, and a
metal badge on his left breast. His slacks were deep blue
with black stripes down the sides, and they were accompanied by a utility belt containing his flashlight, baton, and
empty handcuff pouch—it was technically illegal for him
to detain anyone. At the end of the day, he had no juris-

diction, was just a scarecrow Ted Daniels hired at $10.75 an hour to patrol the aisles, scaring teenagers before they mustered the courage to lift something.

"Hola, Vernon," Hector said to an armed guard who had sneaked past me without my realizing it.

"Oh, good! Right on time!" said Ted, who was walking up right then.

At the end of every month, on the twenty-eighth at 4:00 p.m. sharp, Vernon came to relieve the store of the roughly one hundred thousand dollars in cash it had made in the month. Until then, it was held securely in a Summerfold safe in Hector's security office, right next to the monitors that displayed a closed-circuit security camera feed. With the exception of a few blind spots, the entire store was covered—not only the aisles, but outside too, including the front parking lot and back loading dock where Frank took his frequent smoke breaks.

"How's your day, Ted?" Vernon asked. He was in his sixties, short and frail for his age, with white hair hiding under his work hat and a bit of a limp in his left leg. His partner, Gary, was the one who drove the armored truck. Gary never left his position.

"Well, I'm just fine, Vernon," said Ted. He smiled, his teeth protruding more than ever.

Vernon grabbed the three deposit bags and put them in a locked duffel bag. "See you next month," said Vernon. Ted and Hector waved good-bye and returned to their daily paperwork.

"That guy looked like Father Time, huh?" I said to Frank.

"Who are you talking to?" asked Ted.

"Frank," I said, turning my head to look. Frank was no-where to be found.

"Well, he must have slipped away while you were standing there daydreaming. No more of that, okay?"

"Got it, Ted, sorry about that."

"Can I see you in my office?" Ted said with a smile.

Sitting in Ted's office was never fun. He was always so awkward. He was the boss who wanted to be everyone's buddy, insisting that you come to him if you ever needed anything. But as he pulled his chair up next to mine, the only thing I needed was space, quite honestly.

"Flynn," he said, looking concerned. "How are we feeling today? You've been acting a little aloof lately. Everything all right? Things going smoothly? Anything you need, just know that I'm here."

"No, everything is going pretty okay, thanks," I said. He was right. I was aloof. But that was only because I was preoccupied trying to take mental notes for my book. If I wasn't floating or being distracted by Frank, I was plotting the story in my head, thinking of how these characters would puzzle together. Trying to figure out the rising action and climax.

"All right, well, listen . . . I just want you to know that you're a part of this family now, and if there's anything I can help you with, you let me know," he said with a smile. "Oh," he continued, "the code to the break room is 34652, okay? That's the code to everything else around this place. I made it something super easy that I would never forget. I mean, everything is pretty much unlocked or open anyway, but, you know, just in case!" he explained, pointing at me with one brow raised, as if to say *in case you were wondering.*

I wasn't.

Like that, I was out of his office as quickly as I had entered, with one thought in mind.

I hope this doesn't become a reoccurring thing.

From the corner of my eye I caught the clock on the wall. It was 6:00 p.m. My shift was over. The day had flown by. I was feeling more comfortable with how things operated, but I was still a little disoriented. I clocked out, and said bye to Ronda. Just as I was leaving, Frank stopped me.

"Flynn, where you going?" he said.

"I'm going home, man, it's six," I said.

"You're not doing it right, dog," he said, pulling out a stack of twenties and tens from his pocket.

"Frank, where'd you get that cash?" I said.

"Umm . . . ha, where you think, Einstein? From the fucking cash register," he jeered.

"Frank, what the fuck, man, you can't be stealing like that, that's embezzlement!" I said.

"Bro, I've been tipping myself out nightly for months and no one has said shit—it's easy as pie," he said as he took out a banana from his apron.

"That ain't right, man. Your luck is going to run out one of these days," I said.

I turned and went home.

I got home and poured the day into my Moleskine. It may not have seemed like an eventful shift from the looks of it, but it was the kind of pedestrian, humdrum nonaction I needed to set the stage for the first few chapters. I wrote and wrote and wrote until my hands hurt. I turned a page, pausing momentarily, mentally dazed from the stream.

I turned my notebook sideways and scrawled in all caps:

MULDOON'S

That was it. That would be the title. It was a rare moment of certainty. I closed the book and went to bed.

The next morning, when I came to work, I saw the old black man outside playing chess again. This was already feeling like déjà vu. As I entered through the automatic doors and walked toward the break room to clock in, I saw the crazy-looking dude holding his coffee to his nose. He sniffed intensely.

"Coffee coffee coffee coffee!!!!" he said.

"Hey, what's your name, man?" I asked.

"Coffee? Coffee coffee coffee!" he said.

"Oookkaaayyyyy theennn . . . ," I said, and just kept walking until I was intercepted by Ann from the pharmacy. Like clockwork, yet again, she handed me a couple of multivitamins, which I pretended to ingest, secretly storing them in my jacket pocket.

I reached the break room and hit the keypad above the doorknob: 34652. I went to clock in. Rachel and Becca were sitting inside again, talking about last night's episode of *The Bachelor*.

"Hey, Flynn," Rachel said.

"Hey, Rachel, what's up?" I responded as I opened my locker and put on my Muldoon's apron and name tag.

"Nothing much, just another monotonous day in the grocery store," she said, taking a sip of coffee. Her bright red lipstick stained the paper cup. Before I even had a chance to respond, I heard it.

"Floater to bakery, floater to bakery, please." The voice of a woman with a Russian accent crackled through the static of the dated intercom.

On my way to the bakery the lights went out in half the store.

"What the hell?" I said, stopping in my tracks.

"Oh, that's just the busted-ass electrical system," a voice said from behind me. When I turned around, I was met by a black man in his late twenties.

"You Flynn, right?"

"Yeah, that's me."

"I'm DayDay." He extended his hand and I shook it.

"Nice to meet you, man."

"Yeah, Ted's cheap ass still ain't put the money he should into the electrical system." DayDay, I soon learned, was like the on-call super for the store, the all-around handyman.

DayDay actually seemed like a chill dude. One of the only employees I could say that about so far.

"Yeah, man," he continued. "The lights in this place are always shady. Never really know when they gonna go on you. This white nigga so cheap."

White nigga? I thought to myself. What the hell does that mean?

I mean, I couldn't exactly just ask him what white nigga

meant because, as a white man, I'm pretty sure he would beat the shit out of me. Rightfully so—white people have no reason to use that word. But maybe . . . *white niggas* do?

I guess this is something I will never understand about lingo and black culture as a white kid. Hell, I'd like to think I'm a pretty good writer, but I can't dance for shit. And let's be real: black people have soul! There're just some things people won't ever understand. As for me, the oxymoron of white nigga is one I shall never uncover.

"Okay, well, thanks, DayDay. It was nice to meet you," I said, beginning to walk away.

"Aright, my nigga, Imma get back to fixing these lights."

I was so puzzled. Now he called *me* nigga? What the hell was going on? Was that a . . . good thing? I contemplated this all the way to the bakery, which was located in the back of the store near aisle thirteen. The bakery smelled amazing; all around me were pastries, fresh loaves of bread, cookies, muffins, cakes, and bagels. I felt transported by the aroma.

"Hey, you're Flynn, right?"

And this was how I met Mia Torres.

She was an absolute beauty! A twenty-five-year-old, Spanish-speaking, tan-skinned, 5'6" supermarket model with jet-black hair; an amazing body; a warm, welcoming energy; and a radiating smile. She was the only thing in the entire store that felt real. She was a combination of Jessica Alba and Rashida Jones. Random mixture, I know, but damn, was she gorgeous. Mia was the kinda girl who you see and feel an instant attraction to and chemistry with. I felt light on my feet. I was infatuated. Lovestruck.

She was wifey material. I realized I had just been standing there silently. I fumbled.

"Yeah . . . uhmmm. I, second day," I said, nervously reaching for my Moleskine.

"Awww, yay, you haven't been tainted yet," she said with a chuckle, giving me an infectious smile. "This place is kind of a killer of dreams."

"Why do you say that?" I asked, eager to take micro-notes of key points of our conversation.

"Well, for starters, the—"

She was interrupted by a tiny, pasty white woman with a face that rested in anger—she was like a 5'4" female Robert De Niro, dressed in all white, with a flour-stained apron, a rolling pin, and a disgusting hairy mole above her lip. She opened her mouth to speak, but before the first syllable slipped out, I knew the voice was going to sound like a creepy James Bond villain.

The very same Bond villain who requested my presence in the first place.

"Is this the floater?" she said, not really asking either one of us in particular.

"Yes, I'm Flynn . . . I . . ."

"You—come with me, floater," she interrupted, grabbing my arm.

Here I was, being manhandled by a sixty-five-year-old female De Niro, forced into the baker's den. We stood surrounded by freezers, ovens, and huge baking sheets about three feet long and two feet wide. Counters piled with dough framed the room. "In freezer we keep dough," she said in her thick Russian accent. I looked at her name

61

tag. It read *Bianca*. "Now dough is ready." She pulled out a box and I realized exactly what she meant—none of the donuts, pretzels, or bagels were made fresh. They were outsourced by another company and kept frozen in white paper boxes. So all you needed to do was pop them in the industrial oven, let them cook, take them out, and put them in a pretty package to give them that baked-from-scratch look.

I spent the next few days in the bakery, and over that time I learned a lot. Pretty soon, my notepad was almost full. For example, did you know that when anything new is brought onto the floor, such as pies and any other baked goods, they place the freshest on the bottom so as to move the old product first? So whenever you go shopping, be sure to grab your bread from the back or bottom.

Aside from the Bond villain trying to kill any bit of happiness I might have, there was always Mia. Our stations were right next to each other. I prepared the bagels and loaves of bread on a countertop, like a buffet table with the sneeze guard, you know? I mean, well, minus the sneeze guard. To my right was a gap where we could walk out onto the floor, and on the other side of the gap was Mia's station. Mia would man the ovens. We had enough face time that we built a nice little rapport. We would chit-chat, shoot the shit, joke around. She taught me how to bake and ice a cake. This was straight out of an episode of *The Bachelor*. Contestants having to bake together. Flour was flirtatiously tossed. I really got the feeling she'd taken a liking to me.

Mia told me about her ambitions in life, and how she had been in college studying law. She explained how her family was extremely poor, how her dad had left her family and was a little crazy. She'd entered a contest for a full-ride scholarship to law school, had written a moving essay to a man running for governor. In the end, he decided to donate his own money to a good cause—the good cause being this brown-skinned poor girl. It was a smart move, playing to the young, lower-class female and Hispanic vote all in one shot. That's politics.

Mia didn't mind knowing this was a big reason she received the ride—all she cared about was the fact that she'd be in school and working toward a career she really cared about. She wanted to be an entertainment attorney. She wasn't really musically inclined, but in the shower it was *Showtime at the Apollo* for her! She wanted to be behind the talent, representing their interests, making sure they weren't being exploited, and that they were getting their money where it was due.

The time we spent together was amazing. I mean, she was the girl next door who you just wanted to spend time with and get to know. Her family situation reminded me a bit of mine. I was attracted to her intelligence, ambition, and perseverance. And for whatever reason, she seemed to want to know more and more about *me*. I told her everything. Well, *almost* everything.

I told her about my dad who I never knew. I told her about my aimless youth. I told her about my breakup with Lola and my months of depression. I told her about my ambitions of writing. I told her about how incredible and strong my mother was to have raised me on her own. What I didn't tell her? I was currently writing a book. A book she was now a character in.

She smiled when she spoke to me, interested in everything I said. I couldn't help but feel bad for being a little dishonest. For using her for information, as research for my novel. But pretty soon, it didn't feel that way anymore. I decided I could ethically keep that to myself for the time being. After only an hour speaking to Mia that first day, I didn't need the notepad anymore—I was hanging on her every word. It was all in my memory! After a while, I realized the last time I wrote in the Moleskine was with Frank.

Oh, shit, Frank! I thought to myself as Mia was speaking. By then, I hadn't seen him in a few days and wondered where he had been. And wouldn't you know it? It was kind of a welcome respite, I gotta say.

Just then, a lanky arm by the front of the store near aisle one was waving intensely with a banana peel, trying to get my attention.

The hand was followed by Frank's head, which popped out from behind the shelf like a cartoon. He motioned me over, but I motioned back that I was working and pointed toward Bianca, Russian Villain and Sucker of Happiness.

"Who are you talking to?" Mia said in a *why aren't you paying attention to what I'm saying* tone.

"What? Oh, I'm sorry! My buddy was just trying to get my attention."

"Oh," she said.

"Yeah, sorry about that."

Just as I was searching for a further excuse, we were interrupted by a voice.

"Hey there, Muldoon's employees!" said Ted Daniels, giving us an overzealous wave. He was headed toward the coffee shop with Cara, the full-lipped blonde who worked there.

"Oh, poor girl," Mia said. "Ted is kinda creepy. I'd hate to have to go anywhere with him! And she's so sweet."

"And freaky," I added.

"What?"

"Oh, I just heard she gets a little . . . freaky, haha."

"Who told you that, Flynn?"

"Frank had sex with her."

"Well, Frank is a liar," Mia said. "Because Cara is, like, super Mormon. I've witnessed it firsthand. If she had sex with him, well, then . . . I have a penis."

My eyes glanced down toward the zipper in her pants.

"Flynn!" She giggled, then smacked my arm.

The giggle slap. She was *definitely* into me. I mean, that's like ninth-grade shit right there . . . I was so in!

By lunch I was pretty tired—not from speaking to Mia, obviously, but from working hard under Soul Sucker Bianca. As I was about to take my break, green-haired Kurtis came over, awkwardly trying to talk to Mia while I re-stocked the bagels. Fuck this guy, I thought. As he left, he gave me a menacing look—like he wanted me dead. And as if that weren't bad enough, Bianca would tell us not to speak to each other while we worked. Like, I could under-stand if we weren't being productive, or being loud and unprofessional, but our work areas were feet from each other and this bitch had the balls to tell us *no talking*?

During my break I snagged a few slices of "dead" bread from the bakery, and then went to the deli and swiped some honey ham and Swiss cheese when Kurtis wasn't looking. An impromptu sandwich. After that, I went to the break room, where Frank was filling a paper cup with water from the blue plastic jug.

"Dude, where you been?" he said.

"I could ask you the same thing, man. I haven't seen you in days."

"Bro, didn't you see me today trying to get your attention?" he asked with attitude. "I've been doing that the last few days when that mean bitch who works there wasn't looking."

"Yeah, but I—"

"You were talking to that Mia chick, huh?! She's fuckin' hot, right?" he interrupted.

"Dude, she doesn't even know who you are," I snapped back a bit defensively.

"Man, *all* these hos know who I am," Frank said, opening a locker and taking out a pack of cigarettes and a lighter. "You know, in my locker there's a little cubby under the metal at the base. If you push down on the right side it pops open. It's where I keep the shit I steal . . . and my gun."

Frank shut the locker.

"You don't have a gun in there!" I spewed. "Whaatt?!"

"It's for when the time comes."

"What the hell are you talking about?"

"I'm foreshadowing, man," he said with a smirk.

"Foreshadowing what?"

"The day some disgruntled schizophrenic nutjob employee shows up and stalks the aisles with an AR-15 semi-automatic rifle. Pumping rounds into customers and employees. Or even himself." Frank put a cigarette in his mouth. "I'm gonna be prepared for that fucker. He's never gonna know what hit him. I'm gonna be a thousand moves ahead of him. Like a game of chess."

"You don't really have a gun in there, do you?" I asked, though, deep down, this was the shit I loved about Frank. You kinda didn't know what was real and what wasn't.

"Ever seen the roof?" he said, ignoring me as he walked past.

"No, I haven—"

"Cool, let's go."

As we walked through the store, he continued talking. "You didn't see me because you didn't want to. Just admit it to yourself, man. This really isn't healthy by now, you must realize that."

"Wait, what? What are you talking about?" I replied.

"Mia, man. We were talking about your obsession with her, and how it essentially makes me invisible, dude."

"What do you mean?" I stared at Frank, puzzled.

"Bros before hos, man. But if you wanna get technical—the brain is a very complicated organ, man. If you don't control it, it will control you. You see what you wanna see. And as the saying goes . . . you only had eyes for her, I suppose, lover boy. Every time I tried to get at you, I couldn't because you were so focused on this chick, man. Keep your eyes on the prize, bro."

In some weird way, it's almost as if Frank was speaking directly to the creative inside me—in a way, he was right. I was so infatuated with this girl that I had completely forgotten why I was there in the first place: to finish my novel! I was smitten and it had been a major distraction from my book. But Frank couldn't possibly know that.

"Eyes on *what* prize?" I asked.

"All this fuckin' pussy just laying at your feet, man! You can't get all hot and bothered over one chick!"

I paused for a moment near the exit.

"Look, man," I said. "I'm not here for 'all this fuckin' pussy,' and I genuinely like Mia. Chill on how you talk about your coworkers. These women are just trying to make a buck in the summer. Just because you feel the need to try and fuck everything that walks, don't drag me into your gutter. I like Mia, so what?"

"She's old news, man."

"Old news? What the fuck is that supposed to mean?"

"Bro," said Frank, who was now to the right of me. He stopped and put his left hand on my shoulder, like a blind man walking next to a person with sight. "I'm just saying this place is like a revolving door; there are new girls in and out of here every day. So if you want to focus on li'l ol' Mia, be my guest, brother . . . but you're missing out."

We walked out the back door and onto the loading dock near the trash and recycling. Frank jumped on top of the giant brown Dumpster, reaching for a latch on a ladder that extended to the roof. He released the latch, and the bottom half of the ladder rushed down, stopping about a foot from the ground.

"Hustle up, lover boy," Frank said as he began to climb while holding the cigarette between his lips. I gripped the skinny, rusting bar of the ladder. As I began my ascension, I was quickly winded and realized that, for a skinny guy, I was out of shape.

It was peaceful on the roof of the store. Frank pulled out a joint and tried to light it. But the heavy wind blew out the spark. "Ever try to light a joint with a Zippo? It's the fuckin' worst," he said, though he eventually lit it and gestured for me to indulge with him. I politely declined with a slight wave. "Who are you, Ted Daniels? Hit the goddamn joint!" he said.

"Nah, man, that shit makes me paranoid," I told him.

"Suit yourself," Frank said, raising his eyebrows as if to say *more for me.*

"I'm more of a drinker if anything," I told him. "And honestly, I try my best to stay away from that, seeing as my dad was an alcoholic. Or at least that's what my mom tells me. She said it brought out his schizophrenic tendencies."

"Oh, yeah?"

"Yeah. So it's in my blood, you know?"

Not seeming to care, Frank just stood there looking forward. Our view from the top of Muldoon's faced the back end of the store. It was trees as far as you could see. The sun was starting to set.

"I'm gonna be remembered forever," Frank said. "Immortalized, I can feel it. This is just the start. People will know my name. Maybe it'll be in infamy, but my name will be known."

I pulled out my Moleskine to take note of this quote. I found it a bit creepy how sure he was of this. It was even more unsettling because what he was stating was *currently happening* in my novel. This would be a scene.

And with that, we peered into the horizon. Miles out there were dark clouds punctuated by thunder and lightning. I could feel the storm approaching. Frank's joint

69

had become a roach. He flicked it over the side of the building and reached for a cigarette. He brought it to his lips, lighting the Zippo. "Looks like rain."

I went home inspired. I paced back and forth in my apartment, chewing a toothpick, bouncing my red rubber ball. Different ideas, dialogue, and story arcs raced through my head. Thoughts tumbled over one another; they were moving so quickly. Whenever something stuck, I rushed to my typewriter and went to town. The muses were speaking and I was responding. So many things and people—ordinary people I never thought I would meet—having such an impact on me creatively and personally.

I stopped to ponder. Fuck the literary world. I wanted to write something I'd want to read. And isn't that what art is about, anyway? Expressing yourself the way you want to. Maybe that's why I had been so scared to actually finish and release a book. Because of what others would think. "You should have done it like this" or "You shouldn't do that." A bunch of people, mainly other writers, or people who wished they were, reading your work, telling you why it wasn't good enough. So fuck them and their established rules. I'm gonna break every rule unapologetically for my audience. The only people I'm writing this thing for, anyway. I mean, think about it. One doesn't create art for the people who hate it. Plus, when it comes to other writers, if they think it's bad they'll hate it because to them it's bad writing, and if it's good they'll be covetous, wishing they had done it, and consequently hate on it all the more. So if you're making your art based on others it's lose-lose, and if you say "screw everyone, I'm gonna make something I love," you'll win every time. It was actually Alan

Watts, the late, great philosopher, who said simply, "Anything you can be interested in, you'll find others who are," so this work is for the others . . . like me.

I wrote until 4:00 a.m. As my eyes grew heavy, my fingers slowed down. My head lowered involuntarily. I was asleep at my desk, using my typewriter for a pillow yet again.

CHAPTER 6

PANIC

For the next few weeks it rained. It rained and rained and rained. As dumb as it might sound, Mia was the sunshine through it all.

By then, I was about halfway done with the outline of my novel, and had even written a few chapters. But I was stuck. I'd been experiencing writer's block because I needed something . . . big. I needed a big event to really fuck shit up, you know? Something the reader absolutely wouldn't see coming—an event to have them holding on to every word, eager to reach the next page, and the next, and so on.

Back in the supermarket, things were great, but my time in the bakery was done. That was bittersweet because I missed seeing Mia in the mornings, but I was ecstatic I would no longer be working under Bianca the Sucker of Souls.

This week I was in the coffee shop with Cara, and Mia was right, she was extremely sweet and super Mormon, indeed. But she was also super cute and I could completely see why Frank had said he'd had sex with her. As hot as Cara was, my mind was on Mia. I hadn't had sex, let alone made out with someone, in a minute.

I sat slouched at the counter with the palm of my hand under my chin, allowing the weight from my head to balance lazily.

My mind wandered to visions of kissing Mia, undressing her . . .

Kurtis walked by, with his fucking leather wristband, giving me his usual sneer. It was a look of disdain that I was growing tired of. What a clown. That loser would walk around trying to mack on all the girls at the store. None of them wanted anything to do with his bullshittery. Dude probably subsisted off Monster energy drinks, JUULing, Doritos, and Puddle of Mudd.

His bad energy interrupted my escalating fantasy of Mia. It was a slow day in the coffee shop. And if there weren't customers, there wasn't much to do.

I tried to think of something eventful to write about. Writer's block was the worst. If I wasn't creating, I felt static. Like a failure. I needed to keep going. I sat daydreaming about possible climaxes. If my book was essentially about nothing, how was I going to bring it to a dramatic resolution?

Cara stood idly, scrolling through her phone. "This bra is killing me," she said under her breath, adjusting her T-shirt. "Being a girl sucks, Flynn. You're so lucky . . . Flynn . . . *hey, Flynn!*"

I snapped back to reality.

"Oh, sorry, what now?" I said, only half paying attention.

"Oh, Flynn, you silly goose, something is bugging me. Can you watch the front for a sec?" she asked, her big blue eyes staring into my soul. Hardly listening, I just nodded, continuing to spitball ideas in my head for something *eventful*, something not quite climactic but preclimactic. The big bang before the biggest bang!

I saw Rachel and Becca walking toward aisle nine. Ted was calling them over to restack a pyramid of canned soup that someone's tyrannical child had decided to push over.

"Yo, go tell that girl I like her!"

Frank had popped up from behind the counter, scaring the shit out of me.

"Fuck, dude! Don't do that, man!" I yelled. "Jesus!"

"Hahahahaha, you're a pussy, bro," he replied. "Just tell her I like her."

"What? Who are you talking about?"

"Kat Dennings's cousin over there," said Frank.

"Oh, Rachel? Why don't you go talk to her yourself? Aren't you the self-proclaimed 'pussy slayer'?"

"I need a different approach, man," said Frank, looking at me. "Word is getting around I'm a whore."

"Rightfully so," I said.

"Look, man, when you can . . . just tell her I'm into her, okay?"

Just as I was about to answer, a large white woman with short, thinning red hair appeared. She was wearing a fluffy blue blouse with white flowers, a matching white skirt, and black heels. She cleared her throat in a very authoritative manner. "Yes," she said. "I would like one medium coffee, black, two sugars, and a piece of iced lemon cake, thank you."

I froze, trying to register everything she had said. I looked back to Frank for guidance, but he had gone, most likely sensing the bitchy attitude of this woman and not wanting any part of it. I looked back at her, my mouth open to speak . . . but nothing came out.

"Hello!" the woman said, loudly and obnoxiously. "Can I get some service here?"

"Oh, yes," I responded. "Of course, I'm sorry, ma'am . . . it's just my first day in the department."

"Well, even on your first day, pouring black coffee isn't too complicated now, *is it honey?*"

"WHAT THE FUCK DID YOU SAY TO ME?!" I screamed. But before I had time to register what I had just done, I was already balls-deep in the commitment of standing up for myself and anyone else this woman had ever made feel inferior.

"Bitch, what dimension are you from? You think just because I pour coffee for a living you can talk to me like I'm some piece of shit?! You are such a fucking cunt!"

The woman's jaw was on the floor at this point—she was stunned. Fuming with rage.

"FLYNN!" I looked up. It was Ted Daniels, screaming my name from across the store. But his scream was nothing compared to . . . the child running from aisle to aisle, kicking over stacks of food.

"AND FUCK YOU TOO, TED!" I said, my voice pointed straight into his soul. "You creepy fuck!"

Rachel appeared. Her eyebrows were raised high. She

let out a quick laugh, then covered her mouth with her hand.

"I'm here to help you!" I said, focusing my attention back on the insulting woman. "Not *serve you*, goddamn it!" From the corner of my eye, I could now see the kid jumping up and down, smashing plastic bags of tortilla chips with his shoes. "And if I *were* to help you, I would tell your fat ass that *you don't need the fucking lemon cake*! Why don't you give your arteries a break, woman, damn!"

At this moment, a child began to cry. The same goddamn child who had been terrorizing the store for an hour, the child who knocked down the eight-foot towers of canned soup for his own devilish amusement.

"Listen here," the child's neglectful mother said. "I don't know what you think—"

"—and you, terrible mom!" I interrupted. "Put that fucking kid on a leash or I'll strangle that little shit myself!"

The mother's eyes grew furious. "How dare you," she roared. "My son is—"

Without hesitating, I ran over, picked the child up, and threw him through the plate-glass window, shattering the Muldoon's logo on the glass and immediately snapping me from . . .

"Hello! I said coffee—black—"

. . . my daydream.

"—and chop chop, boy," the overweight woman finished.

Alas, I thought. Another daydream.

"Okay, sure, sorry," I told her, pouring the coffee so quickly I spilled some on my thumb, burning it. "Shit!" I said aloud. The pain was excruciating, but I did my best to keep my composure, holding my right thumb under my left armpit as I rang her up using my left hand. The burning intensified with each passing moment.

"Boy, aren't we forgetting something?" she said. I had no clue what she was talking about. I just wanted to be away from her and out of the store.

"I'm sorry, what?" I replied.

"You forgot my slice of lemon cake."

Goddamn! I yelled internally, sweat dripping from my brow.

"I'm sor . . . I'm sorry," I said, bending down to grab a slice of lemon cake. But as I opened the glass I saw there were none left.

"I'm sorry, ma'am, there are none here." My legs went weak. It was a deathly scary feeling.

"What do you mean? I'm looking at it right there," she said, pointing to a piece of cake.

"No, I'm sorry, that's the display piece, that's not—"

"Display?!" she interrupted. "Well, what about in the back? Surely there—"

At that moment, everything around me began to flicker, as though the lights were being sucked from the room, then instantaneously brought back. My hearing became muffled, then ceased altogether. A high-frequency pitch shot into my head, like in those old war movies when a soldier experiences shell shock. Everything seemed to be moving in slow motion and yet superfast at the same time.

"I'm sorry, but I've got to get my kids to school here," said another woman in line.

"What's the holdup?" asked a man in a suit with a news-paper under his arm.

My chest tightened.

"Hello!" the large woman in front of me said. She glanced at my name tag. "Flynn, is it? Well, Flynn, I said there must be SOME IN THE BACK!" she repeated as though I were deaf.

My breath became shallow and my neck felt numb. Not sure what was going on, I turned around quickly and walked into the back staff area of the coffee shop. I stumbled through the door like a drunk. I glanced around, trying to find a seat. Cara stood in the corner. Topless. Topless and fidgeting with the wire in her bra that had been stabbing her side.

"FLYNN! What are you doi—"

"I'm sorry!" I yelled, transfixed on her breasts. Her body was incredible. I hadn't seen a naked woman since Lola. The excitement only fueled what I had been experiencing.

"I'M SO SORRY!" I yelled "I'M SO—"

"Flynn, get OUT!" she screamed, and I backed out of the room as fast as I could, repeating the same words to myself.

"I'M SORRY, I'm sorry, I didn't mean to! I'm so sorr—"

I stumbled out of the coffee shop. By now, my legs felt as though they would give way at any moment, but I made my way past the line of customers and onto the supermarket floor.

"I'm sorry," I continued to repeat, confused, in a state of panic. I couldn't understand why my body felt this way, because I wasn't freaking out in my mind—it was my body that felt out of control, as though it were about to shut down.

"Flynn?!" a voice said from behind me. "Flynn, are you okay?"

It was Mia.

"I'm sorry," I whispered to her. "I'm sorry—"

I felt dizzy and disoriented.

"Just breathe, Flynn," she said, putting her arm around my waist to support me. "Flynn, breathe!" she said as I slipped from her grip, hitting the cold vinyl floor. My vision blurred. And then . . .

Blackness.

When I awoke I was lying in a hospital bed, staring at the ceiling. A monitor beeped to my left. An IV drip ran intravenously into the top of my hand.

I had full memory of everything that had happened; I just hoped I didn't have, like, a six-year-old coma beard or anything.

Much to my surprise, it had only been about forty-five minutes. Mia was holding my hand and smiling as I came to.

"The doctors took blood and urine samples while you were asleep. They ruled out any serious condition," she said. "But they are pretty sure what it is."

I wasn't sure what I wanted to know first—what *it* was or how the hell they got my urine sample.

"What do you mean? What is *it*?" I asked. "*It* doesn't sound good." My fear was extinguished by Mia's laughter.

"They think you had a panic attack," she said.

"A . . . what? What the fuck is that?" I asked just as a doctor walked into the room.

"Ah, he's awake," the doctor said. He was a tall black man—maybe 6'4"—and skinny. Seeing him, I got that second feeling doctors can give you.

You see, doctors only give off two kinds of vibes, the first being *I don't give a shit about you, where you come from, or where you're going; my job is to diagnose what's going on and collect a check.* And then there are the doctors who genuinely care and want to help people, no matter how many years they've been doing it.

My doctor had a warm energy that seemed to convey the latter.

"Hi there, Flynn," he said. "So, it would appear you have had a panic attack. Do you know what that is?"

"I mean, I've heard about them, but no, not really," I said.

"Now tell me—are you prone to anxiety?"

I had to gather my thoughts.

"Uummmm, I don't think so," I replied.

"Bullshit!" Mia snapped. "Yes, doctor, he has severe anxiety," she said with a half smile. "Flynn, all that shit you've told me about your life? You've got serious issues, boy. I mean, don't get me wrong. You got issues I can handle," she said with a wink, "but issues nonetheless."

The doctor gave me a warm smile.

"Wait . . . what's wrong with me?" I asked.

"Well, nothing is 'wrong' with you, Flynn. You just have a hyperattentive mind." I stared at him for a moment.

"Sooooooo, what . . . I have ADHD or something?"

The doctor laughed.

"No, Flynn. I didn't say hyperactive, I said hyperattentive. My guess is you are constantly thinking, you rarely take a break," he said, then lightly tapped his ballpoint pen to his temple. "And you are always on the go upstairs. Mia says you put a lot of pressure on yourself to succeed. And the pressure is synonymous with worry . . . anxiety. It's incredibly common. People just don't talk about it openly enough." He gave me another kind smile. "I think you need a few days to yourself, and I recommend you see a therapist."

My eyes went wide. "A therapist?! I'm not crazy!"

The doctor sat in the chair next to my bed. "No one is saying you're crazy, Flynn. But panic attacks are serious. They affect a lot of people without them knowing it or addressing it. They're something that should be looked into. In order to treat them, we must find the source. Treatment can come in many forms. There's cognitive behavioral therapy, mindfulness exercises, sleep, and excer—"

"Why do you keep saying panic attack? What the hell is that?" I interrupted.

"Well," the doctor explained, "a panic attack is an involuntary occurrence that happens in the mind. It's—"

"Wait a second," I said, cutting him off. "This wasn't a *mind* thing, Doc. This was a physical thing. Like, this was my legs giving out, and I couldn't breathe, couldn't see straight. This is a *feels like I'm dying, life-threatening event* here!"

The doctor looked at me for a moment, his hand placed over his mouth. Then he removed it and spoke. "The mind is a very powerful thing, Flynn. If you don't control it, it will control you."

I immediately remembered my conversation with Frank, regarding the attention I was giving Mia and not him. The thought of Frank increased the anxiety I was feeling. Frank always blathered on some *Waking Life*–type shit about the power of the mind to create and destroy. "What you believe to be completely physical is actually stemming from your mind. It's a concentrated episode of acute anxiety that manifests itself physically. But it is not life-threatening. A panic attack cannot kill you. This is what you experienced," the doctor continued. "I've got the test results to prove it." He lifted up his clipboard, and pointed at it, as if that were proof. "Look, Flynn . . . just take a few days to yourself. Get your head right and see a doctor sometime. A therapist. It will be good to talk to somebody. In the meantime, I'm going to prescribe Ativan and a—"

"Oh, no no no, Doc," I interrupted. "I don't do pills."

"Well, then you'll have to white-knuckle through your anxiety, but I'm still suggesting you go to therapy. You can leave here whenever you feel ready."

Then, just as quickly as he had arrived, the doctor was gone.

"What's wrong?" Mia said to me. I knew it was the look on my face that gave me away. Like I was pondering something fierce.

"Honestly?" I said. "I just hope this doesn't blow my shot at getting with you."

"Getting with me?" Mia chuckled. "What are we, in seventh grade?" She moved over and sat next to me in the hospital bed. "You wanna *get with me*, Flynn?"

"Well," I stumbled. "I mean, like . . ."

"Flynn, I'm here, aren't I?" she interrupted. "If you want to get with me . . . then *get with me*."

She put her hand on my leg, moving in for a kiss.

It was absolutely incredible—her lips were soft as silk. It felt electric. I held the back of her neck. I was suspended in the moment. The fact that she kissed me like it was no big deal? That let me know just how special she was. But even then, in the middle of our kiss, my mind raced. Thinking of where this could go, thinking that I was still not fully over Lola. That I wasn't ready to move on. Thinking about how Mia had been there for me through this terrifying experience and then . . .

Well, in that very same moment, as my mind raced, as I was in the middle of kissing this beautiful woman . . . I thought about how spot-on the doctor was.

My mind truly was hyperattentive, and I needed to chill the fuck out. Writing this novel was messing with my head.

I mean, even in this moment, I wasn't fully present. I couldn't just enjoy something I had fantasized about for weeks.

As Mia pulled back from our kiss with a bite to my bottom lip, I looked into her eyes and had one final thought.

Maybe I should talk to somebody.

CHAPTER 7

DEREALIZATION

And that somebody was . . . Google.

Ted Daniels had no problem giving me a few days off to myself. Mental health days, if you will. Honestly, I thought he was going to be a bitch about it, but he was fairly understanding. In those days I thought a lot about, well, *a lot*. Essentially the only time I went outside was to walk Bennett. And the biggest thing on my mind, besides my novel? That feeling of not being in my body.

It's hard to explain, but the next day when I woke up, I didn't feel quite myself. My mind felt sharp, and yet at the same time it didn't. It was the same reason I didn't smoke pot, actually.

You see, when I smoked weed, I felt like there was a little person inside my brain watching me live. *Did I really just pick up that glass of water and drink it? Did I really just scratch my arm? Did I really just awkwardly look at the person next to me? Did I really just say "Yeah," while shaking my head no? What the fuck was I talking about? Who am I? What even is I?* You know the kind of feeling, when you are questioning your own existence. When you know you are real but are not exactly convinced. When you feel barely tethered to reality? That's the reason I didn't smoke, and that's the sensation I had been feeling all the time lately. Now I felt it when I was sober.

So as you can imagine, I was alarmed. I wanted to fix myself. I was so sure the doctor was wrong—this wasn't anxiety. This was something else. This felt different.

I began constantly thinking. Thinking *all the time.* Worrying about the things I had never really thought about before, you know? Like death. Obviously, death is going to happen; it's unavoidable. It is what it is. But then it hit me: *YO! You're gonna DIE! One day! It'll be all OVER!* And then I got scared because I didn't know *when* I was going to die, and I began to wonder . . . if there was an invisible ticking clock above my head, would I want to know the number it was counting down to? Or how, or why . . . and it gets worse.

When I took Bennett for walks I would see the world entirely differently. Obviously, at that point in my life, I was scared. Flat-out petrified. When I was around other people, I wouldn't want to be there anymore. I'd be too anxious to speak. I wouldn't want to give a fake smile as they walked by, didn't want to try to pretend. I just wanted to stay inside and do . . . nothing. I couldn't even write. It was different than when I was super depressed. My mind was racing, but my thoughts were stuck in the confines of my head, and they couldn't get out and be turned into actions. I had more panic attacks. But now I knew what they were. That didn't necessarily make them any easier to get through, but I could at least intellectually understand that I wasn't dying. Or was I?

I would force myself to interact with others, even just the slightest interaction. The anxiety I was feeling was not crippling, exactly, but it seemed to hurt more to "white knuckle" through than to just accept myself as a coward— even though, as a coward, no one would know I *was* a coward because I would never have to subject myself to the company of others.

Holy shit. This is pretty dark.

Even now as I'm writing this, it is sickening to imagine where I was in my life. And not to break the fourth wall again, but . . . in some crazy way, these feelings are kind of returning now that I'm writing about it.

I don't want to write about it. But I will because it's part of the process. The process of healing, I suppose. Writing was the only thing that brought me any solace. My creative energy was the same energy that caused my hyper mind and anxiety. It was a cycle. A bad loop. Madness and creativity. Creativity and madness. Writing was both my salvation and my undoing. I got more pages written, but I got further into my panic. When I was writing I felt whole, like myself. Like a stable person. But the minute I stopped, I started to unravel.

To shake it off I would walk my dog, Bennett. But even then I would be constantly thinking of death and the various ways to go. For example, when I was a teenager, I used to skateboard. I would skate relentlessly, and afterward, I saw the world completely differently from before

I'd started. Stairs were no longer stairs, they were called *a set*. A set of four I could kickflip down, or a set of ten to nollie down. A handrail to grind, a loading dock to jump off. The world had become my skate park.

Only now, that imagination and awe I had for my surroundings had turned into something else. A horror film. A TV stuck on Fox News . . . *If a car banks this corner I'm gone*, I would think as I crossed the street. *If I trip and land teeth first on this fire hydrant, game over.* What if there were a tumor in my brain, what if I had an aneurysm, what if that guy in the convenience store wanted to rob the place and I'm the guy who takes a bullet to prove he's *not fucking around* . . .

Where my life used to be an adventure, I now wondered, how was I going to get through the day? Slowly, uneventful, typical, everyday, mundane errands came bearing death. And these constant thoughts, plus the feeling of being out of my body, ripped from reality, isolated and alone even in a room full of people? That is what finally turned me on to the idea of actually speaking to someone. And that someone . . .

. . . was *Dr. Search Engine.*

Why do I feel like I'm not real, slightly off-balance, and out of it?

In an instant, a slew of results came across my laptop screen. Problems with the blood, problems with the brain, problems with damn near every part of my body. Even though I knew all this was impossible, and the doctor had told me my blood results were normal, and I felt in my heart it couldn't be life-threatening, I wasn't myself. I didn't feel like I had before the incident at the supermarket. I typed into the search engine:

Feeling out of my body like life isn't real

After some digging I discovered a condition called derealization. The dictionary results changed everything for me.

Merriam-Webster:

Derealization: a feeling of altered reality (such as that occurring in schizophrenia or in some drug reactions) in which one's surroundings appear unreal or unfamiliar.

The American Heritage Stedman's Medical Dictionary:

Derealization: the feeling that things in one's surroundings are strange, unreal, or somehow altered, as seen in schizophrenia.

Oxford English Dictionary:

Derealization: a feeling that one's surroundings are not real, especially as a symptom of mental disturbance.

I spent hours reading reviews, medical articles, testimonials, and people's personal stories about it. Some people experienced it for a few weeks and it was gone, while others spent years with it. I also discovered that the condition, along with schizophrenia and a host of other mental disorders, is genetic. Fuck. I thought of my dad. How he lost it, left the family, wound up dead by his own doing. I felt a similar fate was inevitable. I felt trapped, shaken to the core. I couldn't focus on anything else.

It seemed apparent that derealization fed off attention like a stripper whose father never gave her the time she needed as a developing child. So you see, in other words, the more one focused on how weird they felt, how out of it, how they didn't exist and the world around them wasn't real . . . the more attention they brought on it. The more they couldn't escape themselves.

And the crazy part? The more I read about it, staring at the screen, the more involved and focused I was. And the more focused I was, the more focused I was on something *besides* what I was feeling. Even though that thing was reading about what I was feeling and why, in those moments, the less I experienced it.

For example, when thinking about my book—or that "big event" I had been searching for—I hadn't felt out of my body. Because I wasn't thinking about my body, or the feeling of not existing. And that was the key to overcoming derealization, essentially . . . *don't think about the pink balloon!* only makes you *think about the pink balloon.*

All in all, in the hours and hours of looking this stuff up, the one thing that made me feel better was learning that feeling that way couldn't hurt me. It was scary, it made me feel uneasy . . . it was annoying and really fucked with me . . . but it wouldn't hurt me! And it couldn't kill me.

Ring!

During one of these deep-dive research sessions, my old-school phone went off. I looked at it, puzzled.

Ring! it went again. I reached out and pulled the phone to my ear.

"Hey, man, how you feeling? Ted said you wigged out or something."

It was Frank; before I could even answer, he continued, "So, yeah, buzz around the store is you saw Cara's tits."

"Who told you that?" I said.

"Doesn't matter who, just tell me about them. Haha, they're nice, right?"

"I . . . yeah. I mean, I, I guess," I said, wrinkling my brow while recalling the event. Since it had happened, I hadn't thought a minute more about how beautiful her body was. But, of course, leave it to Frank to remind me of a woman's naked upper body. As Frank chewed over the phone on what I'm sure was a banana, my mind was thrown back into that instant where I walked in and saw Cara topless. That moment where I froze before either of us frantically reacted. Standing there, back at the supermarket in my mind, I could picture it all—her breasts were so supple, her skin smooth and pale, seeming to have no imperfections. No necklace, no markings, no . . . tattoos.

No tattoos? I thought.

In a fraction of a second I had both realized something insane, and . . . forced myself to forget it for the sake of my book. Frank had said Cara had a cupcake tattoo on her rib.

Ever since I met him, Frank had droned on and on about himself, telling me about the girls he'd been with. His pseudophilosophies and his take on life. I'd been so fascinated by the sharp edges of his personality. So fascinated that I had based my book on him. But this entire time he had just been another phony. Frank wasn't real like he claimed to be. He was a liar, and a goddamn good one.

At that moment, I realized what he was. Or what he *wasn't*. I could see right through him. I was struck with panic at the thought of what this would do to my book. Upset that creating my main character around him was now pointless because there was no authenticity to Frank's words. I no longer knew what was false and what was true.

I almost called it off. Right there in that moment. I was on the edge of scrapping the whole book. Until those words echoed again in my head, just as they had the night in my bathroom. That night before I set foot in Muldoon's to fill out that application.

Finish the book! Finish the book! Instantly, a maddening vision of failure boiled up inside me. *Finish the book! Finish the book! Let nothing stop you!*

Right then, I got that feeling again, as if I were split in two. Just as I had that night in front of the mirror. In that moment of frozen time, a new me had emerged, filled with determination to complete the task and prove Lola wrong. In that moment, ignorance was bliss.

Talking to Frank, my mind just blanked itself to the event. I forced myself to forget his fallacy, instead believing every word he spoke. For the sake of my book's completion, I believed fully in everything he conveyed. I did it so the audience would do the same from page to page! Because how could I sell a book about a womanizing, self-indulgent supermarket employee if . . . he wasn't one?

If I didn't believe it, my audience wouldn't.

91

And just like that, the cupcake tattoo was real, both in my mind and in my book. The cupcake was there and all doubt about Frank's stories was thrown from my mind, and . . . I was inspired again! The writer's block was gone and I could feel all the things I had to write about coming to me!

"Yo, help me fuck Rachel, man!" Frank said into the phone.

"What?" I replied, feeling energized. Feeling the best I had in weeks.

"Go tell her ya boy Frank likes her. We've never formally met, so it will be awesome. Like some seventh-grade shit," he said.

"Okay, sure, man. Let's discuss it at the store."

Frank agreed and I hung up. After the phone call I jumped into bed feeling rejuvenated.

The first thing that came to mind was Mia. I couldn't help but think of Mia and how beautiful she was. How I missed her. How I wanted to kiss her again. I hadn't seen her in the few days I took to myself, so I was very much so looking forward to seeing her. I thought to myself, *I should take her on a date.*

Tomorrow was the last day I had off before I headed back to work.

With that thought in mind, I fell asleep.

I woke up feeling great. I asked Mia to meet me at this Putt-Putt golf spot at seven that evening for a much-needed date. But I had the whole day until then to do whatever the hell I wanted.

I grabbed Bennett's red collar from the top of the dresser and took him on our morning walk. I never left it on him when we were home, figuring it was uncomfortable for him. On my way out, I saw Mrs. Huffle in the stairwell. Like always, she was very sweet and asked how my dog was doing, as if he weren't right there in front of her. She was kinda batty, really.

Like always, people gave me and Bennett super-strange looks on our walk.

I never understood why. I mean, he wasn't exactly the cutest dog, I guess that was it. Man, people can be so superficial.

We walked around, ending up at this park by my house on Bleeker Street, then we played fetch with the red rubber ball—the same one I bounced thinking of ideas to write. It was nice to just chill with Bennett. I don't know why, but whenever we hung out I got the same feeling I did when I hung around Frank—I was definitely entertained, I'll tell you that.

Later in the afternoon, back at my house, I decided to clean up the place. It was pretty messy, and who knew? Maybe Mia would end up coming back later that night if I was lucky.

I had a few framed pictures I had collected in the time I had been living in the apartment, along with busts and other collectables, but I'd never found the time to properly decorate the place. Down the street was this awesome store called Blast from the Past. They had all sorts of amazing memorabilia, T-shirts, and busts—anything collectable. But the thing they had that was super awesome was their poster selection. I had befriended a guy who worked there named Duncan. He was British and seemed to be of mixed race. He was definitely black, but very light-skinned. Super nerdy, but he had a cool vibe about him. I always wondered what the hell he was doing in the States, working at a place like that, but I never asked. I did, however, know he really enjoyed it.

Every time I went there he was pretty stoned. We would talk *Star Wars* and other fun sci-fi shit. Anyway, it was definitely my favorite place to waste my time. That and Fisher's Vinyl Village.

I absolutely love music and vinyl. I mean, even now as I'm writing and you're reading, there's a record spinning next to me. Today's twelve-inch of choice is an album called *Salad Days* by Mac DeMarco. He's one of my all-time favorites.

Anyway, I spent the next few hours hanging up posters of all my favorite stuff. *Futurama*, *Star Wars*, anything Seth MacFarlane—especially *The Orville*. I had quite the collection. *Guardians of the Galaxy, Indiana Jones, Blade Runner, Back to the Future*—all that shit. I actually had a blast turning my bland writing room into an author's sanctuary. When I finished I looked at my watch and did a double take. It was 6:25 p.m.

I had to run or I was gonna be late for our date. I gave Bennett a loving pat on the head and was out the door. My entire way there I was beaming. I couldn't wait to see her.

By the time I got there, the sun was almost down. There was a beautiful vanilla sky, like God himself had painted it just for us. Cheesy, I know, but I must admit the vanilla sky is my favorite sky. Full of pinks and creams. It really is quite the sight. No wonder Monet created a masterpiece from it.

I was pretty out of breath when I showed up. Mia was

sitting on a bench under the huge Putt-Putt sign, which was lit up: *Bobby's Mini Golf.*

She looked amazing. She was wearing a sexy black slip dress and Dr. Martens boots.

"Hey there, cowboy," she said with that perfect smile, her lips a dark red color. Swear to God, she spent all her money on Fenty Beauty and Kylie Cosmetics.

"Hey there, Jessie," I said, gesturing Wild West pistols with my fingers.

"Who the hell is Jessie?" She spit. "Some other bitch you fuckin' on the side?"

"No, no!" I said, panicking. "I mean Jessie from *Toy Story*, you know? 'Cuz Woody, he meets Jessie when—"

"I'm totally fucking with you, Flynn! Haha, Jesus, man."

Of course she is, I thought to myself. That's why she was so awesome, Mia. Because of shit like that.

"Oh, haha. Yeah, totally. Anyway . . . ready to get beat?" I extended my hand and we made our way inside.

We had a blast. Though, to be completely honest, she kinda sorta severely kicked my ass. I had to get a new ball twice because I kept knocking it into the water traps. The windmills really fucked me up too. But Mia just laughed at me and gave me shit for it. On the second-to-last hole, she was setting up to putt, and as smooth as ice, I stepped behind her, grabbed her golf club, putting my hands over hers, and hugged her from behind. I nearly cracked up because the move was so cheesy, but I went through with it.

"Need some help with your game?" I asked, trying to be smooth. She smelled amazing.

"Oh, wait a minute," she said. "Um, I may be mistaken,

but . . . wasn't it *I* who was kicking *your* ass?" She giggled and gave me a big smile, leaving me weak. "You know," she said, "if I wanted to, I could totally kick your ass from this position."

"Uuuhhh, haha . . . what?" I said, tightening my grip on her body just slightly.

"Well, my self-defense teacher—"

"You take a self-defense class?" I asked, intrigued.

"Well, yeah. How else am I supposed to fight off all the hot guys constantly coming on to me?"

"Uh . . ."

"I'm joking, Flynn! Jeez."

"Oh, right. Yeah, totally."

"You're such a nerd," she said, chuckling. "It's true. My defense teacher showed me how to fuck somebody up when they are constraining you from behind."

"Okay, I'm curious. What do you do?"

"Okay, so hold me tight," she said, grabbing my hands. The golf club fell to the ground. She placed my hands around her toned stomach. "Tighter, lover boy . . . not scared, are you?" she said, then giggled again. Her ass was at my waist.

Shit, I thought to myself. *She's so amazing.*

"I'll show you scared," I joked. With my left hand still holding her stomach, I brought my right hand to her throat in a playful, pretend choke.

"Oh, now you're talking, Daddy." Whoa, damn. I'd never had a girl talk to me like this. Certainly not on a Putt-Putt course.

"Jeez, girl . . . you're kind of a freak, huh?"

"Maybe just a little one," she said, gripping my hand around her neck. "Punish me, Daddy, I've been bad."

"Uuhhmmm . . . ," I mumbled, not sure what to say.

"Now," she continued. "Mug me."

"What? What do you mean?" I asked.

"I don't know, man. Pretend you're mugging me . . . what would you say?"

"Hey, bitch!"

"Haha, nice." She laughed. "Keep going!"

"Gimme all your fuckin' money!!"

"CRUNCH TIME!" Mia screamed as loud as she could. She raised her knee high into her chest and slammed the heel of her boot on my right foot, shooting pain to the receptors in my brain . . . along with any blood that might previously have been in my penis.

"Oh, what the FUCK!" I half yelled and half laughed. The pain wasn't excruciating, but it fucking hurt, that's for sure.

"Oh, sorry! Haha, I tried not to do it too hard. Must be muscle memory."

"What the hell, Mia?" I said, laughing despite the pain.

"Well, in the class we used realistic dummy legs connected to feet with this bone-like material. That move, if done correctly, and with all the force necessary to flee the situation, would have broken all the toes in your foot."

"Wait," I said suddenly. "Why the hell did you scream CRUNCH TIME?!"

"Oh, I don't know. The instructor told us to give a war cry whenever we do it. That it would give us more power."

"And . . . *'crunch time'* came out?" I laughed. "I mean,

97

what about *'HI-YAH'* or some other karate-kid shit? Crunch time sounds like you're doing a real-life Cap'n Crunch commercial."

"Haha . . . a *what*?" she asked, moving closer to me.

"A Cap'n Crunch commercial," I said, giving her a puzzled look. "You know Cap'n Crunch, right?"

"What the hell is Captain Crunch?"

"WHAT'S CAP'N CRUNCH?!" I couldn't fucking believe it. "Mia, you work in a supermarket!"

"What are you talking about, Flynn? I've never heard of Captain Crunch."

"It's *Cap'n*, not Captain, Mia. Let's get it right. And it's a cereal. One of the finest ever engineered. How the hell have you never heard of Cap'n Crunch? What planet are you from? I mean, what cereal did you eat growing up?"

"One question at a time, damn," she said, laughing. "I was poor, remember? All I ever knew was the off-brand cereals."

"You're kidding me." I chuckled.

"I mean, I've had Sergeant Smash."

"Sergeant Smash? What kinda shit is that?" I laughed.

"Hey, asshole!" she said, punching me in the arm. "It was pretty good, actually. Better than this Captain Crunch guy, I bet."

"Cap'n, Mia . . . Look, I know we were supposed to get pizza after this, but honestly . . . I say we go pick up some Cap'n Crunch and head to my place for a taste test!"

"Whoa there, cowboy," she said. "First real date and you're already trying to get me to your place?"

"Huh, no. I, well. I didn't mean it like tha—" And of course she started laughing at me and my babbling.

"I'm just pulling your leg, Flynnagin."

"Soooooo, taste test?" I asked.

"I'm so down," she said, giving that amazing giggle once more. "Let's go!"

On our way back to my spot we stopped by Muldoon's to get a cereal medley. Had to put that employee discount to work. All 15 percent of it. We cruised down the cereal aisle, surveying the scene. Each box loudly vied for our attention. Screamed at us, really. Little cartoon characters popped out, threatening us with their sugar-fueled enthusiasm. Lucky Charms, Rice Krispies, Frosted Flakes, Trix, Cocoa Puffs. Poor Sonny the Cuckoo Bird looked like he had just mainlined a speedball.

"I'm telling you, Flynn, the generics are just as good, and half the—"

"I don't want to hear it, Mia. It's time to ball out. Only name brands today. This is the pure shit. Top-shelf cereal shopping. I'm about to show you a whole new world." And there it was, near the end of the aisle. Captain Horatio Magellan Crunch. Casting his watchful eye over a chaotic sea of competitors. A steady hand among the cereal mascot miscreants. He was always there for me in the mornings. Through good times and bad. It brought me joy to show Mia the wonders of the cereal aisle. The intercom interrupted.

"Attention, Muldoon's shoppers, we will be closing in ten minutes. Please select your items and make your way to check out. Thank you for shopping at Muldoon's, and have a good night."

We grabbed our selections and headed to check out.

Mia got distracted as we passed through the produce

section. She brought it to my attention that she was obsessed with pomegranates. The deseeding was rewarding to her. And the pop of the seeds was "exhilarating." She shuffled the pomegranates, disrupting the precarious pomegranate pyramid. A few fell to the ground. I bent down to pick them up, and as I stood up my heart stopped.

It was Lola, pushing a cart our way. FUCK. I panicked. I hadn't seen Lola since the diner, and I wasn't trying to see her now.

"Mia, let's get out of here, the store's about to close," I said.

"Chill, Flynn, we work here, and I need to find the perfect pomegranate," she said.

"Mia, let's go, I'm hungry," I said, pulling her forward with my arm.

"Flynn, Jesus, okay."

I rushed us to the express lane, ten items or fewer, hoping to get the hell out of there before running into Lola. I grabbed a copy of *People*. Brad and Angelina were going to trial over custody. Kanye was doing some Kanye shit. Bieber and Baldwin seemed built to last. I loved *People*. I emptied my basket of cereal onto the conveyor belt and tossed the magazine on top of the pile.

"Flynn?"

I stared dead ahead, petrified by the voice coming from behind.

"Flynn, is that you?"

I turned around.

"Lola . . . heey . . . hi," I said, my voice shaking.

"What's up? How've you been?" she said.

"I'm great, everything good with you?" I said.

"Yeah, I'm moving to Portland in a couple of months," she replied.

"That's great."

I didn't know what to say. I was feeling twisted, confronted by an intense array of emotions, unable to process any of them. Anxiety. Fear. Attraction. Resentment. Happiness. Sadness. Anger. She was gorgeous. But she was cast in a new light. She was no longer mine. I missed her. But I was trying to move on. Mia pressed my elbow with hers, acknowledging the awkwardness of the situation.

"You sure got a lot of cereal there . . . is that for dinner?" Lola said with one eyebrow raised.

"Umm, yeah . . . no . . . ," I said.

"Hi, I'm Lola, who are you?" she asked, turning to Mia.

"I'm Mia."

"This a new girlfriend, Flynn?" Lola said.

"Um, don't worry about it," I said. FUCK. What the hell was I supposed to do?

"I see . . . what's new?" Lola asked. "How's the novel coming?"

I panicked. I hadn't even told Mia about my novel.

"Novel?" Mia said.

"It's going," I said as the cashier told me my total.

"Eighteen ninety-five with your discount, Flynn."

"Discount? You work here, Flynn?" Lola said, now with both her eyebrows raised.

"Umm, yeah. It's for my . . ."

Mia handed the cashier a twenty, pulling me by my waist.

"Lola, nice to meet to meet you, we're running late and are in a bit of a hurry," Mia said, pulling me away.

"Umm, okay. Good luck with all that, Flynn," Lola replied.

I grabbed our groceries. The white plastic met my sweaty hands. My vision became speckled with spots of white light. My chest tightened.

"Flynn, we'll talk in the car," Mia said on our way out of the store.

We pulled out of the parking lot. I didn't know what to say.

"I'm sorry that had to go down like that, Mia."

"Flynn, it's fine, it happens. Exes keep living lives. Run-ins happen. You just . . . you've never said anything about a novel."

"Mia, you're amazing. Thank you for understanding. I was caught off guard by the whole thing. Look . . . at one point I was fooling around with some writing. It was just a juvenile hobby. There's nothing more to it than that," I said.

"That's cute . . . I didn't know you were creative in that way. I want to read some," Mia said.

"Oooh, no," I said. "That stuff is long gone, buried deep in a landfill somewhere. It's for the best . . ."

"Well, you should keep writing," Mia said. "I think it'd be good for you. Could be a sort of therapy."

"I'll think about it," I said.

The drive home was strange. That was a roller coaster. It was crazy how sweet and understanding she was about the whole thing. How she saved me from the nightmare situation. That was grace under fire. We sat in silence for the rest of the drive, windows down, with the radio faintly playing in the back.

We got back to my place, and I had, like, five different kinds of Cap'n Crunch set up for her to try. My record player was spinning "Someday" by the Strokes. Bennett was being shy, I guess. He stayed in my room the whole time, avoiding us.

On the table I had the original Cap'n Crunch. I had the one with Crunch Berries. CoZmic Crunch, Cinnamon Crunch, Chocolatey Crunch, and my personal favorite, Peanut Butter Crunch. She tried them all and fell in love! She was an instant convert. We had a blast, staying up for hours talking about life and the future and everything each of us wanted.

Turns out, we both wanted kids. We both believed in a higher power of some sort, but weren't super religious about it, though neither of us judged others who had those beliefs. We went deep about our shaky childhoods, about growing up with low resources, about our fucked-up dads. About feeling directionless but ambitious at the same time. We both appreciated what we had in life but wanted so much more. She dreamed of passing the bar and joining a firm in New York City. I wanted to tell her about my New York experience, but I held back. I couldn't let her know I had a book deal. Maybe I would tell her after it was actually finished. Surprise her.

After an amazing night, I walked her home. We held hands the entire way. It was a bit chilly out, so I gave her my bomber jacket to wear on the way. Once we arrived at the bottom of the stairs that led to her front door, I grabbed her other hand and pulled her close.

"Thanks for an amazing night, Mia."

"Are you kidding me? Thank you, Flynn! I can't remember the last time I had this much fun with a close friend."

"Close friend?" I said, trying not to stutter. "Close . . . but—but I thought we—"

"I'm just fucking with you! Come here," she said, then she leaned in and kissed me.

It was amazing, even better than our first kiss. Because this time I was completely present and in the moment. I wasn't thinking about anything—not Frank and how he wanted me to set him up with Rachel, not walking in on Cara, not dumb-ass Kurtis, not my anxiety, not my panic, or the derealization or the pressure I had been putting on myself to finish the book. And especially not Lola.

All I thought about in that moment, all I cared for . . . was Mia. I pulled her closer. Her chest pressed into mine. She bit my lip. I gently pulled her hair back and moved my hand to the small of her back. She leaned against her door and raised her leg to my waist, her dress falling back to reveal the length of her thigh. I looked down to see the edge of her black lace underwear. I gently put my weight into her as she thrust her waist forward. Her tongue entered my mouth.

She pulled back from the kiss.

"Damn, Daddy," she said with a smirk.

I looked at her, flushed. "I wanna buy combat boots with you."

"What? Why?"

"Because I wanna kick the world's ass together!"

"It's a deal," she said, shaking my hand.

We parted ways and I went home to get some sleep.

The next day at Muldoon's, things were as dull as they had been since I'd started. It had been about a month now. What a brutal comedown after last night. The same old, balding, white-haired, frail customer holding that cup of coffee over his nose, inhaling, and saying, "Coffee coffee coffee coffee," then repeating it over and over and over again. By now, I'd just named him Coffee Joe, or Joe for short.

I saw Ann, who worked in the pharmacy, and just like always she insisted on making me take multivitamins in the morning. Like every other day, she would go out of her way to find me at pretty much the same exact time, then force them upon me with a smile. Of course, there was lovable Ronda, who worked in the front customer service area; DayDay, who had been working on replacing a fluorescent light near produce; and Kurtis, the green-haired deli dick who seemed to hate everyone. Lately, he'd been claiming someone had stolen his silver Zippo lighter from his locker.

As he passed me, he insisted that I had been the culprit.

There was Ted Daniels, still greeting customers with his yellow teeth protruding from his smile. Then there were Hector and Vernon, who would be coming for pickup that very day. It felt like Groundhog Day around here. Same shit, different day.

"Yo, come here, dude!"

And then there was Frank, of course. Standing by aisle nine.

When I caught up to him, he was grinning.

"Dude, Rachel is in the break room right now! I need you to do this for me."

"I mean, look, I'll do what I can," I told him. "But being the ladies' man you are, why don't you just ask her yourself?"

Just then, the lights on this side of the store went extremely dim.

"Whoa, what the fuck?!" I said.

"Goddamn lights again, man. This place is falling apart," said Frank with a smirk.

"DayDay to the electrical box, DayDay, your assistance is needed at the electrical box," came a voice from the intercom. A disgruntled DayDay headed in that direction.

"Dumb-ass white people," he muttered as he went. "Don't wanna spend the proper money on shit, so a nigga gotta go get the ladder and climb his ass up the top of that shit and fix the lights. Always calling DayDay, and DayDay gotta be all 'yes, massa, be right there, massa.' I oughtta kill these white niggas."

"Make sure you videotape it for me, baby!" Ronda shouted to him. It seemed like she was kidding, but then again, I never really knew.

"See, man, this is why there's a gun in my locker. You never know what a crazy person is capable of. Shit, he might try to shoot my ass right here in aisle nine," Frank said, half joking.

"What the hell is wrong with you, man?"

"You know what's wrong with me? I need to get laid! Now go ask Rachel for me, okay?!"

"I don't understand why you just won't ask her yourself, Frank. Damn!" I told him, a bit pissed off.

"Bro, we've been through this. I'm trying to take a different approach. Rachel is a smart-ass and I'm trying to bypass that side of her, y'know. Play a little hard to get. Tug at those heart strings, fam!" Frank paused and gave me a look that said *do you feel me?*

There was silence for a moment.

"I just don't understand why you play these games with women. I mean, Rachel isn't exactly a nun. I'm sure if you went up to her and were honest and clear about what you wanted, it would work out. Tell her you want a good time, no strings attached . . . especially heart strings! Be straight up. I think she would be about it, man."

Frank snagged a banana from produce and began to peel it. "Bro, you're thinking way too much into this. Just do me this solid and go tell her your friend Frank likes her, okay?"

I was tired of trying to reason with Frank. He wasn't a reasonable dude. I decided just to get this shit over with and move on with my day. With that, I was on my way.

I reached the break room, and sure enough Rachel was there. Only this time, she was not accompanied by Becca. She was completely alone.

"Hey," I said to her.

"Hey . . . Flynn," she said in a tone that said she didn't give two shits about engaging in a conversation with me. She was reading *Cosmopolitan*, her lips red as ever and hair darker than Frank's sense of humor.

"Look, a buddy of mine wanted me to tell you he likes you."

Her face was hidden by the magazine. *26 SEX TIPS THAT WILL BRING HIM TO THE EDGE* was printed in bold on the corner of the cover.

She lowered the magazine, revealing dark eyes beneath her bangs.

"Oh, you have a friend, huh?" she said as she set the magazine down. Her mouth curled into a smile. She stood up and walked over to me. She was close, almost too close. Even in her dorky store uniform she looked fine as hell.

"Yeah, my buddy. His name is Frank." She stared at me, puzzled.

"Oh . . . okay," she said, seeming a little let down.

"Yeah, he works in the store," I said.

"Do you guys spend a lot of time together?" she asked.

"Oh, yeah. Well, at work, anyway."

"So this Frank . . . how old is he?"

I thought for a moment. "About my age," I said, grabbing a paper cup on top of the water cooler. "Look, either way, he wanted me to tell you that he's into you and you guys should hang out sometime. Maybe grab a bite."

Rachel bit her lip.

"Fuck it . . . why not?" she said. She ripped part of a page from her magazine and scribbled down her number. She put her hand on my elbow, and looked up at my face, surveying my features.

"You have pretty eyes, Flynn. You look like a tortured artist," she said.

"Uhmm, thank you?" I said.

"Tell him to call me," she said, handing me the scrap of paper.

Then she walked out of the room.

I looked at the number and put it in my right pocket. I couldn't help but feel a bit annoyed that I just did Frank's job for him. But I was also a little turned on by the whole encounter. Just then, Mia walked into the break room.

"There's my boy," she said with a smile.

"Hey!" I said, feeling guilty for having another woman's number in my pocket, even though it was for Frank. *How will I explain this to her if she finds out?* I thought. Anything I said would sound like total bullshit.

"What were you and Rachel talking about?" she asked.

"What? Who?" I said. She looked at me suspiciously.

"Rachel the cashier. She just left the room smiling. What were you two talking about?" Oh, shit, I thought to myself. When she walked in the room it was all peaches, except for me acting as though nothing had just happened between Rachel and me. My posturing had unintended consequences. Now Mia was thinking something was in fact happening. Maybe I should just tell her about the whole thing.

What are you, fucking stupid? Frank's voice said in my head, like some funny angel and devil scenario. *She's gonna call bullshit immediately!*

The voice was right, but I didn't want to lie to her.

"Flynn!" Mia said, a confused smile on her face.

"Sorry, baby . . . I was literally here daydreaming. Now that I think about it, Rachel was trying to say hello or something, but I didn't even notice. She must have been laughing it off on her way out."

Mia looked at me, and I felt horrible for lying. But it wasn't like I did anything wrong.

And just like that, she let it go.

"Listen, I had such a blast with you last night!" she said. "I was thinking, maybe round two tonight?"

I knew I should work on my book. But at the same time, so much had been going on that I felt I deserved another night to myself.

"Okay! That sounds like fun."

"It's settled, then. I'll see you soon!" she said, departing with a kiss to my cheek.

CHAPTER 8

DISAPPEARING DOG

It had been a crazy few days. My anxiety had been ebbing and flowing. I was falling hard for Mia, and trying to embrace that beautiful feeling. But I wasn't getting anywhere with my novel. I still couldn't figure out how to end the book with a bang, which was nagging at me. It's always something. Frank was being Frank. A burden, a friend. I couldn't quite tell which. The Lola run-in fucked me up, but Mia saved the day and kept me from unraveling into what would have surely been a full-blown panic attack, or worse yet, a spell of derealization.

Things at Muldoon's were fine. I finally felt like I had my bearings straight. I'd spent enough time in each department to have the lay of the land. I wasn't making as many mistakes. Today I was in the refrigerated section, taking care of inventory. Shit was cold in there. I was rocking earmuffs, a scarf, and gloves. It was the section behind the glass when you reach in for your fancy-ass almond milk. Or oat milk. Or cashew milk. Or hemp milk. There were more foo-foo milks these days than I could count. What happened to the classic cow shit?

I ran into Frank while restocking. I told him everything. The conversation between me and Rachel, and even Mia walking in and how it must have looked. "People see what they want to see, man. You should know that better than anyone else," Frank said.

"What do you mean by that?" I asked, wrinkling my face.

"I mean Mia's insecurity was giving her a suspicion that something was going on, so she prodded. Then she let it go because, regardless of what was happening before she walked in that room, she has no reason not to trust you. It's perfect." Frank smiled.

"Wait . . . why is it perfect?" I asked, confused.

"Because you got Rachel's number, man! Now let me see it!" he said, eager to hold it in his hands. I reached in my left pocket, pulled out the torn magazine page with the number on it, and handed it off for him to do with as he pleased.

"I'm gonna call her tonight. Meet me on the roof in five for a smoke."

And Frank was off. I grabbed an AriZona iced tea and headed up to meet him.

On the roof I looked out over the other side, opposite where there was the loading dock and endless trees. On this side, I faced the dreary parking lot and the rest of our shopping center—the record store, the bank, the dry cleaners, and, of course, the diner where Lola had left me.

Reminded of Lola, I took out my wallet and stared at the picture of us. I felt bad. I was into Mia, and keeping a picture of my ex in my wallet? That just couldn't be healthy.

But I couldn't bear to let it go quite yet. I don't know why. I just didn't feel ready. As I contemplated it, I could hear the flick of Frank's Zippo.

"Beautiful day," he said.

I turned around to him sparking his cigarette.

"Even in this shitty little town, we still get some breathtaking views," he said.

Now that I thought about it, it was beautiful. It had been raining for weeks and I hadn't realized the sun was finally out. But then again, with all the shit on my plate, finishing a novel, and trying to forget the pink balloon that was derealization, it was hard to notice what was going on right in front of me sometimes.

As Frank snapped the lighter shut, I realized something.

"Hey, hasn't Kurtis been looking for his lighter?" I asked, and Frank smiled.

"Yeah, I guess so, huh?"

"You swiped it?"

"Yeah, fuck that guy!" Frank said.

"Frank, you aren't that evil. What if it's important to him?"

"Fuck Kurtis and fuck everybody else who works in this godforsaken hellhole. I'm corrupt, Flynn, just face it. You know it's true." He smiled. "Somebody's gotta be the evil villain. But deep, deep down, I'd like to think there's a good man in there somewhere . . . he's an elderly black man named Billy, hahaha."

"Oh, come on, Frank. You should really give it back. It may be more significant to him than you know, I mean, even if he is an asshole."

Frank smirked and lit another cigarette.

"What greater meaning could that asshole's lighter have when it's engraved with the words *Vanilla Sky*? He either loves Paul McCartney or is gay for Tom Cruise." He gave a heavy laugh.

When Frank and I talked like this, it really felt like the conscious and subconscious were battling, the angel and devil on the shoulder. I suppose that was just Frank, though. He was the guy who said all the shit most people only thought about. That was part of why I loved him, and hated him. Maybe he filled out a part of me I wish I had more of. The irreverent, unabashed anti-authoritarian. It's funny how you can have so many perspectives inside one person. How you can feel like one person one day and another person a different day. But Frank was also an annoying asshole who treated women with little respect and stole from his employer. I'm no Goody Two-shoes but I have a conscience.

Once again, I pulled out my notebook to take note of all this, and it occurred to me why he was perfect for my book: Frank was a guy who just didn't give a fuck. Or, at least, didn't give a fuck about what other people thought—their rules and regulations. That's what most people wanted. He was saying "fuck morality." He was an antihero of sorts.

Frank kept talking, going on with his graduate-seminar-in-philosophy ramblings. Talking about the beauty behind the madness, saying that without destruction, blood, and pain, life just wasn't any fun. He was a nihilist, he claimed. The world was without meaning. He was a hedonist, he said. A pure pleasure seeker, and he didn't care about the moral rules broken to get it. He didn't seem to ever show a crack in the façade, a vulnerable side, a weakness. That made me suspicious.

"How can you appreciate the things you have if you've never experienced loss?" he said.

It was this kind of reasoning that made me understand the thought process behind taking the lighter from Kurtis—if Kurtis didn't mourn over the lost artifact, he wouldn't appreciate the next one that came his way.

At the same time, I told Frank that maybe Kurtis *already* experienced mourning over an item or person he had lost in life. Maybe that's why he was so bitter and seemed to hate everything, and maybe because of that it was the lighter that he appreciated more than anything. This inanimate object with more meaning to it than Frank or I could even begin to comprehend.

"Yeah," Frank said. "Or maybe it's just a fucking lighter." He laughed, but I didn't. Sure, I thought Kurtis was a clown, but I wasn't going to take his shit from him.

"Why do you even care about that dude, man? You know he wants to fuck your little girlfriend!"

I turned quickly to him. "Wait, what do you mean?"

"Well, why do you think he hates you so much? Always giving you mean looks, dude? He's had a crush on Mia forever, man."

I just stared at him.

"Look, man," I finally said. "Regardless of any of that, the lighter isn't yours."

"All right, all right, I'll put it back in his locker," Frank said.

I smiled as Frank took a drag. He exhaled a full plume, clouding the length of his body.

"Check it," he said, taking his hand out of his pocket.

"Jesus, Frank," I said.

A stack of hundreds sat in his hand.

"5K right here. I've been taking bills from Muldoon's since day one and they ain't said shit. They're obviously not feeling the hit, or else I'd be hearing about it. And they pay us garbage. We need it more than they do. I'm barely making rent over here," he said.

He pointed to two figures on the ground below. They were leaving the store and approaching an armored truck. It was Vernon and Gary with their deposit bags.

"You know I could rob this place blind?" he said, eyes squinting to evade the sun. "I've been here long enough."

"Bro, you've *been* robbing this place blind," I said.

"Like, I'm not talking petty cash from the register. I'm talking the whole shebang," he said. "I know how to get in that safe and I know how to erase the security footage so they would never know. I wouldn't have to worry about fingerprints either. I don't have any. I'd take the money and dip to Canada. Shit's easy living up there and they'd never find me."

I pulled out a toothpick from the box in my pocket and placed it in the left corner of my mouth.

"What do you mean, you don't have any fingerprints?" I asked.

Frank smiled.

"Our fingerprints are all over the store. They wouldn't

be able to prove it was us even if they suspected it. Trying to use that to convict us would be pointless in a place like this."

"What do you mean *us*?" I said, adjusting the toothpick with my tongue. "This isn't *Butch Cassidy and the Sundance Kid.*"

"I'm speaking figuratively, obviously. Not *us*, dude," he said, motioning his hands between him and me. "It only needs to be one person."

And like a ton of bricks, it hit me! That eureka moment I had been waiting for! The climactic moment in *Muldoon's* . . . would be a store robbery. And Frank would be the culprit! It was perfect. Frank actually was a petty thief. He talked big shit about robbing the store blind—but I didn't actually believe he would do it. That's twenty years in prison. But my fictionalized Frank . . . the exaggerated Frank . . . he actually would. What a brilliant way to peak my novel.

Frank flicked his cigarette off the roof.

"Let's head in, I'm getting cold," he said.

We climbed down the fire escape, onto the loading dock, and past Kurtis, who was also outside smoking, looking as disenfranchised as ever. He just wouldn't quit. Maybe Mia really was the reason Kurtis seemed pissed off all the time. Maybe he was only angry around me because he could sense our chemistry. But the last thing I was worried about was Monster Energy Kurtis stealing my girl. Dude probably went to pickup artist classes. If we were taking bets on who would shoot up Muldoon's, my money was on Kurtis.

That AriZona went right through me and I needed to

piss like a racehorse. I told Frank to wait outside the bathroom. After the much-needed release, I walked to the sink to wash my hands. I stared into the mirror. Tortured artist? I wasn't seeing it . . . I did have some dark circles under my eyes, though. Maybe I needed some sleep. I splashed my face with water and smiled into the mirror. "You're going to finish your book! You're going to finish your book! It's time!" I kept saying it, almost as if I couldn't believe it myself. Couldn't believe the content I had ready to put on paper.

As I walked out of the bathroom, I immediately noticed Frank had left. I headed off to look for him just as Kurtis walked back in from smoking.

"Hey, have you seen Frank?" I asked him.

"No, fuck off," he said seriously.

Shrugging him off, I continued on my way past the aisles near the back of the store. I was excited to get off at six o'clock, which was not far away. I looked down the aisles for Frank only to spot Rachel's friend Becca. I gave a wave. She returned the gesture, smiling sweetly, and continued on her way. As I arrived at the end of the aisle, I realized I was in the bakery. I looked behind the counter and saw Mia. She was so beautiful in her white apron, her hair tied up in a ponytail.

"Oh, hey, Flynn!" she said with a beaming smile. "Couldn't wait until later to see me, huh?"

"Can't wait!" I said. "Hey, have you seen Frank around here by chance?"

"Nope, haven't seen him. When are the three of us gonna hang out, by the way? I spend all my time in the bakery, so I don't get to know anyone else who works here. It would be nice to meet your friend you always talk about."

The truth was I hadn't formally introduced Mia to Frank because he had no manners. It was guaranteed he would offend, outrage, or disgust her. I also couldn't admit to her that I was writing a book, not just yet. And the book was the only reason I was continually and willingly subjecting myself to Frank's presence. It was all to get this novel finished. I needed this bullshit artist to keep the inspiration going for my main character. But even deeper still, there was the fact that I was actually growing to enjoy Frank's energy, his outlook. It was infectious. It made *you* not give two fucks what others around you thought. I was so wrapped up in my own head and my own creative pursuits that his whole vibe was liberating. To live free and think what you want, say what you want!

I turned to Mia with an excuse about not introducing her to Frank.

"I just like to keep work and love separate," I said.

"Flynn, are you saying you love me?" she said, blushing.

"Oh, NO! No, I meant 'life,' not 'love' . . . I'm not saying—" I stopped myself, not wanting to insult her further. "I mean, not that I won't, or couldn't, I just, well . . ."

Mia let out another laugh. "Flynn, I'm just fucking with you! I mean, I really like you, but falling in love in just a few weeks isn't exactly realistic. Especially considering we haven't spent enough time together to do so."

I felt relieved. Though, honestly, I knew I was falling for her. I was just glad she was so levelheaded. The great thing about Mia was that she never played games; she was always honest about how she felt.

"Oh . . . haha, got it! Well, thanks anyway . . . I'll see you tonight at—"

"Floater!" interrupted a voice. It was painted thickly with a Russian accent. "Floater, what are you doing here now?"

It was the Soul Destroyer, Bianca, come to wreak havoc on my moment with Mia.

"Oh, hey, Bianca. I was just—"

"Leaving? Just leaving, yes?!"

My eyes widened and Mia's rolled.

"By the way, my name is Flynn," I said. "See you tonight," I said to Mia, smiling and giving her arm a little squeeze.

With fifteen minutes left before work let out, Ted asked me to clean up some spilled coffee by aisle twelve. I grabbed a broom from the maintenance room and headed over, but just as I began to mop the floor, I looked over and saw Cara headed in my direction. She was holding packs of sugar and creamer, but at the sight of me, they slipped out of her arms.

I immediately dropped the mop and rushed over to help her.

"It's okay, you don't have to," she said in a hurried voice.

"Cara . . . Cara, seriously . . . let me help. It's okay," I told her. She allowed me to help, though she seemed a bit tense.

"I'm sorry, Flynn," she said. "I just—"

"You shouldn't be apologizing at all," I interrupted. "Look, I'm really sorry about what happened last week," I explained, trying to sound as honest as possible. "I didn't mean to walk in on you, there was just so much going on and . . . I didn't realize what you were doing, you know?"

"I know, Flynn . . . I didn't mean to scream at you either . . ." Cara looked down at her boots like an embarrassed child.

"Friends?" she said. She looked up and stuck out her hand.

"Friends!" I said with a smile. We shook, then we both stood up, and I helped her bring the fallen packets to the counter.

After I finished cleaning up the spilled coffee, I returned to the maintenance room to deposit the mop. Frank was there in the dark room, next to a mop bucket, throwing a banana peel into the garbage can.

"Whoa, uh . . . hey, Frank."

"What's up, floater?"

"Hey, I forgot to ask, how did it go with Rachel?" I said.

"Oh, man, I called her and told her to meet me for dinner on Thursday and she was super into it." He smiled. "I'm fucking her then, I bet."

"Sure, okay, whatever, dude," I said. "Hey, Frank, I was wondering if you would tell me more about . . . how you would rob the store."

"Why?" he suspiciously asked.

"Oh, I'm just curious. Your imagination is wild, dude," I added with a laugh, trying to seem like I was only interested for fun. Frank paused and then began spilling out words.

"Well, the .357 Magnum Smith and Wesson in my locker would be a go-to for the job, I mean, with—"

"WHAT?!" I said. "You really *do* have a gun in your locker?! What's wrong with you?"

"The question isn't what's wrong with me, my dear

Flynn, it's what's wrong with the sick fuck who walks in here with a tool forged for death and a taste for revenge. I don't know if you've realized, but this world is fucked up, man! And if we're at work and some fucking psycho walks through that door, one of us has to be prepared, you know what I'm saying?!"

Again, it was one of those moments where Frank's insane logic somehow kinda made sense. I glanced at the clock. FUCK! It was 5:45, and I was supposed to meet Mia in fifteen minutes. I asked him if we could postpone the tale of how he would rob the store for another time. With that, I went to the break room, clocked out, put my apron in my locker, and headed home.

Once I got home, I realized I had forgotten to feed Bennett in the morning, so I put a cup of dog food in his bowl. I grabbed his blue leash, clamped it to his collar, and took him for a quick walk.

I loved walking Bennett after work because it gave me time to decompress and think about my day and how it related to my novel. I would write notes, sketching out scenes and dialogue. For how boring work was, it was at least serving its purpose of giving me good material for the book.

Bennett stopped to piss. I waited for him to finish his business and tied him to the bench. My nose was in my notebook like never before, jotting down things about Rachel, Frank and our conversation on the roof, the revolver in his locker, and his crackpot notions of robbing the store. While writing, I heard a very familiar voice.

"Hey there, handsome." I looked up, and Mia was a few feet away, heading my direction.

I grinned from ear to ear.

"What are you doing?"

"Oh, I was just walking my—"

I looked down and . . . there was the end of the leash, but no dog. Bennett was gone! My stomach dropped.

"Bennett?! Bennett!" I yelled. "Oh, no, he must have gotten loose from his collar when I wasn't looking!"

"Oh my god, Flynn, I'm sorry!" she said, examining the end of the leash that still had the part that clips on the red collar. It was perfectly intact. "I wonder how he slipped out?"

"I don't know, but let's look for him, quick!"

We spent the next hour searching everywhere. I had wanted a dog my entire life and when I finally got one, we instantly bonded. Bennett was my main companion. He kept me sane. He really was a best friend. And now he was gone! I felt helpless, but there was nothing more to be done, so we decided to head back to my apartment with the hope that he may have returned.

When we reached my front door, any optimism I had vanished. Mia held my hand sweetly as I opened the door, and we made our way up the stairwell and into my apartment. After sliding my key in the hole and twisting the knob, we were in.

"Look, I know this sucks," Mia said. "But I'm sure he will come back soon. And you might not want to hear it, but worrying won't do you any good, baby."

Looking into her beautiful brown eyes, I knew she was right. Just then, she peered over my shoulder to my record collection.

"Oh wow, Destroyer!" she said, moving toward the couch and my records. "I love him. He's so weird and different."

I told her I felt exactly the same way.

"Have you heard *Poison Season*?" I asked.

"Of course!" she responded. "Have you heard *Five Spanish Songs*?"

I smiled and looked down. "Yeah, I mean, I heard it, but . . . I didn't exactly understand it, given the language barrier and all." We both laughed. She was getting excited, saying how *Destroyer's Rubies* was their best record. We were nerding out hard. I'd never found a girl who was on my level with music.

"Do you listen to Tame Impala?" she asked.

"No, never heard of them," I said, shaking my head.

"You're kidding me!! You haven't listened to *Currents*?!?" she yelled.

"Haha, nah, I haven't. Is it any good?"

She stared blankly at me.

"Is it any good? 'Is it ANY GOOD?' HE SAYS! It's amazing, Flynn. A true modern classic! I'll have to grab you a copy from the Vinyl Village."

"Oh, I love that place!" I exclaimed, grabbing a twelve-inch from the middle of the pile. I carefully freed the vinyl from its sleeve and set it on the record player, dropping the needle in the groove. "Have you ever heard this gem?"

The music spilled softly from the speakers. "This one's called 'Yeah Right' from Toro Y Moi's album *What For?*," I said. The lamp in the corner of the room dimly lit the right side of her body as she hugged herself, smiling and swaying side to side, her eyes closed. "Mmmmm," she said as if she had bitten into her grandmother's freshly baked chocolate chip cookies. "I like this one," she whispered.

The sun was setting outside the window, the clouds cascading into another vanilla sky.

This reminded me of the lighter Frank had secretly returned to Kurtis.

"Toro Y Moi, he's really special," I told her. "I love his stuff. I wish I could make music like this . . . hell, music in general," I thought out loud. "That would be just amazing."

She opened her eyes and put her arms around my shoulders, and we began to slow dance as if we were in junior high.

"You can do anything you want," she said.

"Yes, you're right. But I suppose I have other ambitions."

"Other ambitions . . . you mean to tell me you don't want to work in a grocery store forever?" she said with a smile.

"Of course not," I said.

"Why are you there, then?" she continued. "You seem like you don't belong. You seem . . . I don't know . . . destined for something bigger."

I wanted to tell her everything. I wanted to tell her about the book, about Frank, about how I was falling for her. But I felt paralyzed. I felt as though I couldn't say anything.

She laid her head on my chest as we swayed to the song's BPM.

"Whatever you want to do . . . whatever you sense deep down, I know you'll be incredible at it, Flynn!"

The song stopped and the needle picked itself up and idly hovered, waiting for another record. I let the silence fill the room, then grabbed a very special one from the back of my box of records. I dropped the needle.

As the crackle from the rotating disc echoed through my apartment, I grabbed Mia. My right hand on her hip, the other interlocked with hers as we began to sway slowly. Her head rested on my chest. I was scared she would feel my heart beating, racing at the thought of kissing her. Even though at this point I already had several times. Every time with her was like the first time.

"I'll be the one that stays till the end. And I'll be the one who needs you again, and I'll be the one that proposes in a garden of roses. And truly loves you long after our curtain closes," I sang under my breath to the music.

"This is beautiful, Flynn, what is it?" she asked. She went from using my chest as a pillow to resting her chin on it staring up at me, our lips inches apart.

"This one's called 'Happiness,' by Rex Orange County," I told her.

"Mm, it's fitting," she said with that smile I knew all too well.

"And why's that?" I asked.

"Because I'm the happiest I've ever been when I'm with you," she said.

Just as I tried to utter something romantic, she kissed me. And the world stopped. With her there was no derealization, no anxiety, no book, no Frank. Just . . . us.

The rest of the night seemed to consist of her in my arms, perfect music, and laughter. It was a night I'd never forget.

That night I knew I loved her.

CHAPTER 9

CURRENTS

In the following weeks Mia and I grew closer than ever. I even introduced her to my mother. My mom and I hadn't seen a whole lot of each other since I moved out, but not because we didn't want to. Outside of Bennett and Mia, my mom was my rock. Always had been. I told her I needed to engulf myself in work and knock out the book, which she completely understood. I also needed some space and independence after living with her into my twenties. She wasn't the happiest about not seeing me as often . . . but she was happy when I broke the rule one evening by bringing Mia over to meet her.

The two naturally took to each other. And after a long night of endless baby pictures, Mia fell asleep on my mom's couch. That was when my mom told me she had a very special feeling about her and not to "fuck it up," as she put it. Honestly, Mia was my only hope for humanity. She was so sweet.

All in all, things were great, aside from the unfortunate fact that Bennett hadn't returned. I stapled posters around my neighborhood with the only picture of us, the one we took together outside the dog shelter. Staring at the picture of my hand on his head, his tongue sticking out, made me sad. It was so strange that he had just disappeared. Even stranger was the look on people's faces when I showed them the picture. They looked at me like I was some asshole bothering them about nothing. One guy even said, "Are you fucking kidding me, buddy?" How could people be such dicks about a lost dog? I still had hope he'd return. I called the Humane Society and told all my neighbors. Bennett was too smart to just leave like that. He was certainly smarter than Frank.

Back at the store Frank elaborated on his hypothetical scheme to rob it. He said he knew all the entrances and exits to avoid detection. He knew the blind spots, the security codes, and the sequence for the safe. He was pretty cocky about the whole thing. It was great for me because he was giving me the details for the biggest scene in my book.

In the same monologue he told me about his time with Rachel—especially the sex they'd had. I felt a little uncomfortable knowing all this private stuff about Rachel, but I was intrigued, as one naturally is. He said she was a freak who was into roleplaying and restraints. Landlord and tenant, boss and employee. Handcuffs, chokers, whips. Apparently she would throw on a black leather latex catsuit! Real *Fifty Shades of Grey* shit. Frank must have been an all right lover, because every time I saw Rachel she no longer had that permanent resting bitch face. She was all perky and smiling now. I remember the first day Frank told me he had had sex with her. We were walking down aisle seven and, sure enough, there she was, walking in our direction. "Hi, Frank," she said, giving a wink as she passed by. It was pretty weird to see her with this new insider knowledge. I guess I could see it.

It had been three weeks since that amazing night at my place listening to music with Mia. Wait . . . *oh shit*!

How could I have left out the fact we had sex?!

It was amazing. It happened the week after that night. We had another great date and wound up back at my crib. At her request we put on Toro Y Moi. One thing led to another and we were making out heavy on my couch. She took her shirt off and to my surprise wasn't wearing a bra. She was stunning. She had perfect B-cup breasts. It made me feel good that she felt comfortable enough with me to do that. Things were getting hot. I was kissing her neck and she grabbed my hands and pressed them into her breasts. I asked her if I could go down on her and she nodded yes. After several intense minutes of that she told me she wanted me. I asked her if she wanted to have sex and she said yes. She took off her jeans and grabbed my face, kissing me. She arched her waist and straddled me, slowly sitting down. I'll leave it at that, but, shit, it was really incredible. She was so sweet and cute and into it. She told me what she wanted and asked me what I wanted. She satisfied all my needs, and assuming she wasn't lying when I asked, I satisfied hers as well. It was mind-blowing. And that wasn't the last time that night either. Things couldn't have been going any better between us.

And to top all that off, it was like I'd never known what writer's block was. I was in a groove with my novel like never before. It was coming out of me with total ease, like breathing. I'd pace around my room, bouncing my red rubber ball. The neighbors underneath me must have hated my guts. But the words were just flowing out of me. It almost felt manic. Because the setting of *Muldoon's* was a fictionalized version of the real Muldoon's, the whole thing felt like second nature. They say write what you know. Couldn't have been any truer in this case. I was weaving Ronda and Ted and Rachel and Frank and Kurtis and the whole gang into the book, under different names, of course. Because I lived it, my novel felt incredibly real to me. Art imitates life. Life imitates art? Was my novel too close to reality? I was a little concerned about what all my coworkers would think when they read the book and they encountered thinly veiled versions of themselves.

I figured I would write the robbery scene on the evening of the twenty-seventh, the day before Vernon picked up the cash deposit from Hector, the security guard. It felt more authentic to write this way. That's when the robbery would most logically happen in real life. I'd be able to write it like a reporter would. It'd be more vivid and alive that way.

For example, I made Frank call me every time he and Rachel went out. They would hang, hit the movies, fuck, get something to eat—and then he would tell me exactly how it happened. Like when they had sex after the movie . . . in the *goddamn theater*! Like, Jesus.

It made me appreciate what I had with Mia. Frank and Rachel were pure animals, just constantly having sex and being sarcastic and negative about life. Mia and I had depth. We loved to do things together. Talk, ride bikes, grab lunch, hit the bookstore, play catch. She played softball in high school so she had a pretty good arm. There's nothing sexier than a sporty girl. Oh, and, of course, shop for records at Fisher's Vinyl Village. The guys who worked there were like if the cast of *Clerks* face-fucked *Superbad.* They were always out of it, especially the owner, Fisher. That dude definitely did a lot of drugs in his day. Straight acidhead burnout. But one thing was for sure—they had an amazing selection of music. Anything you could imagine, they stocked it. Except for Tame Impala's *Currents.* Guess it was that much in demand.

One night I was waiting for Frank to call and tell me about his time with Rachel. Mia and I didn't talk much on the days they went out, 'cause I would need to be home to write. I'd give excuses as to why we couldn't hang that night. All the while I would be at my typewriter writing about what Frank and Rachel were currently doing.

Frank would tell me exactly what his plans were for the night. Then when he called to explain what happened on the date, I could pick and choose between fact or fiction. Basically, I wrote what I thought would be intriguing to the reader, and then I'd pepper whatever actually happened into my story, making it more believable.

Frank obviously hadn't actually robbed the grocery, but he had given me an outlandish scenario for how he would execute it. And I'd taken notes. This scene was going to be realistic as hell. Every night Frank went out with Rachel, I would write and wait for his call. But tonight was different.

I sat down at my writing desk and noticed an unopened envelope. The return address was Darjeeling Publishing. *Shit.* I opened it up:

Dear Flynn,

I hope you're well. I just wanted to check in on your progress. I know you've been hard at work but I also know life happens. I want you to know that I'm here to support you. But I'm also here to remind you that your deadline for turning in your finished manuscript is right around the corner. Remember, we have a deal, a contract, and I need to get this out into the market soon. We've got high hopes for it.

This freaked me out. I was almost to the climax but I was far from having it in a place for my publisher to read.

I started to type out a response:

Hi Ed,

I'm making fantastic progress and am definitely on track to meet the deadline. I'm excited for you to read it. I think it's my best work, it's really a speci—

An aggressive knock interrupted me. It sounded like a cop's knock.

Nervous about the banging on the door, I tiptoed over and looked through the peephole. It was Mia! *What the fuck was she doing here?* I told her I had to help my mom move furniture at home.

She knocked again. "Flynn!" she said. "Are you in there?"

Oh shit, I thought to myself. I was in the middle of writing and waiting for Frank's call. And it was very important, as he would give me a needed last bit of information regarding Rachel.

"Flynn!"

Mia seemed upset, maybe even unsure—I couldn't tell.

"One moment!" I said through the door, then quickly ran through my living room picking up all the papers I had written on about Rachel.

"Flynn, open this door!" Mia yelled as I did my best to shove everything into a drawer under my typewriter. Scrambling, I fixed my shirt and opened the door.

Mia immediately pushed past me and into the apartment. "Flynn," she said suspiciously. "What are you doing? Why are you being sketchy?"

"What do you mean?" I asked, not quite sure what she meant.

"Have you been out tonight, Flynn?"

I had no idea what she thought was going on. "I haven't been anywhere," I told her. "I've been chilling here. What are you getting at?"

She set her bag down. "You tell *me,* Flynn!"

"Tell you what, Mia?!"

"Oh, I don't know. The random days and nights you ignore me. The lame excuse you gave me about how you need time to yourself?!" She looked almost betrayed.

"Wait, what do you think is going on?" I asked, confused.

"Just admit it, Flynn. You're cheating on me! I had my suspicions, but I tried to push them away . . . I didn't want to trust my gut because . . . when you look into my eyes and say the things you do, I want to believe you! I want to trust you. I felt like I could. But I've been cheated on before and I know all the signs. It's so obvious. What a foolish girl I am!" she said, heading for the door. I grabbed her arm.

"Wait, Mia, please! Whatever you think is going on . . . obviously isn't!" I said.

"OBVIOUSLY!" Mia repeated sarcastically. "I wasn't trying to be the 'crazy girlfriend,' the 'needy girlfriend'! All clingy and annoying. I told myself the days you spent to yourself, well, you must have been doing something special. Working on yourself. Something that would get you out of that fucking supermarket. And then I find out from Kurtis that—"

"Wait!" I interrupted. "What the fuck does Kurtis have to do with anything?"

I was suddenly pissed.

"I find out from Kurtis that . . . *you're cheating on me*!" As she said the words, Mia burst into tears.

"WHAT?!" I asked with such unfathomable incomprehension that there was laughter beneath my words, even a slight smirk. "Frank was right!" I said. "Kurtis does fuckin' like you! Baby, this guy is lying to you . . . he obviously has feelings for you and is trying to sabotage what we have, okay?!"

Mia ripped her arm from my grip.

"Frank! FRANK, FRANK, FRANK! Is he all you care about? You seem to think about this guy more than me. Why are you so secretive, Flynn? Why can't I meet your best friend?!"

"Don't try to change the SUBJECT!" I yelled. "Kurtis obviously has feelings for you. Why would you believe that joker over me, Mia?"

"He told me he was walking past the record shop and saw you and Rachel in there . . . kissing. *IN OUR PLACE!* I couldn't believe it when he told me . . ."

Her tears were falling faster than ever.

"Baby, I would never do that! It's me, okay? . . . It's me, Mia! I mean I fuckin' love . . ."

I stopped myself quickly, but it was too late. Instantly, Mia's eyes changed. She looked confused, dismayed, scared, and a little stunned. Her tears subsided.

"You . . . . you *what*, Flynn?"

No going back now.

"I love you, Mia."

"Flynn, fuck you. You don't love me. You're fucking some random girl at work," she said.

"Mia, listen to me. I would never think of it. I love you. I know Kurtis . . . unfortunately. He's a bitter man-child who gets off on trying to ruin people's lives. He likes you and wants to see us fail, that's why he's making up absurd lies. Trust me, baby. I love you, I would never hurt you like that. I'm sorry you've been hurt in the past, but that doesn't mean all men are amoral assholes. Let me love you," I said.

She looked into my eyes, cracking a smile. She hugged me the hardest she ever had.

"Oh, Flynn, I love you too! I'm sorry, I . . . I guess I've just been in my own head, you know? This time you've been spending alone has just gotten to me because . . .

135

I've never met anyone like you. And I love spending time together. I think I've fallen for you harder than I thought. I get paranoid because of what my shitty ex-boyfriend did. He was fucking some girl for six months before I found out. I'm sorry I rushed to conclusions. Wow, I love you, Flynn! I can't believe I'm breaking down that wall . . . I love you! And I really want to—"

She stopped suddenly. Slowly, she began moving away from me. Here I was, beaming, thinking it was time to rejoice . . . until her pained gaze ripped that smile right from my face. She looked even more hurt than before.

She pushed me away, tears falling and head shaking as she pulled out part of a piece of paper protruding from my desk drawer. Already in midread, she continued, eyes glued to the text as she pulled it free.

I immediately knew what she was reading.

She was reading a scene from my novel about Frank and Rachel—written from Frank's perspective. Worse still, it was a sex scene.

"Rachel was a pro. Her pussy was the best I've ever had," Mia read out loud. "The wettest my dick had ever been. I would watch her ass bouncing in the mirror. She could get it. And she did."

I couldn't believe it. "No, baby, it's not what you think!" I said desperately.

"It's not what I think? Well, Flynn, what the fuck am I supposed to think? You're keeping a badly written sex diary about the girl you're cheating on me with. The man I just professed my love for lied when he told me he loved me . . . obviously, he doesn't love me if he's fucking some other girl from work! I see how she looks at you, Flynn.

I'm not stupid. And you know what? It all makes sense now. YOU PIECES OF SHIT DESERVE EACH OTHER!" she screamed.

I grabbed her by the arm again, desperate to explain. "Mia, I'm writing a novel!" I admitted. I told her everything. I had to. This was my last chance at salvaging this relationship. I told her I had a book deal. I told her I was working at Muldoon's because I needed a normal place to base my novel on. I explained that I was basing my main character on Frank. And that Rachel had been with Frank, not me. I told her that the only thing that would get me out of the supermarket was this novel. I told her that's why I was ignoring her. That I needed time at home to get this novel done. That my publisher kept bugging me about turning it in. I poured my heart out about how Lola dumped me because I never finished any writing projects. That I was depressed and felt broken and that creating this piece of work was the only thing that was bringing me peace besides her. I told her about my terrifying feelings of derealization. I told her how that feeling had ceased with her.

No matter what, *she had to believe me.* She had to understand it was all for my book.

She stared at me, unsure whether to trust the conviction in my voice or smack me for me thinking she was stupid enough to believe this. And just then the phone rang.

Instantly, I knew it was Frank! And I knew that Frank would be able to set all this straight. Even though I hadn't told him about the novel, he would at least be able to tell her it was he who had hooked up with Rachel.

"The phone, it's ringing . . . it's Frank!"

That's when Mia gave me a look she had never given

me before—complete horror. She stared at the phone as I picked it up.

"Frank, Frank . . . you've got to help me, Mia is here right now and she thinks *I've* been with Rachel! Please, Frank . . . tell her that it's you who's been with her!"

With that, I handed Mia the phone. She shook her head no, eyes wider than ever.

"What do you mean? Take the phone, baby, please! He can tell you the truth!"

Finally, she extended her shaking hand, gripped the phone, and raised it to her ear. A few seconds later, as if she'd been told everything she suspected was true, she dropped the phone. Tears continued to fall.

"Please leave me alone," she said, walking backward toward the door. "Don't ever come near me again, Flynn." Her voice was cold, distant, and definitive.

"What do you mean?! What are you talking about—"

"Don't you ever fucking come near me again!"

The door slammed shut.

I stood frozen, staring at the closed door. Beside it was a bag she had left. Peeking out was a psychedelic-looking twelve-inch that read *Tame Impala,* Currents. It had a note taped to it:

> Flynn, I hope you love this record as much as I love you—xoxo, Mia

I started to cry, thinking of who I had just lost. But then the tears stopped. I started to feel numb. My head felt cloudy, my stomach hurt. I couldn't think. I felt like I was floating out of my body.

I leaped for the phone.

"Frank! Frank, are you there?!" A few seconds later, I heard chewing. Frank eating yet another banana, I was sure. "Frank, what the fuck did you say to her?!"

There was a pause.

"Nothing, man," Frank said nonchalantly.

"WHAT DID YOU TELL HER, FRANK?" I yelled, holding the phone out in front of me.

"NOTHING, FLYNN!" Frank yelled back.

"Don't you fuck with me!" Outraged and unable to think clearly, I kept going. "What did you tell her on the phone?"

Another pause, then Frank finally spoke.

"What she needed to hear."

And the line was dead.

CHAPTER 10

CLIMACTIC EVENT

I was at a loss. As I saw it, there was no way to recover. Two days passed and Frank didn't come into work. I kept my distance from Rachel, as I didn't know if she was in on whatever Frank had been up to. For all I knew, she would try to cause a scene in front of Mia, making it look as though something was actually happening between us.

It was like the fucking *Twilight Zone*. The whole place had changed. It was a radioactive toxic zone now.

As for Mia, well, she was still coming to work, but I couldn't bear to speak to her. I almost wanted to quit to avoid the whole situation. Every time I tried to muster up the courage I just remembered the look in her eyes when she left me. I tried to stay to myself, which wasn't easy as a floater. I was feeling low. I'd find myself staring into the distance, zoned out. Outside the plateglass window, the old man sat, playing chess against himself.

SUPERMARKET

Walking through the aisles, I came across old "Joe" clutching his cup and repeating, "Coffee, coffee, coffee, coffee." *Again!* He hadn't missed a day since I had begun to work there. And then, of course, there was Ann with the multivitamins. And as much as I wanted to bark at her to stay the fuck away from me, she was just so damn sweet I couldn't bring myself to do it. Instead, I said hello with as big a smile I could, took the pills, pretended to pop them, and placed them, yet again, in the right pocket of my brown jacket.

Under the weight of my own thoughts I headed to the loading dock to get away from things. I needed some fresh air. On my way there, I passed by the deli. Kurtis was smiling—a mocking smile that came with a side of pride. By now, he had gotten wind of me and Mia's breakup, a breakup I know he caused because he had feelings for her. I wanted to bash his head in. But in that moment I remained calm. I didn't act, I didn't do anything. I didn't even dream of doing so.

I couldn't risk harming Kurtis, or even verbally scolding him, in the off chance it would get back to Mia.

I just kept walking, making my way to the roof. I truly needed to clear my head and there was no better place. The last time I had been up there was with Frank, when we discussed Kurtis's lighter. I should have told him to never give it back to that fuck! I wanted to kill him for ruining my relationship with Mia. With that thought, I pulled out my wallet once more to stare at the picture of Lola and me.

Why could I find love, but not keep it? I asked myself, and then I heard a voice in my head.

Stop feeling sorry for yourself, pussy!

It was in Frank's voice, of course, but Frank wasn't there. Frank had gotten so inside my head that he had become the devil on my shoulder. The one telling me to just do it. My better-thinking subconscious was the angel. But to be honest, this time, the devil was right.

With that, I stared at the picture of Lola.

I will finish this book! I will finish this book!

I mean, that's what all this was about! It wasn't about Mia or falling in love or any of this other bullshit! It was about finishing something I started. It was about committing to something greater than myself. Something bigger than me or Frank, Lola, or Mia. It was about overcoming my fear of failure. It was about making myself complete through my art. It was about something unexplainable.

The picture had become a burden. A weight I carried around at all times. A symbol of my inability to move forward. It had to go. I had to go. I needed to free myself.

I took the picture and tore it in half. Then I tore it again. Lola was gone. And maybe so was Mia. It was time to rid myself of the things that were holding me back. It was time to do this on my own. Do it my way. I threw the shredded picture over the side of the building. The pieces fell gently like leaves in the wind, rocking to and fro as they approached the ground.

It was nearly seven, which meant I was off. Off to finish the last chapter in my book. I would give it that final, climactic event. In about five hours' time my main character was going to rob the very grocery store I was standing on top of.

I had to prepare.

On the way home, I stopped by the liquor store and grabbed a bottle of Macallan, Frank's favorite single-malt Scotch, at least that's what my notes said. My Moleskine had so many entries I couldn't remember half of what I'd written down. Good thing too, because it helped me with the details and nuances about the characters—articles of clothing, facial features, mannerisms, voice tics, surroundings, weather, and just about anything else I needed to create a real, moving, spinning world for readers to lose themselves in.

After grabbing the booze I stopped at the thrift shop to snag a ski mask and duffel bag. If I was gonna do this, I was really gonna play the part! Fuck method acting. This was method writing.

Back at my apartment, I prepped my typewriter and poured a glass of Scotch. I took a shot. *Fuck that,* I thought to myself, then threw the glass. It shattered on the floor.

Frank would drink it straight from the bottle.

I opened the Tame Impala record that Mia had left at my place and put it on my turntable. I set the needle down. As the crackle from the record echoed through my apartment, I looked at my attire—black jeans, black shoes, black T-shirt, and empty black duffel bag on the floor, to the left of my chair. Ski mask in hand. "New Person, Same Old Mistakes" by Tame Impala blasted through my apartment.

I was ready. Frank was ready.

I put my hands on my typewriter, closed my eyes, and began to type. Frank strutted up to the closed grocery store. With every word I wrote, every step I spelled out on the page, Frank followed. I could feel the energy. This

143

would be the most propulsive scene I'd ever written. I was fully in the character's head. I was Frank! I was robbing the store!

As I sat in my chair, I pulled down my ski mask, as did Frank. I took a swig from my bottle of Scotch, and Frank took a swig from outside the front doors of the grocery store. Then Frank wielded a giant metal baseball bat and swung furiously at the front sliding glass door, shattering it.

Walking in with no regard for the law, Frank strolled from aisle to aisle, picking out snacks at will. He opened a bag of chips, ate one, and threw the rest away.

I took a swig, he took a swig.

Over by the self-serving bulk candies, he grabs a handful of jelly beans and throws them into the air above his head one by one, aiming for his mouth. He strolls over to the produce department, grabs a banana, and begins to peel it. Twirling his small black duffel bag, he heads over to a shelf of pasta sauce, grabs a jar, tosses it in the air, and swings, connecting bat to glass for an explosion of red sauce across the aisle floor. Moving to the front of the store, he stops in the middle of aisle twelve, the fluorescent lights flickering in and out just like they always do. With all his might, he kicks the entire shelf, tipping it over. It collides with the shelves in aisle eleven, which repeats in aisle ten . . . all the way down to aisle six, like dominos, where they come crashing down with immeasurable force. With half of the aisles in the store demolished on the ground, Frank cracks a smile, continuing his walk to the front of the store.

Smashing the vending machine open, he retrieves the PayDay he'd been eyeing.

"What kind of grocery store has a vending machine in it?" he snickers, then continues on his way.

Arriving at Customer Service, where Ronda is usually stationed, Frank swigs from the bottle because I, in my apartment, do the same. Hot, I remove the mask, wipe the sweat from my brow, and pull it back down over my face. Drunk, my fingers begin to move slower than usual along the typewriter keys.

Frank jumps the Customer Service desk and slides across it like it's the roof of a sports car. Landing his feet flat on the ground, he knows what he needs to do next.

He needs to break through the door in front of him, into Hector's security room. He needs to rewind the tapes and then press record, so none of what he did would be caught on camera by the security monitors. The tapes would go from a perfectly fine, ordered store straight to . . . the aftermath. Straight chaos. There would be no explanation of how it happened.

After fixing the tapes, he would retrieve the money and be on his way.

Frank kicks in the door, revealing the inside of the security room. It's illuminated by bright screens displaying a live video feed of the entire store. To the right of the monitors, on the floor under a desk, he sees the safe. He knows what to do.

Frank ducks down and locates the keypad. A small, square red light above the three on the keypad signifies it's locked. Frank plants his left knee onto the floor, removes his black duffel bag from around his shoulder, and downs the rest of his Scotch, throwing the bottle, watching it shatter.

My bottle, however, does not shatter. To the right of my typewriter, it sits in perfect condition, still half full.

As if he'd set the code himself, Frank smoothly dials in 34652. A shrill, high-pitched tone sounds off, the red square above three on the keypad quickly turning to green. The safe pops open. Frank grabs the safe door and opens it, revealing . . . it's *empty*!

Nah, I'm just fucking with you. It's completely packed to the brim with ones, fives, tens, twenties, fifties, and one-hundred-dollar bills; money orders; and checks payable to Muldoon's Grocery. From what Frank can tell, there's damn near two hundred thousand dollars in there.

With that, he puts the money in his duffel, laughing at how easy it was to pull the whole thing off. At the same time, I sit there in my apartment thinking about exactly how I should end this part of the book.

In my book, Frank had planned to rob the store. He always had the idea of robbing Muldoon's blind and running off to Canada, just the way Frank had told me in real life.

He knew the store had no alarm system, just the fire sprinklers, which would automatically alert firefighters and the police station in case of an emergency.

Nobody would know what had happened until morning.

Frank takes his time collecting the money, savoring the process. Once he has it all, he stands up and reaches into his pocket, pulling out a single cigarette and the silver Zippo he had stolen.

He lights the cigarette through the hole in his ski mask and strolls to the front of the store.

Now, originally I was going to write it that he erased

the videotapes . . . but in that moment, sitting behind my typewriter, something overcame me.

I decided to end my novel another way.

As he steps in front of the shattered glass of the automatic doors at the entrance, he looks up into the camera and rips the ski mask from his face. Staring into the lens, he flips off Ted Daniels and everyone else who would be walking into the store the following day. Everyone who would review the tapes would see it was him. And he doesn't care, because he will be long gone, already at the Canadian border with Rachel.

Frank looks over his shoulder to take one last look at the supermarket and the havoc he's wreaked. He walks outside, opens the passenger door of a red Mazda RX-7, throws the bag inside, jumps in, kisses Rachel, and drives into the darkness . . . never to be seen again.

As though he had never been seen all along.

The End.

CHAPTER 11

THE END

I had ended my novel. In a moment of exasperation, my head collapsed onto my typewriter.

The next morning, I awoke, hungover, to the crackle of a needle spinning at the end of a record. I had fallen asleep at my desk. I lifted my head, revealing the letters RDFGTVCSEGHAZXQ and W on the side of my face.

I saw all the tools I'd used to accomplish what I had— ski mask, black jeans, T-shirt, and a bottle of Macallan. I had never written anything in such a manner before. Actually dressing up and truly writing from the perspective of my novel's protagonist, it had felt so . . . right! Like hard-core literature! Like fieldwork for an author.

Wow, I thought. *I . . . I'm an author! I am a real life author!*

Then I looked at my watch and saw the time. "Oh shit!" I said aloud. I was late. That day I had the earliest shift and was supposed to be there by 8:45 for the doors, which opened at 9:00 a.m.

It was 8:50.

I hurriedly changed into a white undershirt but tripped over the duffel bag. Once on my feet, I changed and ran down the stairwell of my apartment building, heading toward Muldoon's.

It was 9:01 when I arrived, so I entered through the side door of the break room—the one that was open during business hours. As soon as I walked in, I went to my locker to clock in and put on my brown button-down and black apron. When I opened it, I noticed a few things I hadn't before, and my eyes grew wide in realization of what was in front of me.

It was Frank's .357 Magnum, a pack of cigarettes, and Kurtis's silver Zippo lighter.

At first, I was angry that Frank would put these items in my locker, but then I wondered, *How the fuck had he gotten the code to my lock?* I pushed down on the metal bottom inside the locker, and sure enough, Frank was right: there was a hidden cubby.

I put the items inside and quickly shut the locker.

"Flynn!"

I jumped at the sound of my own name.

When I turned, I saw Ted Daniels. And he wasn't smiling.

"What's wrong?" I asked.

"Come with me," he said.

He rushed me outside. We moved into a circle with Ronda, Kurtis, Mia, Becca, Rachel, a few other employees I didn't really know, and . . . Frank.

"This is very, very unfortunate," said Ted Daniels.

149

"Someone robbed the store last night. The police are here now reviewing the tapes. Whoever the culprit might be, at least we'll get a good glimpse of what happened."

"I wonder who it was?" Frank said to me with a wink and smirk. The kind of smirk that said *I did it.*

"Oh my God, you guys, did someone get shot?" said Cara, who had just walked through the front door. "There's like a million cop cars out front," she added, stepping over the broken glass.

"Somebody robbed the store," Frank replied. I was staring at him so hard that it seemed to make Rachel, who was next to him, uncomfortable.

"How could you do this, Frank?" I whispered to him.

"Because I wanted the money," he whispered back.

"That's not what I mean! How could you lie to Mia on the phone? How could you ruin my relationship with her? She thinks I had sex with Rachel!"

Rachel, who had heard her name in the conversation, peered over. As did Mia.

"Why the fuck would she think that?" Frank said.

"It's not important," I said. "All that matters is that you go over there and *make it right*!" I said, beginning to raise my voice.

"What are you talking about, Flynn? Why are you yelling?" Mia asked me. This was the first time Mia had spoken to me since she slammed my door.

"You know what, Flynn?" Frank said. "You're such a pussy, man. You brought this on yourself. It's not my fault you can't keep a woman . . . no wonder Lola left you!"

"What did you say?!" I yelled. By then, everyone in the area was staring at me.

"You work in a supermarket, man! You're a nobody and you always will be. You're a NOBODY, BRO!" Frank said, then kept repeating it.

"YOU MIGHT THINK I'M A NOBODY, BUT YOU DON'T EVEN FUCKING EXIST!"

The entire store went quiet.

My head began to feel heavy. My vision blurred. I couldn't breathe. I started to see double. I stared at Frank. The outlines of his body began to radiate out. He started to flicker. He disappeared. Then reappeared. Frank tried to speak.

"You pussy. You're never going to finish that—"

His voice trailed off and cut out altogether.

In that instant it hit me! Everything came back to me! Frank wasn't real.

And I don't mean he "wasn't real" in that he had no substance as a human being, I mean he *wasn't a human being*, he was a made-up delusion. A false character I had created in a desperate attempt to realize my novel. The mind *was* a powerful thing. Terrifyingly powerful. Powerful enough to convince you that a character of your own invention was real. I was forcing myself to finish this book by any means necessary. I had allowed my imagination to fully take over for a greater cause.

It all made sense now.

"Flynn, what are you talking about?" asked Mia.

"This guy has issues," said Kurtis.

"FUCK YOU, KURTIS!" I screamed.

"I exist! What the fuck are you talking about, Flynn?" said Frank, with an uneasiness in his voice.

"Well, Frank," I said with a cocky attitude. "I hate to

151

break it to you, but I created you to help me finish my book. You're a tool. You're something I utilized for the sake of creativity and *nothing more*," I finished in a loud voice, smiling.

"What about all the girls I fucked?" Frank said desperately.

"That never happened!" I retorted. "I fed into the delusion so much I forgot what I had done. I first gained knowledge of what you really were after I walked in on Cara topless," I explained, pointing to Cara.

"Hey!" she said, flushing red and looking around with embarrassment.

"You said you fucked her and that she had a cupcake tattoo under her left breast," I told him. "Right above her rib cage. But she didn't! And I knew then . . . that you were fake. I could *see right through you* . . . I could *see you for what you really were*. Or what you weren't. You were just something I made up to help finish my novel about a guy who works in a supermarket."

Frank looked around, desperate, struck with panic.

"None of what you're saying makes sense! I'm real, Flynn!" he said.

"Then tell me your last name!" I said. "What's your last name? Huh?"

Frank stared down at the floor, then up at me, about to answer . . . and paused.

"You can't tell me your last name, BECAUSE I HAVEN'T WRITTEN IT DOWN YET!"

"I'm real!" Frank yelled. "I'm so real!"

"Then tell me your last name, Frank!" I demanded.

Once more, Frank went to reply, paused, looked at the ground . . . then back at me, puzzled.

"I'm the king of this place! I've slayed so many of the college bitches who have come out of here," he said in a panic.

"That's not true, Frank. I've disproven that!"

"What about Rachel?" Frank asked. "I know I've bent the truth with other girls, okay? I admit it. But I've been fucking Rachel's brains out for, like, a month!" he said, desperate to prove himself.

"I hate to break it to you," I said, "but the only way you technically could have had sex with Rachel is if *I* had sex with Rachel! And I most certainly have never . . . ever . . . had sex with Rachel!"

"How can you say that?" Rachel said, speaking up. "Did our time together mean nothing to you?"

"I fucking knew it!" yelled Mia, storming off.

"You're sick in the head, man," said Kurtis, before chasing after Mia.

And right then, what started out as a cocky realization ended in another realization: I had been arguing with a man who didn't exist in the middle of the supermarket.

This meant I *did* cheat on Mia. Those nights I sat writing on my typewriter about what Frank and Rachel had been doing . . . I was actually *living* those moments myself and writing about them later. How much had I tricked my brain? How much had my brain tricked me?

I looked to my side. Frank began to fizzle, looking staticky, like bad reception on an old-school television. My chest grew insanely tight. I felt like I couldn't remember where I was, or who I was. Time seemed to slow down. Then speed up. It felt like I was in a waking dream.

And in a matter of seconds, everything came back to me. Every moment I blocked out of my mind. Every time I lied to myself for the sake of completing my book suddenly revealed itself. I felt piercingly lucid.

It all started with Bennett.

I pulled out the photo of me and my dog. There was no dog in the photo. Bennett didn't exist. I went to the shelter, imagined a dog in an empty cage, bought him food, a red collar, and a blue leash. I asked a guy to take a picture of my dog and me, and he freaked out because there was no animal by my side. He must have thought I was a crazy person!

Oh, my God, I thought in this instant of realization. *Have I been a crazy person? Oh no . . .*

All those walks after work with Bennett, I had just been dragging around a leash. Posting photos of a lost dog with no dog in it! Asking people if they had seen him, showing them nothing. No wonder that guy asked if I was "fucking kidding."

And then the repressed memories started to pour out, unlocking all at once.

Frank never said anything to Mia on the phone that night. He didn't tell her I was fucking Rachel. He told her *nothing.* There was no Frank to say anything. When I claimed the phone was ringing and Frank was on the line, she knew something was wrong. Because not only did the phone never ring . . . not only was there no one on the other line . . . the phone wasn't even plugged into the wall.

Oh my God, it was all so twisted to realize. This meant

when Rachel walked down the aisle toward us, winked, and said hello to "Frank," she actually meant me. Because . . .

I had been Frank all along.

Of course. When I received Rachel's number, I put it in my right pocket—but retrieved it from my left pocket when giving it to him. I had only done it for the action of doing so inside the delusion. There'd been no reason to hand it over to Frank, because . . .

I was Frank.

Frank was me.

I made Frank up and made him real in my own head. He was a complete illusion, a hallucination, an apparition.

It went all the way back to that first day at Muldoon's, when he thanked me for *being the only person who acknowledges my existence in this place* . . .

In midpanic, I fell to my knees, scared to death. I tried to run but was disoriented, and every time I tried again I fell over from a spell of vertigo. It felt like slamming into the cashiers' conveyer belt.

Then I noticed all the shelves from aisles six through twelve were on the ground, essentially destroyed. The sight of this only confused me more. As I struggled to get up on my feet, something stopped me.

Someone.

I was being held by my neck by a large man in a dark room, looking into a bright screen.

I heard the word why over and over.

"Why, Flynn?" The voice became clearer. "Why would you do this, Flynn?"

It was Ted Daniels. I rubbed my eyes, making out the image on the monitor. The video on the screen was grainy footage of someone in a black ski mask flipping off the camera. The man was me.

A police officer put my hands behind my back, locking handcuffs tightly around my wrists.

"Flynnagin E. Montgomery, you are being arrested for felony burglary and grand larceny in the fourth degree. You have the right to remain silent. Anything you say can and will be used against you in a court of law. You have the right to have an attorney. If you cannot afford one, one will be appointed to you by the court. Do you understand these rights as they have been told to you?"

"I do," I mumbled. I looked forward, and the walls began to disappear. I felt split in two.

"Good job, Flynn, you did it," Frank said.

PART TWO

CHAPTER 12

ASYLUM

I opened my eyes, and much to my surprise, I wasn't laying on my side or my back. I was sitting on a cold metal table staring at my crossed hands.

Imagine, if you will, that you are peering through my eyes. You see what I see. And all you see are your hands in front of you on a metal desk with your fingers interlocked.

As I looked up, I saw a woman in front of me. A beautiful blond woman, dressed in white. The room I was in was totally white, maybe eight by ten feet. I examined myself. I too was dressed in white.

I knew this woman. But how?

Where am I?

And then I realized it. The woman in front of me was Lola!

"Lola, what are you doing here?"

"I'm not Lola, Flynn," she replied. "My name is—"

"What the hell are you talking about, Lola? Why are you dressed that way? Where are we?"

I began to panic. One minute I was being arrested, and the next I'm in a white room with—

"Dr. Olivia Cross," she said. "And you, Flynn, are at the Mayberry Psychiatric Hospital."

I stood up as quickly as possible, launching the examination table against the wall. Pieces of drywall fell to the floor.

"This doesn't make sense, Lola! Why are you saying this?"

"Flynn, we've been here before," Olivia said, rising calmly to her feet.

"I want out right now!! Where's Lola? Where's—"

"Calm down, please," she said, as two men—also dressed in white—entered the room and grabbed me by my arms. "Please be careful with him," Olivia told them.

"Get the fuck off me! What's happening?! Lola, please . . . why are you doing this?" I said, flailing my arms.

"Don't fight it!" one of the men said just as my elbow collided with his nose. Blood was everywhere.

"No, please!" Olivia yelled. "Be careful with him!"

The enraged man picked me up, slamming me on the metal table. The searing pain in my skull was a harsh realization—this wasn't another one of my daydreams, this was really happening! And just then, I felt a prick from a needle in my ass. Everything began to fade.

I was jolted awake by the sound of a mug shattering on the ground.

"Goddamn it!" Frank said. I looked around. I was in the break room.

"Now I gotta pick this shit up! Oh, sorry, dude . . . did I wake you?"

"Hey, guys," said Cara, who was walking in, dragging her leather boots on the ground.

"Guys?" I said. I was coming to.

"Yeah, *guys*, that's what I said," Cara informed me. "You and Frank, duh. Anyway, Frank, I just came in here to tell you Ted needs you to help Rachel with something. I can't believe he doesn't know you guys are hooking up," she added with a chuckle.

"Okay, thanks Cara," Frank said. As she left the room, he stared at her ass and said, "Damn that little Mormon girl is sexy."

"Wait a second," I said, still processing the dream I had just had. "You and Rachel are dating? Since when?"

"Since you did me the solid of getting her number for me. Did you hit your head or something?" Frank asked as he started to walk out.

"Nah, I just had a dream . . ."

I continued as Frank kept walking, almost to the door.

"I dreamt I was going crazy, but . . . I don't know. You ever have those dreams where it felt so real you weren't sure if—"

"Look, man," Frank said. "I've been there. And I can tell you from firsthand experience: sanity is what you're currently dreaming."

Trying to process what he was saying, I couldn't tell what kinda joke he was playing. "Sanity is what I'm currently dreaming?" I repeated.

"Flynn to aisle nine for a psychiatric evaluation," said a voice over the Muldoon's intercom.

"You're eyes-wide crazy, Flynn!"

"What the fuck are you talking about?" I said, starting to feel that all-too-familiar tightness in my chest.

"You can't leave, Flynn. This supermarket is my home. It's *our* home. And if you let this bitch doctor back in, it's over, bye-bye. And I can't have that now, can I?"

Was I in the supermarket or was I in a hospital? Was I a character inside of some book? Was I some asshole on a typewriter writing my own fate, solely for the entertainment of readers? Solely for self-validation? Self-preservation? Self-worth? Was I just some creative who was destroying my life for accolades and achievements?

"I won't stop until you're back here in Muldoon's, Flynn. I won't stop until we're together again like old times. I need you to believe in me. I need you to believe in me so I can live."

Suddenly, the floor was made of wax, melting by the second. I was drowning in the tiles. Struggling with every breath, using all my might to stay afloat until . . .

I awoke, unable to move, held down in a bed by leather restraints. The room was dark, yet familiar. As I looked around, tears fell from my eyes.

"What the fuck is happening to me?" I cried.

I was alone, and the clock said 4:17 a.m. I drifted off into sleep, or delusion, or whatever was to become of my weary mind. In that moment, I let go of everything, and then . . . all of it came back.

I woke in the same bed, but the restraints were gone.

The lights were on. The clock read 7:14 a.m. When I opened my eyes, I could see Lola.

Or, rather, Olivia Cross.

"Do you know where you are?" she asked.

"The nuthouse," I replied.

She laughed.

"How do you feel, Flynn?"

"I feel okay . . . but I have a lot of questions."

"I'll tell you everything after breakfast. Get yourself something to eat. Let's meet in my office after," she said with a smile, putting her hand over mine in a very comforting way.

As I made my way toward the cafeteria, I walked past a man clutching a cup of coffee. He was mumbling to himself, staring at a wall.

"Coffee, coffee, coffee," he said.

He was the same man from the supermarket—the one I would see every day. Joe! I walked around the place; it wasn't what I imagined a nuthouse to be like. Instead of it being full of crazy patients rocking back and forth, screaming and drooling over themselves, it was actually pretty quiet. The part I was in looked like a freshman dorm common area. Patients were reading and talking among themselves.

There was a Christmas tree lit up in the corner, decorated with ornaments. White lights were strung around the perimeter of the room. The windows were frosted. Passing a calendar, I saw that it was mid-December. There was a TV playing lightly. A group was watching soap operas, and a circle of people on the other end were making homemade stockings. There was an area full of board games, and right there sat an old black man who resembled the guy from outside Muldoon's. He was sitting alone by the window playing chess. Against himself, it would appear. His pieces were red, and his invisible opponent's were white.

The place reminded me more of a rehab center or old people's home than an insane asylum—but I guess that's just because of how mainstream media depicts lunatics in film and TV. Like soulless raving madmen held captive in an asylum.

As I neared the cafeteria, I was met by a woman with a familiar face. It was Ann, the same woman who worked in the pharmacy. Just as she had done a million times before in the store, she gave me my daily dose of multivitamins.

"Hey there, sweetheart, don't forget your pills!" she said, planting a bevy of pills in the palm of my hand. Only here and now, I realized they weren't multivitamins at all. These were *pills*. Like hard-core psychiatric medication. All shapes, sizes, and colors. This freaked me the fuck out.

I pretended to consume them. After she left I quickly took them out from under my tongue and put them in the right pocket of my favorite brown jacket . . . which had an alarming amount of the pills already in it.

How long have I been here?

In the cafeteria, I saw so many familiar faces from the supermarket, including the doctor in the white coat. I made my way to where the food was being served and grabbed a tray. They were serving eggs with bacon and a side of toast. I got some orange juice, which was dispensed from a machine, the same as some hotels have. As I looked for a place to sit, I noticed it was pretty crowded, and everyone was kind of divided up into cliques like high school. Looking around, I noticed the black man and his chessboard sitting at a table for two, with no one accompanying him. I walked over and placed my tray in front of his chessboard. The pieces were worn. They had a life of their own.

"Where are you today, kid?"

"Uh, excuse me?"

"Here we go again," he said.

"Pardon?" I replied.

"Have a seat."

He definitely had a Morgan Freeman–vibe going on—midsixties, black with gray hair. He was tall, was calm, and had a distinguished-looking face. To be honest, he didn't seem to have anything wrong with him at all.

As I looked around the place, everyone else seemed to have some kind of telling sign. A tic, if you will, that gave away the reason they should be in here.

But not this guy.

As I looked around, judging everyone by their flinching or stuttering, I stopped and wondered: What is my tic? If I even had one.

"So where are you today, kid?" the man said.

"I'm sorry, I don't know what you mean," I said, stabbing the scrambled eggs on my plate with the silver fork in my right hand.

"Kid, look around. Where are you?"

"Uh, I'm in an asylum of some kind," I told him.

"Okay, that's more like it. You know, so many people don't appreciate the moment. Appreciate where they are. Appreciate the here and now."

"Well," I said, "I'm not exactly sure what's going on, but I certainly don't understand why I should appreciate being in a nuthouse."

"No, boy," the man said. "You are alive. And in this moment, you are well."

"So," I said to him. "What's your name, old man?"

"You know my name, Flynn. You've known it for some time."

I stared at him, trying to find my bearings. What the hell was this guy talking about?

And how did he know my name?

"The name's Samson, William Redding Samson. But friends—like you—just call me Red. Pleasure to make your acquaintance," Red said, extending his hand to be shaken.

"I'm, well . . . I guess you already know who I am," I said, shaking his hand. "How do you know my name?"

"Well, it's not the first time we've had this conversation. But, if I do say so myself, I've never seen you like this. You seem more present, cogent, and certain this time."

"More certain of what?" I asked.

"Finishing it." He took a sip of his coffee.

"Hello there," said Olivia as she walked up to our table.

"Hello," Red and I said in unison.

"I do hope you don't mind, but may I borrow you for a moment, Flynn?" she asked, beginning to walk and motioning me to follow.

"Oh, of course not!" I rose to my feet. "See ya around, Red," I said, walking a bit faster through the halls of the facility to catch up with Dr. Cross.

We didn't say anything on the way to her office. And

166

even though I had a million and one questions, I just enjoyed the walk. Outside the window, there was a faint snow on the ground—a snowfall that must have been a few weeks old.

"And here we are," Dr. Cross said as she motioned me into her office.

As I sat down, before she even had a chance to make it behind her desk, the questions just poured out.

"What the hell is going on? Why does that old guy know who I am? Why am I in an asylum? What happened to my job, my book, where's my mom, and why do I keep thinking you're Lola? Where's Mia? And is there even a Mia?"

"Flynn, calm down," she said. "I know all this must be a lot to take in, but I need you to remain calm. I need you to trust me, listen to me, and accept what I'm about to tell you as the truth."

I nodded my head and she began.

"You are a patient in the Mayberry Psychiatric Hospital, located one hundred and forty miles north of where you live. You had a psychiatric breakdown more than two years ago."

"TWO YEARS!" I shouted.

"Now, Flynn, I told you to remain calm. I need you to bear with me. Everything I'm about to tell you will alarm you. There's no way to sugarcoat it. Just please let me finish and then we can get into it, okay?"

I nodded my head in agreement once more, only this time with greater conviction.

"You were on trial for the robbery of Muldoon's Grocery. Seeing how small the town is, it was all over the news—it made national news, in fact. When I saw you

167

on TV, and heard about the trial, I knew your statements were from someone who wasn't mentally stable. I signed on to the case pro bono after contacting the attorney representing you. After several meetings, we agreed that you should plead insanity and be admitted to our facility for treatment. We are the most well-regarded institution of our kind in the Northwest. The judge agreed, and you've been here ever since."

I processed the information as calmly as I could. "So, what's real?" I finally asked. "What happened, what didn't, what's happening to me now?"

"You never went to jail. You've been in inpatient treatment here. After a full psychiatric evaluation, you were diagnosed with several mental disorders. Schizophrenia, multiple personality disorder, bipolar disorder. Entwined in those are anxiety and depression. You've been making terrific progress, through cognitive behavioral therapy and medication. But you still have extended episodes of dissociation, where you get stuck in imagined worlds. These are loops, essentially. Your memory doesn't function properly. Flynn, tell me what you know."

"Well, I was working at a supermarket to find inspiration for a novel I was writing. I found a guy who worked there, Frank, who became the basis for my main character."

"Only he didn't work there, did he?" she said.

"No, he didn't."

"What else can you recall?"

"Well, this man, he wasn't flesh and blood. He was an illusion I created in order to finish my novel. If I didn't finish my novel, dark things would have happened. My deluded mind made Frank real to me. But Frank became a part of me. He was me. He was another identity in my mind, an alter ego. I guess originally I created him because of Lola, my ex-girlfriend. Or ex ex, I guess. Lola broke up with me because I never finished anything. When she broke up with me, something snapped. I became so desperate to finish a book that it literally drove me insane. I created a main character I believed in so much that he began to take control over me. And before I knew it, my mind had split into two. I was no longer just me." I took a deep breath.

"I had become the character I created. To prove her wrong."

"To prove *who* wrong, Flynn?" she asked.

"Lola," I said. "Wait a minute . . . why do you look like her? I don't understand."

"Flynn, everything you remember happening . . . happened. Lola did break up with you, which triggered your meltdown, and fueled the fire to finish your novel, which you did after creating Frank. You see, Flynn, the reason you look at me and see her is the same reason you saw so many of the people in this hospital at the supermarket where you used to work." She paused, her face calm. "Because you've been living in a loop, Flynn."

Trying to process everything she was saying felt like letting a stranger tell you who you are. Letting them tell you that your identity is a lie, and then accepting it.

"It's a defense mechanism to avoid trauma. You come in and out of reality, in and out of your own delusions. You see, the loop starts with you and me sitting in that white room. You recite the same series of events in your head. You go over the breakup exactly as it happened, all the way down to the waiter pouring your coffee. Then you go into your getting a job at Muldoon's, meeting Frank, writing your novel. And when your mother comes to visit you—"

"My mother has been here?" I asked eagerly.

"Of course, Flynn. She loves you, and she plays her part."

"What do you mean, 'she plays her part'?"

"You see, that's just it. You spend months here reliving everything from the breakup to the meltdown after the robbery, over and over. You give everyone here at the institution roles to play, Flynn, so you can return to the supermarket in a deluded state. You slip out of reality. You're here but not *here*."

"This isn't the first time we've had this conversation, is it?"

"No, it isn't. But this is the first time we've had such a breakthrough. As head doctor in the facility, I monitor all patients on the premises. I only work closely with some— and since you were admitted, I felt an obligation to help you." She gave me a small, knowing smile. "You've gotten close before, close to breaking through and gaining a sense of reality, but you would shut down after reawakening, entering the loop again before we could make any sustained progress."

I was silent for a moment. "What do I do now?" I asked.

"I believe we can beat this, but you mustn't let Frank drag you back. Frank is still a voice in your head. He still affects your actions and your take on reality. I really think you can make it out of your psychosis, but it's going to be a fight. I can help you . . . I'm here to give counsel. However, I can't tell you how to defeat Frank."

"Defeat? What exactly do I have to do?" I had been thinking more along the lines of intense group therapy, but the way she was describing it, it seemed I would be literally battling this fucking guy.

"Everyone has demons, and no one can be told how to deal with their personal ones, Flynn."

"Man, this is heavy, Doc."

"Rome wasn't built in a day," she said, "so we can't just destroy the world you built in one either."

As I sat contemplating everything we had just discussed, I still had so many questions.

"That's it for today," she said, as though reading my mind. "We will resume tomorrow."

"Wait, what about—"

"There is only so much the mind can handle," she said, rising from her desk and walking over to the office door. She opened it.

"I understand," I said. Then I got up and started walking out. "Oh, wait! Doc, just one more thing."

"Yes, Flynn?" she said.

"What about . . . Mia? Whatever happened to Mia?"

"You can ask her on Tuesday," she said, smiling. "That's when she visits you."

With that, she shut the door.

Walking down the bright hallway, I spotted a calendar and saw that Tuesday was only three days away. I couldn't believe Mia was still visiting me here! After two years. After everything that had happened, and everything I inadvertently did to her. All I could think about was Mia. I was getting so excited. But my excitement was turning into anxiety, into a sense of dread. My hands began to sweat. I noticed the floor changing shades of gray right under my gaze. The hallway lights began to flicker, like the fluorescent lights in the supermarket.

As I looked up, the hallway grew darker, my heart beat faster, and my head started to spin. I was shaking. I began to run, trying to make it to my room as soon as possible, but with every step, the hallway began to transform into . . . an aisle at the supermarket.

"You can't escape it, Flynn!" Frank yelled from behind me. He crept toward me, like Jason Voorhees approaching his victim. The muscles in my legs began to burn. With every leap, an item from the supermarket entered my periphery. Shelves of bread and cereal popped toward me, crashing through the hospital wall. The farther I ran from Frank, the closer I got to the supermarket.

"Never again, Flynn! Don't you understand, man?! WE'RE THE SAME PERSON. GET USED TO IT!"

"I'm nothing like you!" I screamed.

"We've already been through this, man! This isn't the first time, but it will be the last!"

"Just leave me alone!"

"You don't get it! If you don't come back, I won't exist anymore!"

"Good!" I yelled.

"I'll never stop, Flynn. Not ever. I'm taking over this time, Flynn. I'm taking over this time for good," Frank said. He began to laugh menacingly.

His laughter struck fear into me. My head started to feel dizzy and my legs started to wobble. Trying to escape,

I tripped over my shoelace, smashing my head on the tile floor. But just as my skull connected, it pushed through and met . . .

. . . a sweat-drenched pillowcase. I had awoken from the nightmare. Tears ran down my face. Why? Why was this happening to me? I couldn't escape my own mind. I wanted out. I was exhausted. I fell asleep, not sure what to expect upon opening my eyes.

CHAPTER 13

PAWN

I woke in the morning to the sound of sobbing. I was scared to open my eyes, not sure of what was awaiting me.

"My baby!"

It was my mother. She was beaming with one of those huge crying smiles. But I could tell from her dubious tone that she wasn't sure just how long I'd stick around this time. My mother was kinda like the mom from that cartoon *Bob's Burgers*. I don't know if you've ever seen it, but the mother on the show is extremely loving, yet she can be claustrophobic, almost stifling, with her love.

"Mom! How are you?" I said.

"How am I? I'm fine, my Flynnagin! How are you, baby?!" she said, kissing my cheeks. I wanted to give her the usual *Stop, Mom!* but I missed her so much and it was comforting. My nightmare lingered and I was still unsettled.

"I'm okay. To be honest, I'm freaked out. I mean, it's been hard to take all this in."

"Oh, believe me," she said. "As soon as I heard you were awake again, I couldn't believe it. This was the longest you were inside."

"The longest I was inside?"

"Well, that's how Dr. Cross always put it for me. Whenever I would come by to check up on you, she would express you were still inside . . . your mind. Confined to the delusion. So I would play my part."

"What do you mean 'play your part'?" I asked her.

"Well, honey," she said as she continued crying, and this cry was even more sad than before, "even though you weren't here, I could still be your mother, there . . . in the supermarket. That's what Mia does when she visits you as well."

"So Mia really does visit me? But why?"

"Because she loves you, you idiot," she said with a smile.

"Even after all this time? After everything I did? After two years of being a basket case?"

"Flynn, you're a good young man and she loves that man deep down. The man who Frank buried. And I'll admit it's hard because . . ." She grabbed a tissue and continued, "This isn't the first time you've awakened. And the thought of losing you is too much to bear for us all."

"When did you talk to her?" I asked.

"After Dr. Cross called, she was the first person I let know. But enough of this, let's eat some breakfast."

Instead of bombarding her with more questions—questions I'd probably asked her a hundred times by now—I decided to drop it and just spend some quality time together.

After getting out of bed and brushing my teeth, we headed to the cafeteria. My mother told me to find a table and that she would grab the food.

"Coffee, coffee, coffee," Joe said as I walked past him.

And like clockwork, Ann approached me and plopped five pills in my hand and handed me a paper cup of water. After drinking the water, she bid me a good day. I spit out the pills, placed them in the right pocket of my brown jacket, and continued on my way.

"Up for a game, Flynn?" I heard a voice say from behind me. It was old man Red, sitting in front of his chessboard.

"I don't know how to play," I said.

"Ah, horseshit, of course you do. I taught you myself."

Not sure exactly how to process this, I sat down and surveyed the board.

"Whites first," said Red.

"Hey, man, no need to bring race into this," I said.

"I'm talking about the pieces, boy. White pieces move first, then my red pieces go. Your move."

Not even trying to come up with a joking reply, I just moved, picking up a pawn and placing it forward two spaces.

"So, we've done this before, huh?" I asked.

"Oh, yeah," Red said with a half smile, his eyes locked on the board, trying not to break his concentration.

"I ever beat you?" I said.

"Well, no, not yet you haven't. Not at the game I'm playing."

"So, are we . . . friends? I mean, you seem like a nice guy."

"Yeah, kid, we're friends. Been friends longer than you realize, apparently." He leaned over, patting me on my shoulder.

"Can I ask you a question?"

"You just did," he said, moving his horse forward two spaces and one space to the left.

"Why are you here?" I asked. "You don't look like you belong here."

"Truth be told, young man, I don't belong here. But I don't belong in the outside world either."

"Well, what the hell is that supposed to mean, Yoda?" the smart-ass in me replied.

"Me and you, we came here for the same reason," he said.

"How long have we known each other?" I asked.

"Olivia brought you to me about three months after you were first admitted. So I'd say about a year and a half."

"What do you mean, she *brought* me to you?"

"Well, you see, kid, we've got similar issues, similar conditions. For years I lived bouncing between two worlds. There was my 'reality,' then there was reality. I'd loop between the two endlessly, living inside my own illusory world for weeks at a time. There are a few others here like us, but I'm the only one in here who has fully escaped the delusion."

"How . . . how do I escape?" I asked, unsure if I was prepared for the answer.

"Well, every time we seem to get near that point, that son of a bitch Frank pulls you back in the loop. He needs you there in order to survive. Then we start over," Red explained.

"What's the longest I've been outside the loop?" I asked.

"Two weeks."

"Two weeks! Two weeks, that's it? Are you serious?"

"If it's any consolation, I've never seen you awaken so well. Something about you . . . you seem more centered this time."

"Hey there!" my mom called. "Come here, Flynn . . . you can play chess later."

"But Mom, I was—"

"We'll talk later, son," Red said. "Enjoy breakfast with your mother. I ain't going nowhere."

After breakfast, my mom gave me a big hug and a brown paper bag with my lunch in it.

"Mom, can't I go home with you?" I asked.

"Honey, the court ordered you here and you haven't been discharged. Until you have it in writing from the doctor that you can rejoin society, you have to stay. I'm sorry. I know you can do it this time! I just know it!"

"I understand, Mom. I love you."

Deep down, I hated the situation I was in. Who wouldn't?

"I love you too, baby! Oh, and we are coming up on a year since your book was released, so . . . I baked you a cake!" she said, grabbing a cake from her tote bag. It was iced in blue frosting with the word *Congratulations* written in red on top.

"Wait, WHAT?!" I shouted

"What do you mean *what*?" she said.

"What book?" I asked.

"*Muldoon's*, dummy. The book you wrote. The entire reason you're in this place to begin with!"

In all this time, taking everything in, I forgot the whole fucking reason I was in here! For pushing myself to my breaking point to finish a novel. And I succeeded . . .

But therein lay the question.

"Who released the book?" I asked.

"Ed Nortan at Darjeeling Publishing! Remember him? He wouldn't stop calling and I figured it wouldn't hurt. I knew how hard you'd worked on it, so I gave him permission as your legal guardian. He gave me your back end, which has been sitting in your account along with . . ."

She paused, as though not sure how to explain.

"Along with what, Mom?!"

"Along with . . . just under nine million dollars. After taxes."

"WHAT?!" I screamed. "Holy shit, what the fuck?! Oh my God, I can't believe it . . . are you serious?!"

"I'm dead serious, son! I'm so proud of you!"

"How did this happen? I don't understand!"

"Well," she said, "after you had your breakdown I went to your apartment to gather your things, and I found the draft of the book you had just finished. I mailed it to Mr. Nortan. In just a few months the book was out and published. Your trial attracted a lot of attention. It was televised and written about extensively. People became obsessed with the case and with you. The book became a cultural phenomenon. They couldn't believe someone was so dedicated to their craft that he *drove himself crazy*!"

"Moooooommmmmm!" I said, sounding like an annoyed child.

"Oh, sorry, honey . . . but you know what I mean! Anyway, the release of the book was a smash success, an in-

179

stant *New York Times* best seller. It blew up. It's even being made into a movie by a big studio."

I couldn't believe it! She was blowing my mind. Everything I could have ever wanted had happened, and I wasn't even in the same fuckin' universe when it did.

"Who's playing me in the film?" I asked.

"Joseph Gordon whatever-his-name-is," she said, trying to remember.

"Holy shit, I love that guy!"

"And some hotshot screenwriter named Brian is writing it. Apparently you two randomly met on a plane a few years ago? He's been great. He remembered meeting you and followed your case. Once the book came out he immediately attached himself to the project as a writer."

"Jesus! That's crazy. What else have I missed?"

"Well, everyone wanted to congratulate you after the book came out. Including Lola. That's when she came to visit you."

When she said this, everything stopped. Right then, I couldn't hear a sound in the room except her voice.

"She wanted to come celebrate and apologize for how things ended. She wanted you to know that she was proud of you, but . . ."

My mom didn't need to finish. The memory returned and I knew exactly what had happened. Lola showed up while I was in a loop at the diner with Dr. Cross a few months back. When she showed up, I couldn't process Dr. Cross and Lola in the same room, and because of this I was sucked even deeper into the delusion.

But not this time. This time I was gonna make it out. I had to.

"Anyway," Mom said. "Thank God she sent that synopsis to the publisher, huh?"

I sat there frozen. No wonder I'd never heard of the publishing company . . . it was Lola all along! She submitted my synopsis to the publisher before we had even broken up. She was the reason I got a book deal in the first place. She was not only the reason I was in this place, but the reason I was now a successful author.

"Congrats, baby," she said. She handed me a copy of my book. It was a slick-looking cover. Minimalist design with only type. It looked so dope.

MULDOON'S: A NOVEL
Flynnagin E. Montgomery

I couldn't believe it. It was real. Tears welled in my eyes.

"I'm going to let you sit with all of this." My mother kissed me good-bye and said she would be back tomorrow for another visit.

Still trying to process the fact that I was an acclaimed, bestselling author, I heard an announcement over the intercom.

"Flynn Montgomery, please report to Ted Daniels's office. I repeat . . . Flynn Montgomery to Dr. Olivia Cross's office."

I did a double take.

"Hey, whose office did they just say on the intercom?" I asked the man in front of me.

"BLUE ANGELS LIVE IN SIN!" he yelled. "It's the mice that will rule once the pirate returns! Am I right?"

"Rriiiggghhttttt . . . ," I said, sneaking away and heading to Olivia's office.

Once I got there, I raised my hand to knock on Olivia's door but she answered before my knuckles connected with the wood.

"Flynn," she said, the door opening suddenly. "Just the man I was looking for! I figured it's such a nice day out; we should have our session in the fresh air . . . what do you say?"

Even though it was December, I agreed. It looked great outside—the sun was shining, the air was crisp, and the outdoor heaters radiated warmth throughout the garden.

Dr. Cross took me on her favorite walk around the property. It was a gorgeous tree-lined walking path. I started to open up, telling Dr. Cross about my nightmare the night before—how Frank was chasing me down the hallway, and as I ran it turned into an aisle from Muldoon's. I didn't tell her about what I heard on the intercom, though. I was too afraid. I didn't know what to make of it.

"Let's sit, Flynn," Dr. Cross said. We took a seat on an old bench.

"You have made incredible progress with your treatment. Your conditions are some of the most complex mental conditions there are. Psychotherapy seems to have helped you the best. You have bravely examined your own mind, untangling a complex web of thoughts, emotions, experience, and behavior. You put a huge amount of pressure on yourself. And while you maybe thought that pressure was coming from other sources, it was nearly all self-imposed. You have worked to find self-love despite your challenging circumstances. Schizophrenia typically begins to show up in men during their early twenties. The emotional trauma of your breakup, the extreme creative pressure you put on yourself, the change in your environment—all these factors exasperated your latent schizophrenia. What you saw during your breakdowns—the panic attacks and out-of-body moments—were early warning signs. It's a condition that changes your perception of reality and reroutes your memory. It creates delusions, hallucinations, and paranoia.

"You pushed through the early warning signs, and buried yourself in your novel. Your novel became its own altered state. In it you created a character, and that character became 'real' to you. So real that Frank became a distinct personality inside your head. Your multiple personalities were antagonizing one another. Frank is a powerful entity in you. He still lingers, as you saw in your nightmare. But you seemed to have broken through in a major way lately.

"You must do everything in your power to stay in the real world. You must do everything in your power to not allow Frank to undo your progress. Because he will try. His existence depends on it," she said.

"But, Doc, I mean . . . I've been here before. If I go back I can make it out again, right?"

"I'm not so sure, Flynn," she said. "The last time you retreated it was for so long. I thought perhaps we'd lost you for good."

"How do I end this, Olivia?" I asked. "How the fuck can I just be normal again?!" I yelled to the sky. Birds scattered from the trees into the cold air.

"By getting rid of him, Flynn, once and for all."

"How the fuck do I get rid of a man who doesn't exist?"

"I can only give you encouragement and tools, Flynn."

"What tools, Olivia?" I asked in anger.

"Do you like chess, Flynn?"

"What the fuck does that have to do with a guy living in my head? A guy who wants to trap me in a world he's created?"

"Knowledge is half the battle. The answer is inside of you. You know where you've been, and deep down, you know where you are." She gave me a small smile. "This story is your own. And only you, Flynn, can write the ending."

"Nice writing pun . . . 'cuz I'm a writer . . . you get it?"

"Don't be an asshole, Flynn," she said, and I could tell she was holding back a smile.

"I'm sorry, Doc," I said.

We finished our walk through the garden in silence. And then I told her something I hadn't thought of since the morning after the robbery.

"You know, when me and Frank first had our argument in the middle of the store . . . in front of everyone . . . I demanded he tell me his last name. But he couldn't do it. He went to reply, paused, and stared into the floor. Then he looked back up at me, puzzled. I told him if he was real he should tell me his last name! And again he went to reply, paused, looked at the ground for a moment . . . then back at me, totally puzzled. That's when I explained in front of everyone that he couldn't tell me his last name for one reason: I hadn't written it down yet."

Olivia sat down on the bench we were passing, and I joined her.

"Go on."

"The truth is, the day Lola left me at the diner, there was a man waiting on us. His name was Frank. 'The'

184

Frank, I suppose. The young guy who I completely based my character's physique on . . . the physical projection that fuels my delusion. So you see, Doc, I never gave Frank a last name, because . . . I never knew it."

Olivia paused a moment, then she took my hand. "Well," she said, "I suppose you will just have to go back to that very diner and find out what it is. That's what you'll do when you beat this thing, now, isn't it?"

CHAPTER 14

CHECKMATE

The next day, I woke up refreshed. I was excited because it was Monday, and you know what that meant? It meant Mia was visiting the next day. There were so many things I wanted to tell her, so many things I had kept inside and couldn't wait to let out.

On my way to breakfast, like clockwork, I walked past Joe.

"Coffee, coffee, coffee, coffee . . . hi, Flynn!"

"Oh, shit," I said, turning toward him. "Did you just . . . talk?"

"Coffee, coffee, coffee," he replied.

"Joe, did you say something?"

"Cofffeeeeeeeeeeeeeee . . ."

"Okay, Joe," I said with a little wave. "See ya tomorrow."

"Hey there, Flynn," said Ann, approaching with a smile. "Here are your happy pills!"

We did our usual morning medication mambo—she

was my dealer: she supplied the pills, I pretended to take them, and then I spit 'em out and slipped them into my jacket pocket.

This morning I wasn't that hungry, so I snagged a bagel and cream cheese and went to see what old Red was up to. He was always an interesting conversation. He was the only person in here who I could just chill with. I went to his usual spot, but he wasn't there. I searched around the hospital, but I couldn't seem to find him anywhere, so I decided to go for a walk with hopes of finding him.

As I strolled through the garden, lo and behold, who did I spot? Red, sitting in the grass in front of an old oak tree, right under one of the heaters. He was plopped down, Indian-style, in his white slippers and robe, a cup of coffee in his hand, I watched as he arranged his pieces on top of the chessboard.

"There you are," I called over to him.

"Hey there, kid! Know where you are?"

"Why do you keep asking me that?"

"Just checking is all . . . I need to know which *you* I'm talking to. Join me for a game, will ya?"

"I don't know how."

"Kid, we've been here before. Sit down."

I sat down in the grass and crossed my legs. Taking a bite from my bagel, I examined the board. I picked up my knight and moved it two spaces forward and then one to the left.

"There we go," said Red.

"But how?" I asked.

"The brain is a powerful thing. The information it can

187

retain is astounding. But that's not what you really came here to discuss, is it?" Red smiled.

He was right, so I decided to get to the point.

"I need your help. How do I beat this thing? How do I get rid of Frank?"

"How do you get rid of the king?" Red replied.

"I don't understand."

"You play the game," Red said as he moved a pawn forward. "This is all in your head, kiddo, and Frank lives in your head. He controls the game, so you control the game. It's just like chess. There are an unfathomable number of ways to win a chess game. But there are only two possible results. You win or you lose. Chess is like consciousness. It's finite yet infinite. It's logical yet illogical. It's knowable yet unknowable. It's hard. It's part art, part science, just like any creative act. You play against your opponent, but really you play against yourself. You are your toughest challenger. Only you have the power to defeat yourself."

"Look, Red, I'm sorry, but . . . I just don't get what this has to do with—"

"Years ago, I had a wife. Her name was Veronica. She was the greatest thing that ever happened to me. I was addicted to heroin when I was your age. I had demons. And I blew it all. Stopped painting, started stealing, you know how the junkie story goes. And at rock bottom I found myself in a rehabilitation center. There I met the woman who would one day be my wife. She was a nurse there, and she helped me through the agonizing withdrawals. The night terrors, the loneliness. I don't know if I would have made it out of there alive if it weren't for her. She believed in me when no one else did, and somehow . . . we fell in love. We spent the next few years on top of the world, boy. I returned to my work as a painter and pool player, and she continued helping those who needed her care." He looked into the distance, as though he was seeing those days in front of him. "She was adventurous. She loved to hike and ski and explore. One Christmas, we went away to a resort to have some fun on the mountain. After a wonderful weekend, I returned home. The day I got back, I was painting a picture of Veronica, who was posed in the window, and my family came to visit me. When my family arrived, though, their eyes were full of tears."

My heart dropped. "What happened?" I asked.

"I just knew it," Red said. "Someone had passed. So my mother told me to sit down, and I told them I was in the middle of painting a portrait of my wife . . . and then I called her into the room and told her we would finish later. That's when my mother asked me if I was ready for the funeral. I didn't understand and called to Veronica again, asking if she knew what was going on. My mother held my hands, tears running down her face, and said, 'Red, Veronica's gone, baby.' I couldn't register what she was saying, so I turned back to my wife . . . but she had vanished. 'Red, she's gone,' my father said. Then I began to panic. I became violent, thrashing about. My brother and a cousin restrained me." He paused for a moment. "I came to in a hospital bed a few days later. Veronica was there, tending to me. I was in rehab again, and she was my nurse. Or at least that's what I saw. What I believed. The truth is, Flynn—"

I sat there, staring at Red as he wiped the tears from his jaw.

"The truth is . . . I spent years in this facility living in a loop much like your own, Flynn. I gave the nurses roles to play, and all of them were the role of my wife. Here I was, a drug addict . . . and she was my angel. Outside of here, I was a nutjob with no way out of his own delusion, and so I let it consume me. Your move."

I looked down at the board.

"And when I faced my wife," he said, holding back more tears, "when I really faced my wife, I realized that it was only me, myself, and I who was holding her captive. That I was the one who couldn't let go. And so I had to face myself—battle myself. To regain my freedom. It was painful and treacherous, but I did it."

"Did what?" I asked, then moved my pawn.

"I played the game I created and got rid of him."

"Got rid of who?"

"The part of myself that refused to let go. *I killed him.*"

"What?" I said. "How can you kill a man who doesn't exist?"

"Therein lies the question, kiddo," said Red, bringing out his bishop.

"Wait a second, Red. If you did it—if you made it through your delusion—why are you still here?"

"I tried, kid, I really did. I went back out there into that world after ten years of living in my mind. I went out into that world and I realized . . . it wasn't a world worth living in without her. And so I came back. Because here is all I really know now."

I stared into Red's eyes as he looked at the board.

"Your move, Flynn."

"How do I kill a man who doesn't exist, Red?"

"Don't you get it? Even if I told you how to do it, it wouldn't register. I can only help you, show you the way. But *you* have to step through the door!"

My forehead wrinkled in confusion. "Okay, Morpheus, how the hell am I supposed to do that?"

"Flynn, think of it like this: it's like depression. Nobody can cure your depression for you. Pills only suppress the real issue. They force the mind into a synthetic state of happiness, which is immediately undone once the substance has left the bloodstream."

This made me think of my jacket pocket full of pills.

"So what then?"

"I'm saying he's real because you've made him real. And yet, there's the part of your brain that refuses to believe the impossible."

"Because you can't kill a man *who does not physically exist*, Red!" I shouted.

"Oh, you can't?!" He pulled out a straight razor, flipped it open, and sliced the palm of his left hand diagonally from the bottom of his index finger down.

"Jesus Christ, Red! What the fuck are you doing?" I yelled, the deep gash making my stomach churn.

"Can I heal the wound with my mind?" Holding his hand out in front of him, Red clenched his fist, hiding the wound. Drops of dark blood began to fall on the chessboard. "Can I heal this wound?"

"What the hell are you talking about?" I said.

"Can I make this wound go away with my mind?"

"Of course not, you crazy son of a bitch!" I said, our voices only intensifying.

"Why the hell not?!" he shouted.

"Because it's . . . just impossible, Red! You need stitches!"

"You're telling me it's impossible for this wound to heal using the power of my mind?"

"That's exactly what I'm saying!" I told him, starting to stand. "I'm getting you a doc—"

"Sit the hell down!" Red demanded, pulling me back to the ground with his right hand. "Do you know what an ulcer is, Flynn?"

"A, wait . . . what?"

"Just answer the fuckin' question, kid."

"Yes, okay?"

"And do you know what creates ulcers?"

"What the fuck are you talking about?!"

"Do you know what creates ulcers?!" Red repeated.

"Stress! I don't know!"

Red smiled. "Exactly! And do you know what creates stress?"

"What the fuck does this have to do with anyth—"

"Do you know what creates stress, goddamn it?!"

"Yeah! Old guys slitting their fucking hands open, okay? You need a doctor!"

"DO YOU KNOW WHAT CREATES STRESS?!" Red screamed, forcing my hand over his clenched fist.

"I don't know!"

"What creates stress?"

"THE MIND!" I screamed as loud as I could. "The mind . . . ," I said again, finally coming to a realization.

"Yes, Flynn," Red said calmly. "The mind."

As I sat there frozen, Red slowly turned his fist over

192

and opened his hand. When he did, blood drained onto the chessboard. My eyes fixed on his hand, Red grabbed the handkerchief from his front robe pocket with his right hand, then wiped his palm, revealing a healed hand. There was no visible wound. Only a faint scar from where the gash had been.

"Holy shit, man!" I screamed, shooting to my feet and backing away. "What the fuck was that?! Who are you, David Blaine?!"

Red began to laugh.

"Do you see what I'm trying to show you, Flynn?"

I slowly sat down.

"Still your move," Red said, gesturing to the blood-stained chessboard.

"If you think I'm touching that shit, you're fuckin' mistaken," I said with a laugh.

"Do you see, Flynn? Do you understand now?"

I thought about how I'd been running from Frank, telling myself he wasn't real. And the denial of his influence had given him the advantage. It made him stronger. But now I knew the truth—Frank's existence had real-life implications. He was real. Maybe not flesh and blood, but real in my mind. He had a distinct personhood in my head. By denying his existence, I hadn't been able to get rid of him because . . . I had no way to fight him.

Until now.

"I have to kill him, don't I?" I said. "But how?"

Wiping his hand with the handkerchief, Red smiled.

"Kid, you're asking a guy who killed a piece of himself to stay alive. This is the part I can't help you with. But look at it this way: you can't go to jail for killing a man who only exists in your head."

"Have you told all this to Dr. Cross?" I asked.

"She can't see me."

"What do you mean?" I asked.

"I'm not her patient."

CHAPTER 15

THE LIBRARY

I couldn't sleep that night. There was too much on my
mind after Red's talk. The next day seemed like the slow-
est day of my life. It was the day Mia was finally going to
visit me.

I couldn't stop pacing. I constantly checked the clock,
waiting for 3:00 p.m. to arrive.

Regardless of everything going on in my head about
the future and Frank and whether I would win this battle,
I would do my best to put that all aside today. To just enjoy
myself.

I played a few games of chess with Red, then spoke to
Olivia in therapy about my excitement about seeing Mia.
I didn't mention Frank, though, or even the conversation
I had with Red.

Deep down, I didn't think Olivia would even understand or believe what had happened between Red and

me the day before. And in many ways, neither could I. It seemed surreal and out of a movie. However, the knowledge I gained from it had been vital to the mission at hand. The whole incident with Red and the wound was powerful. I knew it would change the course of my life.

In the afternoon, I couldn't eat. I just wasn't hungry. I was far too nervous, so I walked around the hospital people-watching and trying to take my mind off Mia. I headed to the one place that brought me some peace: the library. It's where I spent most of my free time. I didn't yet have the mental stability to write, but I could read. The stories in the books transported me to other worlds. They let me become someone else. Not that I needed any help with that, but the stories in the books actually grounded me. It was the power of literature.

The library was beautiful. Especially for a nuthouse library. It was older, with mahogany shelves, worn-in reading chairs, and comforting low light. It was a sanctuary of sorts—wall-to-wall, floor-to-ceiling books, both fact and fiction. As a writer, being surrounded by literature made me feel at home. But it's ironic, because, see, the funny thing is . . . so many books just don't *do it for me*. I know, I know, "You're a writer, how can you not like reading?" you're asking. It's not because I don't want to, I really try, you know? Like legitimately, I've spent so much time trying . . . but most books just don't grab me.

Take, for example, *The Lord of the Rings*. I just can't stand it! Let's be real here—I know the books are hailed as masterpieces. Tolkien goes into such detail, I mean, he has created an entire world with various races of living things inhabiting it. But fuck, dude, by page eighty

I'm like, "Shit, you could have legit said this in ten pages, bro!"

But you see, that's the type of reader I am. I need adventure, I need something fun and fast-paced. I need the pages to turn—suspense, drama, sex, violence, murder, whatever it takes, just keep it moving. I didn't really get into reading until my early twenties. I actually started with Indiana Jones novels. Not sure what it was about them, but I just really enjoyed the reading experience. Maybe it was the fact I'd seen and loved the movies, so it was so easy to imagine Harrison Ford jumping off the page and doing all the cool shit the author was making Indiana Jones do.

Another series I absolutely loved was Jurassic Park. Like most, I had only seen the movies, but holy shit, the books are incredible! The author, Michael Crichton, was literally born to write. Damn near all his novels ended up films—some great, some not so great. But either way, the books were awesome.

With that in mind, I went to Crichton's section of the library and came across one of my all-time favorites, *Sphere*. The movie was great, but, wow, the book! Okay, so—*spoiler alert*—long story short, the book is about these people who are brought together by the government and taken to the bottom of the ocean to investigate what appears to be a spaceship—a spaceship that's been there for more than two thousand years. In time, they open the ship and find a *huge* golden sphere. After they exit, those who entered the sphere can summon things with their minds.

That's kinda how I felt. I felt like my mind was so powerful it could summon things, even subconscious things. Things I didn't want, like Frank.

I hadn't seen Frank since my awakening with Dr. Cross a few days ago, but staring at the book reminded me how more than any book, more than any worries about Frank, all that was really on my mind was Mia, and how I just wanted to be with her. I couldn't stop thinking about her, just hoping she would show up soon!

But it was only eleven o'clock. Since I had a while to go, I decided to keep browsing the fiction section.

I came across a heist thriller about the most successful bank robber in U.S. history. For decades he had never been caught. But when he is falsely imprisoned, he must do anything to survive. It was titled *The Glorious Five.* I was the kinda guy who would read the first line of a book, and if I wasn't intrigued I wouldn't really keep going. So I opened it and read.

CHAPTER 1: TALES FROM THE CRYPT

First things first. You should know I die at the end of this story.

But we'll get into that later.

Oh, I was hooked. That was all I needed. I grabbed the book and put it underneath my arm like a businessman grabbing a newspaper from his front porch before speeding off to work.

Farther down, I stumbled upon another one of my all-time favorites. It was a science-fiction epic called *The Maker,* which takes place in the future. I picked it up, turned it over, and read the synopsis.

A mind-bending adventure that pushes the bounds of reality, <u>The Maker</u> is the dramatic tale of an ordinary man who discovers he isn't a man at all, but a computer program. Created to occupy a simulated existence, the man's existence only serves one purpose—to entertain users longing for adventure in a synthetic world. The man learns of the individual responsible for his very creation, The Maker. Only one question remains: can he find The Maker, gain freedom, and enter the real world?

Reading this got me excited, even though I already knew the story. But there was so much that I forgot that I got psyched. It was like I was falling in love with the story and characters all over again. Time for my third reading of *The Maker*. As I made my way to the checkout counter, I saw another patient waiting in line. She was a woman in her midfifties, overweight, and wearing a cream-colored sweater. Looked like she knitted it herself.

Standing behind her, I began to grow impatient—not because she was taking forever, but because every time my mind snapped back from the distractions I tried to feed it, all I could think about was Mia. I was so excited I couldn't contain myself—she was the light at the end of the tunnel.

I wasn't sure what I would talk to her about. Should I be honest? Should I just lay it all out there? Should I tell her about Frank and really explain what I'd been through? Do I tell her about Red, and did she know about my newfound fandom status? The wealth? I began to wonder if she had only stuck around because of that. Could she be playing me? Maybe she was. I mean, who in their right mind would stay with some philandering schizophrenic psycho? Even though, technically, it was Frank who cheated.

The longer I stood behind this woman, the longer I thought Mia must be in it for the money. There's no way, after all this, she . . . or *anyone* . . . could love me enough to deal with all the shit! Thinking this over for several minutes, I realized *this line hadn't moved.*

"Excuse me, ma'am," I said to the woman in front of me. She just stood there, blankly staring into space. "Hey, lady!" I said, snapping my fingers by her ear. Still, she didn't move. I waved my hand in front of her face. Nothing.

"I'll be with you in just a second!" came a woman's voice from behind the counter. She had a country accent with a smoker's rasp. Her voice was pretty fucked up, and since she was tending to something under the counter, I couldn't see her face.

"Okay, no problem," I replied.

I was staring at the back of the woman's head in front of me. I put out my hands, rested them on her shoulders, and slowly moved her to my left. She was in front of the register now—to my left but looking away.

You know, even as I write this, I'm questioning if I should even be telling you. Not because it isn't an important part of the memory, this woman in a sweater she probably knitted herself, but because it is not exactly vital information.

Sorry, I don't mean to fuck shit up, making you remember that you're reading a book again. But who cares, am I right? I mean, who cares what books I read, or how

I felt about waiting in line? I suppose the only reason I'm describing these things is because that's what you do in novels, am I right? I mean, obviously, we all want to jump to the part where I sit down with Mia, because she's the hot girl we hope I end up with in the story. Even if I am a fuckin' whack job.

But I can't just do that. I'm literally stuck here racking my brain over every detail. Trying to recall every step I took just to paint the picture for you, the reader. I suppose I could tell you what happened in five minutes. I mean, hell, this whole story could have been told in five minutes.

Hey kids, Flynn here. Years ago my girlfriend broke up with me because I was a loser who couldn't finish anything, and it drove me literally insane. So you know what I did? I decided to go work at a supermarket. But wait, there's more! I only worked there to get inspiration and material for a novel I was writing. And I got so immersed in my main character that I started to think he was a real person. But he wasn't! He was an illusion in my mind. Then I realized that we were one and the same. And somewhere in there I fell in love with a girl I worked with and then unwittingly cheated on her, and then she left me. And then I robbed the store, thinking it was all just a scene in my book. Then I had a psychiatric breakdown and woke up in a mental hospital! And . . . and . . . and . . . what if I told you I wanted to skip all this shit and get to the end, because I can't bear to go through it all again? That I spent years of my life living in a loop, and to me, that's what these pages feel like? Or maybe that's all bullshit. Maybe in some sick and twisted way, I'm going through this in great detail because, deep down, I love it. Because these were actually the best times of my life . . .

I'm sorry. As I write, it's clear these things still weigh on me. And even though I've obsessed, and in many ways still do, over the events that have happened . . . it was like going back to a place I never want to visit again. And doing it just for the reader.

It's kinda fucked up, right?

Call it closure, call it whatever you want. All I know is that whatever happens to me at the end of this, deep down I know I can't bullshit you, the reader. I can't cut corners. I have to tell you exactly what happened. Every detail, every memory.

I wasn't sure how much time had passed, but it had been a while.

"What do you need, darlin'?" said the woman behind the counter.

"Just checking out a book."

"Is that so?" said Frank, standing up from behind the counter dressed as a woman—lipstick, a wig with curlers, and a lit cigarette stuck between his lips.

"Oh, shit!"

"Ssshhhhh," Lady Frank said, gesturing to a sign that said *Quiet in the Library!*

"You can't be here!" I said.

"What do you mean, Flynn? I'm clearly here, man."

"I need you to leave me alone," I pleaded. "I need you to get out of my head."

202

"Flynn, baby," Lady Frank said in that fucked-up country accent. "You're just gonna have to accept the fact that you can't get rid of me . . . cuz we're *the same person.* We're in this thing together, to the very end."

"Bullshit! We aren't the same, Frank! I'm real, Frank! You don't exist!"

"If I don't exist," he said, his voice now dark and serious, "then why does this hurt?"

He smacked me across my face: smacked me so hard my bottom lip split and started to bleed. Shocked, I raised a few fingers to my lip, revealing the blood on my middle and index finger.

"This doesn't make sense!" I yelled. "You can't do this because you aren't real!"

"Flynn, you fucking idiot, how many times am I going to tell you this . . . I am real!" He put another cigarette in his mouth and lit it with a silver Zippo.

"Then . . . tell me your last name!" I demanded.

Frank stared down at the floor, then up at me, about to answer . . . and paused.

"Is this real?" I asked, looking down at the blood again.

"If it is," Frank replied, "then how can I not be?"

I looked at Frank, then at the blood on my fingers . . . and then back at Frank.

Only he was gone, like a ghost.

"You say Frank did this to you?" said Olivia, gripping my jawline with her left hand and dabbing a cotton swab on my lower lip.

"Yes. Twenty minutes ago. Right after breakfast." Dr. Cross looked at her watch.

"This happened after breakfast?"

203

"Yes. Olivia, listen—"

"Explain what happened," she demanded.

"I was in the library and—listen, this is gonna sound weird, but . . . Frank is real!"

"No, Flynn. We've been through this. You made him up in your mind."

"Yeah, I know, but . . . my mind has made him real." I winced as she put her hand on my lip, dabbing the wound again.

"Red said . . . ," I muttered under my breath, then paused before continuing. "Frank is real," I said with determination. "Because I've made him real."

"So what?" said Olivia. "You think you can physically extend your hand and touch Frank? Is what you're saying?"

"Yes. I do," I responded, my tone serious.

"Flynn," she said, throwing the cotton swab in the trash. "Come with me."

She turned and headed out of the room. I spit into the can and followed her.

As we walked, I saw Joe drinking his coffee, and I saw Red walking in the garden through the window. As I followed Olivia down a hallway toward a wing I'd never been to, I extended my hand, tracing the wall with my fingertips as I walked behind her.

"Where are we headed?" I asked.

"Here."

She swiped her key card in a door and pulled it open. Inside, the room was dark but illuminated by dozens and dozens of monitors.

"Hey, Henry," she said. A middle-aged, heavyset, balding man in a white security outfit turned around.

"Hey there, Dr. Cross. Haven't seen you in a while."

"Henry, I need you to show me surveillance footage of the library from around one thirty p.m."

"Right to the point, I see, Doctor."

"Look, Henry, just pull up the footage," she told him, putting both palms on the surface of his desk. "I'm not fucking around."

Henry began typing on his keyboard. After a moment, he pulled up the footage.

"Here it is," he said.

"Can you show me the checkout area, please?" Olivia said.

Henry typed on his keyboard and the camera moved around, showing different parts of the library.

"Right there!" I said.

The video showed me in the checkout line, standing behind the zombie woman. Standing there, I realized the last time I saw myself on a monitor, I'd been robbing Muldoon's blind. And the hardest part? Trying to process the fact that a few days before, when I'd been arrested . . . that wasn't a few days ago at all.

It was years ago.

My life was literally slipping away from me. Terrified as I was to lose myself, I somehow felt I was on the right path. At the same time, Olivia was making me feel like my goal was to prove her wrong.

"That's not the right—" said Olivia, then stopped herself as she saw me approaching the older woman. "Why are you touching that patient, Flynn?"

"Because she was just standing there. She wasn't moving or anything."

"So why were you standing there if no one was around to assist?" she asked, a confused expression on her face.

"Because I was waiting for the woman *behind* the counter."

"Uh," grunted Henry, "what woman behind the counter?"

"Look, man, just play the footage, will you?" Olivia barked at him as I threw my hands up in frustration.

That's when Frank popped into the picture on the monitor.

"See, there he is!" I said excitedly. Olivia stared at the screen. "He and I were having a conversation about how he wasn't real."

"I agree," she said.

"No, see . . . that's what I was telling him! That it was bullshit and I was over it. I asked him to tell me his last name and—look, right there!"

On the monitor, Frank stared down at the floor, up at me . . . and paused.

"Did you see that? Just like I told you! Same thing he did when I confronted him in the supermarket."

"Flynn, there's no—"

I quickly pointed at the screen.

"Wait, wait, watch, here it comes . . . BAM!" I said.

"Oh, shit!" yelled Henry.

"You see, I told you," I said, looking at Olivia.

"Flynn, there's no one in this video."

"What?" I said.

"Flynn," she said. "Are you okay?"

"Of course I'm not okay, but not—"

"Yeah," Henry inserted, motioning to the screen. "I mean, this guy is slapping the shit out of himself—"

"Flynn," said Olivia, ignoring the security guard. "I believe you are reverting." She turned back to Henry and ordered him to replay the video.

"No, you don't understand . . . Frank slapped me."

"What do you see when you look at this video, Flynn?" Olivia asked.

"I see Frank and me arguing."

Olivia's eyes widened, the look of concern growing on her face. "Frank isn't in the video, Flynn. Frank doesn't exist!"

"No, I know he doesn't exist, but . . . he is real, Olivia! He's real because I've made him real! Red said that I had to fight him, and the only way I could fight him was to believe in him. Because if I *made* him real, then . . . he could actually be killed!"

Olivia stepped back. "Flynn? There is no one in this video."

I tried to process what she was saying.

"You're reverting," Olivia continued. "You're giving Frank power again, and he is pulling you back into the delusion!"

I refused to believe this. I mean, she couldn't possibly understand. I knew in my heart she was trying to help me, but she wasn't going through it. She hadn't experienced it like me. Red had.

Red, I thought to myself. *I've got to tell him about this.*

Deep down, I felt so conflicted. Dr. Cross was trying to help me erase Frank from my mind; Red was urging me to make him a real man who could be killed.

I needed to speak with Red. I turned around, heading toward the garden where I had last seen him.

"Flynn, wait!" Olivia called after me, but I ignored her. Only Red could help me with this, and I knew it.

In the garden, I sat with Red at a table and told him everything. He explained to me that Frank showing up wasn't a good sign. That Frank was going to do everything he could to bring me back into the delusion, back into the supermarket loop. However, Red told me, the fact Frank was growing more and more real in my mind was actually good.

I remembered the story Red told me about himself. *If Frank were real, he could be killed.* I said this to myself as a reminder. Reminding myself not to forget that epiphany . . . that moment in the garden the day before, when Red showed me the power of the mind over his chessboard.

"Dr. Cross is a good woman who means well," he said. "But in the end, she's the doctor and we're the patients. We are the ones who must suffer. And as someone who has made it out of the delusion, you must heed my advice. Because it is the only way to beat this thing, Flynn."

As I thought about what Red was saying, Olivia walked into the garden and stood in front of our table.

"Hello there," she said.

"Olivia, I—"

"Listen, can I borrow you for a moment?" she asked, placing her hand on my arm for comfort. It worked.

"Okay," I said, standing up. "I'm coming back after," I told Red, then pushed my chair into the table before following Olivia.

We walked slowly, quiet for a moment. "I don't believe you are thinking clearly, Flynn," she finally said.

"Listen, you don't know what this is like." I kicked a pebble in front of me. "This has been hell. I'm fucking living in a psych ward. I've got some alter ego trying to ruin my life. Half the time I can't tell what's real and what's fake. I'm present for no more than a couple of weeks at a time, then I'm back in the mind trap. I know I've been working hard in therapy and all, but damn. When will it end? Is this thing going to go on forever? Am I going to wind up on the streets, stark raving mad like my dad? I can't take it anymore. I've got to beat this thing. The suffering is cruel. I know you're only trying to help, but you're not the one living it, you can't feel what I'm feeling in here."

"Yes, that's true. I cannot feel what you feel. But . . . I've seen this before in you. And I don't want you to fall back into Frank's grip. You are at a tipping point."

"You know what, Dr. Cross? He isn't real. And I know that, but it's just difficult and sometimes . . . sometimes I think it's hard for me to let that thought go. Because that feeling is all I've known for so long."

"Frank isn't real, Flynn. Frank is something your subconscious conjured up as a last resort to aid you in the completion of your novel. Now he's taken on a life of his own. And now, you must let it go. You must let *him* go."

"You're right!" I said. "I will fight this thing, Olivia! I will let Frank go and let go of his power over me."

"It won't be easy," she said.

"I know. But I have to give it my all."

After our talk, I returned to the table I had been sitting at with Red. He asked me how the talk went, and I told him that when speaking to Olivia, I told her everything she needed to hear. I couldn't tell her the truth. She just wouldn't understand.

Instead, I pretended she was right. That I needed to let Frank go. But the truth? That hadn't worked in the two years since my breakdown.

Red had been right. He gave me vital information that day under the tree—that day when he showed me the power of the mind. In order to destroy Frank, he had to be real.

He just had to be.

CHAPTER 16

THE LETTER

I sat on my bed, checking the clock.

2:30 p.m.

I stood up and began to pace.

2:35.

I did push-ups. I never did push-ups.

2:40.

I ate a stick of gum and turned the wrapper into an origami swan.

2:45.

I couldn't take it anymore, so I left my room and walked around the place. I still didn't know what I was gonna say. And what would she say?

I slowly walked toward the entrance of the facility, where Mia would arrive. I started getting nervous. Maybe I shouldn't greet her at the door? *Too weird,* I told myself. *Too needy.*

Instead, I walked back to my room.

2:50.

I'd been cooped up in this place so long, constantly obsessing over Frank and regaining my life . . . I needed a break. And Mia was the only thing I wanted. Deep down, I knew she was a huge reason why I was fighting. Because even if I did get my sanity back, get my world back . . . what's the world without anyone to share it with?

3:00.

She would be here any minute now. I couldn't contain myself.

3:05.

Running a little late, but it was okay. I just couldn't wait to see her.

3:10.

I started throwing my red rubber ball against the wall of my room.

3:15 . . .

"Traffic. Has to be traffic," I said out loud, the ball bouncing off the wall in front of me. As I extended my hand to catch it, Frank intercepted the catch.

"Traffic in the middle of the day?" he said. "Unlikely."

"What are you doing here, Frank?"

"I'm doing my part, man. I'm being the only real friend you've ever had. You let this bitch get between us from day one, man."

"Don't call her that!" I shouted.

"Jesus Christ, bro! Sorry, damn."

"Please leave! You can't be here when she shows up," I said, snatching the ball from his hand.

"Jesus, you're fuckin' rude!"

"Well, excuse me if I'm not laying down the red carpet for the guy who *ruined my fuckin' life*."

"Look, man," Frank said. "Whether you want to believe this, I'm your only friend." He leaned against the wall with a James Dean swagger.

"That's not true . . . I . . . I've got Red!"

"Haha, that old man is feeding you bullshit. You can't trust anybody here. You're in a fucking insane asylum, Flynn. Nothing is as it seems."

"Well, it *seems* like you need to *get the fuck out of here before Mia shows up*!"

"She's not showing up, man!"

Just then, there was a knock at the door. Frank and I looked at each other, then back at the door. The handle turned, and the door slowly opened. It felt as though it were taking an eternity, like there was someone on the other side who didn't want to come in but felt compelled to.

And then there she was, standing in front of me.

I felt a number of emotions. But the strongest one? Anger. Not at her, but at the situation. I knew deep in my heart why she had come here.

All I wanted was Mia. All I wanted was someone to escape into, to love. And instead of the woman I wanted to see, here stood Dr. Cross.

"I'm sorry, Flynn, but—"

"She isn't coming, is she?" I interrupted, then turned around to sit on the bed. As I did, I noticed Frank had gone.

213

"She . . . she left this for you," said Dr. Cross, walking toward me with a note in her hand.

She sat on the bed next to me, her hands in her lap gripping the piece of paper.

"She said she was sorry. She thought she was ready to see you. But she, well . . . she didn't want to open up just to have you slip away again. She couldn't bear to . . ." Olivia sighed. "Well, I'm sure everything you need to know is in this note."

She took my hand and placed the piece of paper in my palm. With that, she rose to her feet, wiped a tear from her cheek, and left the room.

The last thing I wanted to do was read the letter. The only thing I wanted to do was read the letter.

As I opened it, I noticed Mia's familiar handwriting. I began to read aloud.

My Dearest Flynn,

I thought I was ready for this. I thought I was ready to see you. The real you again! But I'm not. I've grown so accustomed to living in your loop. Coming to the hospital, entering those doors, and seeing this place through your eyes. Watching it transform into Muldoon's right in front of us.

You've broken free from the delusion before. And having you, the real you, in my arms . . . that was amazing. But that was only once, and I wasn't prepared in the slightest for what I felt after. The emptiness I felt when Frank pulled you back again.

I went from dating you in the real world to you

214

losing your mind, then I regained you and lost you all over again. I'm sorry, but I just don't think I can do this anymore. I just don't deserve this. And that makes me feel terrible. It's so selfish of me, because <u>you</u> are the person who doesn't deserve this most of all! You are the one living with this. The one haunted by Frank.

I was there, Flynn. I was there and helped you escape the supermarket that time. And then he came . . . he took you from me! I just can't do that again.

I love you, Flynn. I'm sorry. I'm truly sorry.

With remorse,
Mia

Tears rolled down my cheek onto the letter. I lifted my head, dropping my hands in my lap. "I told you she wasn't coming," said Frank.

And with that, I threw my head back onto my pillow and I slept . . .

And slept . . .

And slept.

When I came to, I was coughing. The room smelled of smoke. I checked the clock. 4:00 a.m. I looked around, squinting into the darkness.

The room wasn't on fire.

Frank was sitting in the chair next to my bed, softly illuminated by the moonlight entering the window. He was smoking.

215

"Come to the supermarket, Flynn."

"Dude, we've been through this a million times. I'm not letting you suck me back."

I sat up and swung my legs over the edge of the bed, my hands gripping my knees.

"No, man, that's not what I mean," he said, dragging on the cigarette, then exhaling a plume. The smoke was beautiful in the moonlight.

"Then what do you mean, Frank?" I said, my voice tired.

"I mean meet me at the supermarket. Leave this fucking place and . . . meet me at Muldoon's in town."

I didn't understand. "What?"

"Just agree to meet me this Friday. If you do, I'll leave you alone until then."

"You want me to break out of here? This place is like a fuckin' fortress, man."

"Meet me there Friday," Frank repeated, "and I won't bother you at all until then. I promise."

I thought about this and wondered . . . why? Why the hell would he want me to go there? But in that moment, I thought of Red and suddenly realized two things.

If I accept, that gives me three days to prepare . . .

. . . and this just may be the opportunity I need to end Frank once and for all.

Finally end him, in the very place he was created.

"Okay, Frank," I said. " You win. I'll meet you there on Friday."

"At midnight, buddy."

"Wait . . . midnight on Friday? As in Friday morning at twelve a.m.? Or Friday at midnight, which is technically Saturday morning at twelve a.m.? Just to be clear—"

216

"See you then," he said. He put out his cigarette on the nightstand, right next to the classic-looking white alarm clock. As he lifted his hand, I stared at the butt of the cigarette, bent and withered.

When I looked back up, Frank was gone. I started tripping.

When I woke up coughing on the smoke from Frank's cigarette, was that me choking on a figment of my imagination? Or was I the one actually smoking? And was I even in my bed? Or was I sitting in that chair, the one in front of the window?

And the scariest thought of all . . .

If Frank and I shared the same mind . . . was I ever really alone?

Did Frank know my thoughts, my moves, and even my subconscious ideas before I did? All of a sudden, all these questions raced through my head; the entire thing was such a mind-fuck. I couldn't believe everything I had, and was, going through. It felt like something out of a twisted movie . . . but I guess even the craziest movie concepts stem from real life.

With that I coughed, stood up from the chair, laid down on the bed, and drifted asleep.

I woke up Wednesday morning feeling refreshed. Everything I'd gone through was draining, taking a tax on my mind and body—but they told me that was common in schizophrenic breakdowns.

The clock read 9:25 a.m. However, I noticed that next to the clock there wasn't a cigarette butt.

Instead of the usual—racking my brain trying to figure out what the hell that meant—I decided to start my day.

Walking to the cafeteria was peaceful. Good ol' Joe was drinking his coffee; Ann and I did our little antidepressant dance. And then I was sitting next to Red, eating pancakes, arguing about an episode of *Friends*.

"They were on a break!" Red said.

"Yeah, a *break*. As in, like, not together *temporarily*!" I retorted. "Just because they weren't together, that doesn't give Ross the right to go fuck whatever girl he pleases!" Red shook his head, obviously unconvinced. "Look, man." I laughed. "We're just gonna have to agree to disagree."

"So," said Red, finally bringing up the Big Subject. "How you holding up? I heard Mia couldn't make it yesterday."

"Who told you that?"

"I know what you know, kid. It's my job to stay in the loop. These are serious times."

"I'm okay, man," I said. "I get it. It's tough . . . I can only imagine how hard it must be for her."

"I hear ya, kid."

I thought about telling Red about the encounter with Frank last night, but for some reason I had a bit of hesitation. Not because I couldn't trust him, but because I was enjoying my morning so much I really didn't feel like discussing it.

Red was my first real friend since Frank, and we all know how that ended. In that moment, I was less concerned with the mind-bending events ahead of me, and more focused on having a laugh with the only person who'd really been able to help me. He was such a great old man, Red. It made me sad his wife had been taken from him.

But I still had time.

With the things Red had taught me, I could still get my life back.

CHAPTER 17

RED

It was almost 5:00 p.m. when we linked up to play chess.
It wasn't looking good for Red. In five moves I had check-
mate. I was lifting up my queen when I saw her.

She was standing by the soda machine at the front door
of the rec room, wearing a chunky cream-colored sweater.
It was the kind with a loose turtleneck. Black jeans hugged
her long legs, amplifying her amazing body.

With a nervous smile on her face, she waved.

I stood up, tipping the board in the process. The pieces
scattered across the floor. I walked toward her, my hands
in my pockets. So many things raced through my mind.
I wanted to talk to her about everything, yet I didn't. I
wanted to tell her everything I'd been going through, but
also wanted to escape it all in that moment with her.

"Hey there," she said, biting her bottom lip.

"Hey yourself."

"I . . . I'm, well . . . you think we can talk?" she asked, clearly nervous.

"Of course," I said. "Why don't we head to the West Wing? There's a pretty quiet area with a table we can sit at."

"Sounds good."

We didn't say a word to each other on the way. Luckily, it was only a short walk. Out of everything that had been going through my mind, all I could think about was this moment. That this was real and Mia was here. I wanted to pour my heart out but I didn't want to scare her off.

As we arrived at the table in the West Wing, we sat opposite of each other in low, comfortable chairs in front of a small coffee table that was also low to the ground.

"I'm sorry, Flynn."

"No, please don't. I know you've—"

"Flynn, please. I need to say this." She gave me a stare that said *I've been thinking about this for a long time and now's the time for me to talk.* Then she adjusted herself in her chair.

"I didn't come yesterday for obvious reasons. But I've also come today to tell you that . . . I graduated law school."

This wasn't what I had expected. Obviously, she had been in school to become an entertainment attorney but . . . well, what can I say? I'd quite literally been living in my own world.

"The reason it's so hard to be here is because, as much as I'm still in lo—" She stopped herself. "As much as I care for you, I can't continue to wait for you, Flynn. I have to live my life and I feel so horrible saying this, but—"

"No, Mia. You're totally right. As hard as it is to hear, I

221

completely understand. With everything that you've been through, I can only imagine how you must feel."

"But, Flynn," she said, tears welling in her eyes, "that's the worst part. My life goes on. But you're here dealing with this insanity! I wish I could help you, but I just don't know how." And that's when it hit me. That's when I knew exactly what needed to happen.

"Mia, what if I told you . . . I knew how to escape this." She wiped her eyes with both hands before the tears had a chance to fall. "What do you mean, Flynn?"

"Well, there is this old man I've befriended who is a patient here. His name is—"

"Red. Yeah, I know." I was taken aback. "You know about Red?" I asked.

"Flynn, this isn't the first time you've woken, remember?"

She was right, though it was crazy to think she could remember Red but I couldn't. Memories from my previous awakenings were extremely blurry or completely nonexistent.

"Well, if you know about Red, then you know he's been a great help to me."

"I can only imagine," she said. "I remember when you first told me about him, and you explained how he had struggled with his own delusions. And even though he made it out, he was never the same."

How many times have I awoken? I thought. *How many times did Red have to put himself back there in that pain, explaining the death of his wife over and over, all in the hopes that it would help me heal and fight my own delusion?*

"Mia," I said, sitting up straighter. "Mia, I think I know

how to beat this thing once and for all. But I'm gonna need your help."

"Flynn, we've been here a million times."

"Not. Like. This," I said, more serious than ever. "Mia, I'm so in love with you. And after the news about my career from my mother, success of my book . . . what we had and the future we could have . . . I can't let this go."

"Flynn, I'm moving to NYC."

My heart sank.

"I've got an entry-level position at a law firm as soon as I pass the bar. I can't wait anymore. I've put it off for too long and . . . I'm sorry."

I tried to process this information.

"I've done all I can do, Flynn. I've been patient, I've been persistent, I've been aggressive. I've spent days and nights here. I've given you my time, my energy, my thoughts, my emotions. I've done anything and everything to help you, but I'm sorry. I've run out of patience. I have to live my own life now." Holding back tears, she started to rise from her seat. "I hope you understand."

She turned to walk away.

"No, Mia, wait! Listen!" I said, running after her and grabbing her by the arm. "I can kill Frank!"

She stared at me, taken aback.

"What the fuck are you talking about, Flynn? Do you hear yourself?"

"Look, I know how it sounds . . . but Red told me that."

I thought about my next words very carefully, and the whole time, Mia waited, looking as though she were in emotional limbo, hanging in anticipation of the words I would utter next.

"What's another day?"

"What?" she said. "What are you talking abou—"

"Look." I put both hands on her shoulders. "I need your help. I need you to trust me, utterly and completely. I need you to just . . . help me. You don't owe me shit, okay? But do this one thing, and if it doesn't work, then you go . . . you go live the life you deserve in New York. You get a great job, find a guy who isn't out of his mind. Get married, start a family, and live happily ever after." I took a breath. "But if it works, and I feel deep in my heart it will, then I go to New York City with you and we live that ending . . . together."

She thought about what I was saying and seemed totally lost. She didn't know what to make of the situation, and, to be honest, neither did I.

"You're fucking crazy. No way," she said.

"Mia, please. Listen to me. Just this one thing," I said.

"What do you need from me?" she asked.

"Your help. I need you to help me break out of here."

"What the fuck, Flynn!" she erupted. "Are you serious?!?! I can't do that."

"I need this. Trust me, please."

"Flynn, you're asking me to be an accessory. I can't help you break out . . . of a mental facility!!!"

I put the palm of my hand over her mouth. "Ssshh-hhh!!!!!"

Mia pushed my hand from her mouth. "What the fuck? Get the hell off me!" I could tell she was getting really angry.

"Listen, Mia, I'm fucked up, okay? There's no way around it . . . I've got fuckin' problems. And to be quite honest, you've got problems too, or you wouldn't be standing here with such a mess!"

"I came here to tell you I'm leaving, remember?" she said with a smart-ass tone and smirk to match.

It was *so hot*.

"I can kill Frank." She looked at me, and I knew that expression from memory—confusion, but also intrigue. "Frank is real," I continued. "I mean, look, I know he doesn't exist in the physical sense but he does because . . . he's real in my mind. I tried to run from him for so long, and that's what kept him alive. It's like all the problems we face, or rather don't have the strength to face . . . we run from them. But that doesn't make them less real. Emotions, sadness, anger, depression, financial debt, physical insecurities . . . *Frank*. All real things that we, as human beings, are constantly running from. But these things that frighten us can be dealt with if we accept their realism and deal with the problem. *Head on*." I stared into her deep, brown eyes. "I kill Frank, I kill the problem."

Then, in the moment, I wondered . . .

"Mia, have we had this conversation before?" I asked.

"No," she said softly.

"Then you see that's why this has to work . . . because I've never tried it."

"You're going to kill the fictional character and protagonist of your novel?"

"Yes," I replied.

"Do you have any idea how that sounds?"

"One day, Mia," I said. "What's another day?"

225

She paused, looked at the ground, then at me . . .

"What's the plan?" she said.

"To be completely honest, I hadn't really thought of one yet."

"What the hell, Flynn? Why would you ask me to commit to such a thing without thinking it through? Jesus!"

"Look, honestly . . . I didn't exactly think you were gonna agree, okay?"

"Well," she said, moving closer until her body was lightly pressed against mine. "I did."

For a moment, she was silent.

"Why one day?" she asked softly.

"Because that's when Frank told me to meet him," I said, reaching for her hand. I held it loosely, the fingers of my right hand interlocking with her left.

"Where?" she asked, tightening her grip a bit.

"The supermarket."

She looked at me with a blank stare. I wasn't sure what to expect.

"Okay. But listen. None of this run-off-into-the-sunset craziness. I'll support you through the next twenty-four hours, because I care for you. And if this gets you straight, then I'll agree to a date. Okay?"

"Okay?"

"Yes, Flynn, okay!" she said, eager to move on to more important things. "Now, what's the plan?"

I thought for a moment.

"Listen, give me some time to gather my thoughts. Really think things through. I'll call you tomorrow and explain."

Our bodies were so close. Our lips almost touching.

"I really want this to work," she said.

"I really need this to work," I replied.

I could feel the warmth of her breath on my face, and as we inched closer, she tilted her head down ever so slightly . . . planting her lips on my cheek instead.

"Talk to you tomorrow," she whispered in my ear.

Later that evening, I found myself lying in my room, thinking of all the possible outcomes. After an hour of throwing my ball against the wall, ricocheting back into my hand, I realized I was only psyching myself out.

I decided to take a stroll. It was quarter to ten, which meant I had fifteen minutes before lights out. I decided to make my way over to Red's room, and on the way, I tried to think of ideas. Ideas of how to break out of this joint.

I thought of dressing up as a guard . . . but where the hell would I get the clothes? I mean, all we wore was white. The doctors wore white coats, the security guards wore white pants and T-shirts, only the black shoes and badges proving their authority. And we, the patients, wore what looked more like white pajamas. Sweatpants, long-sleeved shirts, and robes to match. I did, though, convince them to let me rock my jacket. It was my security blanket. As similar as the color was to a security guard's, the actual attire was unmistakable.

I had just under twenty-four hours to devise a plan that would get me the hell out of here.

Snatching a security guard's outfit wasn't happening.

I finally made it to Red's door. I raised my hand, fingers clenched in preparation to hurl my knuckles into the door's cold metal surface—but before I made contact, the door swung open.

My hand fell limp from the absence of contact, and there was Red. It was as if he knew I was coming—he had a smile ready on his face.

"Hey there, kid," he said.

"Hey, Red. Mind if I come in?"

"Not at all." He gestured for me to come into his room. "How about that Santa Claus they have coming here, huh? It's a trip. They've only started doing that the last few years."

He was right. The week of Christmas a group of actors would come play Santa, Mrs. Claus, and some helpful elves. They would put on a play and then hang out with some of the patients. In the days leading up to it, patients would talk about it day and night, all excited. It was sweet in a way.

"Listen," I said. "I've been thinking."

"You want a drink?" he asked.

"What? You have alcohol here? How the hell did you get that in here?"

"Kid, when you've been here as long as me, you know how to get things in and out of this building."

I froze, the statement giving me the boost of confidence I needed.

"I hope you like Scotch," Red said as he grabbed a bottle of Hibiki from underneath his bed. Hibiki was a type of Japanese Scotch—I'd only had it once before, years ago. Accompanying the bottle were two whiskey glasses with the words *Bobby Billiards* printed across them. It was the same place Red used to shoot pool back in the day.

"I love Scotch, actually," I said, still thinking about what he had just said. Maybe Red would know the best way to get out of this place.

"You know," he said, "the first time I ever had Hibiki was actually in Japan at the Ritz Carlton. Years back. I was there for a pool tournament."

"You don't say."

He gave a graceful pour and handed me a glass. Raising his in the air, he said, "To sanity." I looked down, then we clinked and took our sips. Delicious. Smoky and full-bodied.

"Eyes, eyes!" he said.

"What?"

"Eyes, boy! You never take your eyes from another when making a toast before you drink! It's bad luck."

"To sanity," I said, staring right at him. Our glasses collided and I downed the entire thing.

"Damn, Flynn!"

"What?"

"Scotch is for sippin', boy . . . not for pouring back! This ain't tequila now!" He chuckled.

"Hey, Red?" I said, extending my hand for another pour.

"Yeah?" He gave me a much heavier pour this time.

"You said you can get things in . . . and out of this place?"

I was already feeling tipsy. Now that I thought about it, I hadn't had a drink since I wrote the ending of my novel.

Since the night Frank robbed . . . I robbed the super-market.

"Yeah," he said. "I can get pretty much anything in this place."

"Red, I gotta tell you something."

"What is it, Flynn?" he said, face full of concern.

I told him all about the previous night, when Frank visited me in my room. I told him about the planned meeting at Muldoon's. I told him about the conversation I had with Mia and how, deep in my heart, I felt this was the end.

Or, at least, the beginning of the end.

He clutched his glass as I told him my plan. I was prepared to get rid of Frank by any means necessary.

To kill him in cold blood.

I still didn't know exactly how to do it, but I figured it would all work out in the end . . . or, at least, I hoped it would. Or it wouldn't . . . then I didn't know what would happen.

Red sat on his bed, listening. His face was blank. He checked the clock—five till ten.

"This is heavy, kid," he finally said. "Listen, I have an idea but, just . . . just give me some time to think it over. Let's meet tomorrow for breakfast, and I'll have a solid plan in place. Okay?"

I realized Red was the father figure I'd always wanted. The man I would make up in my head as a kid, the kind of dad I dreamed of having. A guy I wanted to be like. A guy to go fishing with, or play catch with in the yard. Red was everything I wished I had growing up but didn't. And yet . . . he was here now. When I needed him most.

"Okay, Red. I'll see you in the morning for breakfast."

This was different. I could feel it. Something wasn't normal here . . . and normal for me had been living in a series of delusions inside a psych ward. This was different, and different was good.

I really felt, for the first time in a long time, that I could beat this thing.

"Flynn, I know it's hard. I've been there, but you're ready now, I can feel it." Red stood up. "I'll meet you in the cafeteria."

He took my glass and gave me a hug.

"Thank you, Red," I said as he walked me to the door.

"Now get outta here. If we're gonna put an end to this, I got shit to plan . . ."

CHAPTER 18

BREAKOUT

I awoke Thursday morning to the sun on my face. I must have forgotten to close the blinds before falling asleep. The sun's warmth blanketed my skin. It was the most at peace I'd felt in a long time. As I opened my eyes I realized that today was the day.

Today was the day I would kill a man.

I still wasn't sure how you killed a man, especially one born out of a chemical imbalance in your brain. But I'd figure it out with Red's help.

I swung my legs around the side of my bed and looked at the clock. 8:37 a.m. I felt an inner calm. A certain tranquility. Somehow, I just knew Red was gonna pull through. It was as if I already had tonight's escape laid out in my head. It was like some kind of emotional foreshadowing. You know that feeling you get when you know something is going to go down a certain way?

I put on my clothes and walked toward the cafeteria.

In the hallway, I saw things differently. Looking at the other patients, I didn't see people who were stuck in this facility. I saw people who were stuck within the confines of their own minds. The key to their escape lay deep beyond the layers of their subconscious. In a way, as I stared at them, I was staring at myself.

"Coffee, coffee, coffee!" Joe said yet again this fine morning as I walked past.

"Hey there, Joe," I said, and like clockwork Ann came to give me the antipsychotic pills I would pretend to ingest and put in my right jacket pocket. As I placed the pills atop the mountain of others just like them, something hit me—I had officially run out of space to place any future pills. There had to be hundreds jammed in there. That eerily made me feel like it was a sign. Like this would be the last time Ann and I would do the medication mambo.

On the walls were pictures I never really noticed. Every year, the hospital gathered its patients for a yearly Christmas photo. Along the wall was every picture they had taken since the hospital had been built more than a hundred years ago. As I walked past the pictures, I came to the most recent ones. Looking deeply at a photograph, I spotted myself in the crowd. Looking at the photo even closer, all I saw was a shell of who I was.

I didn't even remember taking these photos. I looked totally vacant. I had a hollow expression across my face. I could see everyone from the hospital in them, lined up like those class pictures in elementary school. While scanning a photograph's surface with my fingertips, part of me was looking for Frank. In doing so, I noticed there was someone missing in the picture.

Red. Not only was he missing from this photo, he was also missing from the one from last year.

As I retraced my steps, walking backward, I noticed he wasn't in a single Christmas photo taken during the entire decade he had been at the facility. I found this strange, but only for a moment . . . then I realized it.

His wife had died on Christmas, while skiing. To be honest, if something that traumatic happened to me on Christmas, I really wouldn't want to take a photo either.

I continued on my way to meet Red for breakfast.

He was already sitting. He smiled and waved as I walked up.

"Okay, kid," he said as soon as I sat across from him. "I got it. You know what today is, don't you?"

"I don't know, man. Thursday?"

"No, boy, well . . . I mean, yes, but it's also holiday season!"

He was right! Man, I'd been so absorbed in trying to end this I'd been oblivious to everything else. Including the holiday!

"Okay, so it's Christmas Eve, but . . . I don't get it?"

"Flynn, it is the most lenient day of the year as far as security goes. There's only a quarter of the staff working, which means fewer guards patrolling the hospital at night."

He was right, and it filled me with even more promise.

"Okay, but how do we get out, Red?"

He took something out of his left robe pocket and held it in his hand. Placing the back of his hand on the table-top, the object lay there hidden behind his fingers. As he unclenched his fist, opening his hand, I saw it.

"Holy shit!" I yelled.

"Quiet now, boy, quiet now!" he said, looking around the cafeteria.

It was a key card for our wing.

"How did you get this?" I asked, trying to keep my voice low.

"Now, old Red has his ways. G'on now, take it." I stared at the object in awe. Finally, I was going make it out of this place! Nothing could hold me back. Slowly, I reached for the key card. I grabbed it, exposing Red's palm.

The scar on his left hand reminded me of our conversation a few days ago. So much had happened since then. Since my awakening, I thought.

"Red?" I asked hesitantly. "Have I . . . well, have I ever . . . made it this far before?"

"No, Flynn. It's different this time. Tonight's the night."

He held my hand and smiled, which made me feel better.

"I have to go call Mia," I said. As I stood up, Red grabbed me by the arm.

"Kid, wait."

I sat back down.

"Listen, you know no matter how slim the staff is tonight . . . you can't just walk out of here dressed like that. You'll need a disguise."

"What kind of disguise?" Red glanced under the table, gesturing with his eyes. I scooted my chair back and took a peek. There was a large brown paper bag on the floor.

I grabbed it and put it in my lap.

"Go ahead and take a look," Red said with a smile on his face. I opened the bag and saw two costumes.

A Santa outfit and an elf outfit.

"You're kidding."

"Hell, no, I ain't kidding! Best disguises we could possibly have."

I paused. "What do you mean we, Red?"

"What do you think I mean, we? I'm gonna help you get out of here."

"I've already got Mia involved," I said, feeling a sudden burst of worry. "I just wouldn't feel right dragging you along, Red. We both know I need to do this alone."

"Well, too bad," he said. "The Santa outfit is mine and the elf one is you—"

"First of all, you're not coming. And second, if you *were* to come, you wouldn't be Santa."

"Oh, yeah? And why the hell not?" Red asked.

"Uh, isn't it obvious?"

"Isn't what obvious?"

"Dude, Santa isn't black."

"What you're telling me is that there can't be no black Santa Claus?" he said in a half-joking, half-serious tone.

"I mean, maybe in Compton, old man . . . but the last time I checked, we were in the middle of Oregon. This is, like, *the whitest place on Earth*," I told him, chuckling.

"Well, you might be right about that, but—"

"But nothing! Please, Red . . . you've already helped so much, and you said it yourself. This is something I have to do alone." Red took a deep breath and exhaled. "And I'm not gonna wear this, by the way. I'll look ridiculous."

"Look, kid, I just want what's best for you, is all. And I

do understand. I suppose you do, in fact, need to face this demon yourself. But . . . you are going to wear the Santa outfit."

"But why?"

"'Cause Jeff is off at nine p.m."

"Who the hell is Jeff?" I asked.

"The Santa the hospital hired last week," Red told me, saying it like I was an idiot.

"Well, shit, I didn't know his name was Jeff! I just called him Santa. What does that have to do with me getting out of here?"

"Because!" Red replied. "If you get spotted, the guard will just think you're Jeff on his way home."

"Holy shit, that's pretty smart," I said.

"Damn right."

"Wait, how did you get this key card?" I asked, crossing my arms.

"You know Henry?"

"The guard who mans the security monitors?"

"That's the one," Red said, taking a sip of coffee.

"He's the one who showed Dr. Cross and me the footage of Frank punching me in the library. What about him?"

"Well, he's a younger guy . . . let's just say I took care of him."

"Oh my God!" I said, shocked. "You killed him?"

"No, you idiot!" said Red as he raised both hands in the air. "Who do you think I am? I gave him some money, Jesus!"

"Oh," I said. "Sorry about that. Well, okay . . . that's good," I said, trying to sound like I didn't just accuse my best friend of murder.

"I paid him off," he said, motioning to the key card. "He's playing hooky tonight." He grinned. "He called in, and due to such short notice on a holiday, nobody will be monitoring the cameras this evening."

"Red, you're a genius, man!" I said, smiling wide. "This seems pretty fail-safe!" I high-fived him, my eyes landing on the wall clock over his shoulder. "Oh shit, I gotta go!" I said.

"Where you off to?"

"I have an appointment with Dr. Cross. Hopefully my last one."

"That woman seems like such a good doctor," said Red. "I wish she could see me."

"She's a good therapist, that's for sure. You should put in a request and try to make an appointment." I stood up. "Thanks again for everything, Red," I said, patting him on the back as I rushed off toward Olivia's office.

In my hurry from all the excitement, I realized I had forgotten to call Mia and tell her the plan. Down the hallway from Olivia's office, I saw a phone attached to the wall. I was late, but I picked up the receiver and put it to my ear. Just as I was about to dial . . . I heard him.

"Hey, dude, listen. Don't forget you gotta be there at twelve sharp, okay?"

It was Frank.

"Frank, what the fuck are you doing, man? You said you were gonna leave me alone!" I said, my voice rising.

"Well, look, man, I'm keeping up my end of the bargain, aren't I? I mean, I didn't just appear out of nowhere this time, huh?"

"Fuck you for ruining my life, man."

"Oh come off it, you pretentious motherfucker!" Frank barked into my ear. "I'm just checking in to make sure you're not gonna puss out!"

"Look, I'll be there tonight, okay!" I said into the phone. "Just leave me the fuck alone until then!"

With that, I slammed the phone down.

BLLRRRRINNGGGG.

I jumped at the loud sound and picked up midring.

"Hello?" I said.

"Don't you ever fuckin' hang up on me."

This time Frank sounded calm, but his tone was unsettling. "I'll see you tonight, Flynn. But just know you can't win everything. You know, *I know.*"

The phone went dead. But right then, I knew the phone had been dead the entire time. The whole conversation was in my head.

I was shook. Terrified. I couldn't let myself overthink it—even if he knew my plan, he still didn't know how I was going to kill him. Because *I* didn't know how I was going to kill him.

Therefore, my plan could still work. I picked up the phone again. Reluctantly, I placed it to my ear, bracing myself. It was just a dial tone.

I punched in Mia's phone number. The phone rang . . . and rang . . . and rang . . .

After the third, I was greeted by her voice mail.

Hey, this is Mia, why don't you leave Mia message! Hahaha, get it? No? Whatever . . . just leave it at the beep.

"Hey, it's Flynn. Haha, you still have that message, huh? Anyway, listen . . . I've got a plan. Call me back."

I hung up the phone and headed to Olivia's office. I

239

stood at the door for a moment, not knocking. I was so shaken by everything going on. Damn, this was literally insane.

"Hey, Flynn!"

"Holy shit!" I screamed, jumping. It was Dr. Cross, coming up from behind me.

"Oh my God, I'm sorry. I didn't mean to scare you!" she said, looking extremely concerned.

"Oh, no . . . don't worry about it. To be fair, I was pretty zoned out," I said, wiping the sweat from my brow.

"Okay, well, I am sorry. I'm running behind today. So, let's get started, shall we?" She opened the door and motioned for me to enter. "Have a seat."

I sat down, but I was so jittery I could hardly bear the confines of a chair. So I stood up. "I'm sorry, but do you mind if I pace? I just feel really wound up."

"Of course not, by all means."

I removed my red ball from my left jacket pocket and began to bounce it. This calmed me some.

"So, what do you want to talk about today?" Dr. Cross asked me, already writing in her black notepad.

"Dr. Cross," I said sincerely. "Do you think you have all the answers?"

"Certainly not, Flynn."

"So, well, I mean . . . so your method of trying to get rid of Frank could, in fact, be flawed?"

"Well, sure. I have a great deal of training and experience, but schizophrenia is a complicated and multifaceted condition. Scientists still don't understand it fully. It's behavioral, biological, neurological, environmental, and genetic. There is no known cure. There is no unified theory to explain the condition, so each case is treated on its own terms."

The term scared the living shit out of me. Me . . . *schizophrenic?* I mean, how do I even process that? I knew it was the truth, but her putting it so bluntly just cut me deep.

"You've been receptive to many different treatments. A combination of group therapy, medication, psychoanalysis, even yoga. These have been greatly beneficial to you. I think you should continue on the path we've set forth for you," she said.

"What if I felt I needed to do something . . . unorthodox to fight this. Something I knew that, if I didn't try, I would always regret it. Worse yet, I might not even have the memory to regret it." I'd be permanently gone.

"Flynn, what are you trying to say?" she said, and stopped taking notes.

"Olivia, I just think you and I may not see eye to eye on how to get rid of Frank."

Just then, Dr. Cross's phone began to ring.

"So what are you saying . . . you don't want to move forward with treatment as I've explained?"

The phone rang again.

"No, well . . . I mean, I think it's really just—"

The phone. Again.

This time, Olivia picked it up. "Yes," she snapped into the receiver. "What is it?"

She paused.

"Oh no! Is he . . ."

I knew something was wrong.

"Oh, thank God," she said, then started sobbing. "Thank

241

God! I'll be right there." Dr. Cross hung up the phone and grabbed her purse. "I'm sorry, Flynn, but . . . something has come up," she explained, fighting back tears.

"Are you okay, Dr. Cross?"

"My husband, he's been in a car accident."

"I'm so sorry . . . is he okay?"

"They said he would be, but he's broken some bones," she said, unable to keep the tears from coming. "And he has . . . a gash on the back of his head."

"Oh, my God, I'm so sorry!" Seeing her like that, everything I had been going through seemed to vanish.

"I hope you'll understand, Flynn, but I must be going. Let's resume this conversation later. Keep up the great work and stay focused. I know you can do this," she said, already headed for the door.

"Of course, Olivia! I understand completely," I told her, jumping up to open the door.

"Flynn, I really am sorry. And I'm here for you, I really am. But whatever you are dealing with, we can discuss after the holiday. I'll be back in a few days, okay?"

"Of course, Olivia. I understand. I'll see you then," I said, feeling bad for lying. Who knew if I'd still be around when she got back? "And don't worry . . . your husband will be okay, I'm sure. He'll be fine and . . . I'm sorry."

"Thank you, Flynn. You're so sweet." With that, she kissed me on the cheek and left.

As I stood there in her doorway, I felt empty. This woman had only wanted to help me, and all she had asked of me was to listen to her—to try to fight Frank by pushing him out of my mind and envisioning a life without him in it. She had told me that he would go away naturally as I continued to work on myself over time.

And I'd done the opposite.

I mean, I knew she was the doctor, but she'd never *experienced* this shit. I was the patient. I was the crazy motherfucker in the thick of this shit.

"I've got to do this shit!" I said out loud. "Once and for all!"

I couldn't second-guess myself anymore. I was going through with my plan, ending this shit once and for all. *Tonight.*

But first, I had to reach Mia.

I walked back to the phone and reluctantly picked up, fearing Frank would be on the other end. This time, I didn't put my ear to the phone before dialing.

Ring . . . Ring . . .

Hey, this is Mia, why don't you leave Mia message! Hahaha, get it? No? Whatever . . . just leave it at the beep.

"Hey, Mia, it's me again. Listen, call me back . . . I've gotta explain how it's going down tonight. I'll be waiting for you in the back parking lot around nine p.m. Please, Mia."

I hung up the phone, thinking about the outcome. I needed her. I needed Mia to end all this. I headed down the hall.

I hope she comes through.

CHAPTER 19

THE END OF THE BEGINNING

It had been all day and I still hadn't heard from Mia.

Does she have cold feet? I thought to myself. I was starting to panic a little. I didn't have a backup plan. It was
this or nothing. Whatever it was, it wasn't good. I left a
few more voice mails, then hung out with Red. We went
through every detail of the security guard's route and
what the best time to slip out would be. We hashed it out
over a few games of chess.

The hours flew by and suddenly it was 6:00 p.m. Santa
and his elves had arrived. The stage was set up with a fake
sleigh and reindeer. Even good old Rudolph was in the
building. The patients were loving the show. It was like it
turned them into excited little children.

Six turned to seven, seven to eight. Eight turned to
nine p.m. and . . . still no word from Mia. I could only
hope she would be parked where I told her in the voice

mail, near the hospital. I paced in my room, bouncing my red rubber ball and going over the plan again and again in my head.

I put on the Santa outfit and waited. I thought about the life I could have after this, the things I would do and experience with Mia, especially with nine million in the bank.

And I would get back to writing. This time, fact instead of fiction.

What a fucking story. I could write about all I had gone through and maybe, in turn, help others through their own struggles in life.

But I couldn't get ahead of myself—I was still in the here and now. At the Mayberry Psychiatric Hospital.

But not for long.

The holiday play wrapped up, and after mingling with the patients, the costumed actors packed up their things.

"Lights out!" the security guard said, his voice echoing throughout the wing. It was time.

My stomach fluttered with nervousness. He made his round down my hallway. Just after he passed my door I slipped out, not making a noise. Using Red's key card, I scurried through a maze of locked doors. I had the whole floor plan committed to memory. I was feeling like James Bond, stealthily trailing the guards as they made their last checks of the night. I followed the moving light from their flashlights, bouncing from wing to wing, making my way closer to the back exit.

I was careful not to make a sound.

Nearing the East Wing, I walked slowly but confidently. *I was almost out.* Red said there would be no guard here. As I entered the wing, I picked up my pace. Nearing the door, on my way to freedom, I heard . . . another door open.

A flashlight shone *in my direction.*

I quickly hid behind a trash can, the light growing closer and closer. The trash can was only a few feet from the door leading to freedom and, assuming she got my message and came through, Mia's car . . .

"West Wing, this is East Wing," the guard said into his walkie-talkie as he made his way closer to me. "Thought I saw something down here. Checking it out now."

Godammit, Red! I thought. You said nobody was gonna be on this route tonight!

The security guard was now only feet from me, the trash can shielding my body. But if he continued to walk just a few more steps, then turn to the left, he would surely spot me—

"Hey, who are you?!" the guard said.

Oh, shit.

"I'm an elf, obviously!" said another voice. "I forgot my wallet and have to get home or my wife is gonna kill me. I'm already late."

"Oh, I see," said the guard. "Okay, well, did you grab it?"

"Yes sir, just on my way out now! Thank you."

"Well, be more attentive next time, will ya?"

"Yes sir," the voice said. "You got it."

"West Wing, East Wing here," said the guard, speaking into his walkie-talkie again. "It was just one of those actors from Santa's play. Never seen a black elf before."

I watched as he walked through a door and shut it. I couldn't see anyone and it was dead quiet, so I got up and began walking quickly toward the door until . . .

I was grabbed by both arms.

"Oh, shit!" I said, looking around. It was so dark, I couldn't see anything.

"Hey, kid," said a familiar voice. "It's me!" I could barely make out the goofy elf costume in the dark.

"Red? What the hell, man?! I thought you said there wasn't gonna be a guard in this wing tonight? And why are you—"

"That's just why I'm here," he interrupted. "I had to tell you. I overheard the guards saying that even though Henry called out sick, another guard ended up covering his shift. In the East Wing."

"Well, yeah . . . I can see that."

"Look, Flynn, I'm sorry, okay? I mean, I'm here, aren't I?" Even in the dark, I could make out his smile.

"Yeah, but that's just the thing. You're here now, so how are you supposed to make it back?"

"Well, damn, I hadn't thought of that," said Red.

As much as I wish it weren't true, at this point, he had to come along. If he didn't, there was a chance the guards would catch him heading back to his room, and once they did . . . they would search every wing, making sure every patient was accounted for. And that's when they'd discover . . . I was nowhere to be found.

Game over.

We were already at the exit. No turning back now.

"Come on, old man," I said, swiping the key card and opening the door.

An explosion of freezing air smacked me in the face. I wasted no time, running fast as I could. I was finally out of that damn place! There was a guard patrolling the grounds outside, so I ran as fast as I could, passing the Mayberry Psychiatric Hospital main sign and . . .

An empty parking lot. Fuck. My heart sank. I stood in the cold air, out of breath.

This was the end of the line. Mia hadn't come through.

"Red, what do we do?" I said.

"Well, boy, this ain't good. Let's jet to the trees over here and regroup."

Feeling defeated, we shuffled into the wooded area bordering the parking lot.

"Red, I really thought Mia was going to be here. I guess this is how she really feels. I felt so sure about this plan earlier. I don't know what ha—"

"SHHH—Get down, boy!" Red whispered. A car turned off the road into the parking lot, coasting in as though in neutral. Its headlights turned nearer and nearer to our location in the woods. The car suspiciously parked itself. The headlights turned off.

I could see it now. It was Mia! She'd actually come!

This would be it. This was the night all of this would end! I ran to the car, holding my Santa pants up with my left hand. I opened the passenger door and jumped in.

"About time, holy shit! I've been freaking out!" Mia said.

"I had to sneak out, and there was a guard, but Red helped me and—"

Mia interrupted me with a passionate kiss, her warm hands covering my cheeks.

"Wait," she said. "Where's Red?"

Shit! I thought he was right behind me. I opened my door and peeked my head out . . . "RED, LET'S GO!" I hissed. As I saw Red jogging forward I spotted a security guard exiting the building.

"Security, who's there?" the guard said.

Red jumped into the car. Mia started the engine and we were off.

"What the hell happened? Why were they chasing us? Someone must have been sloppy," I said like a smart-ass, all the time looking at Red through the rearview.

"Hey, I did my part, okay," said Mia.

"Kid, I'm not as fast as I used to be," said Red, still out of breath.

"Yeah, I hear you," I said.

"It's about an hour and a half drive," said Mia, putting her right hand over the heater.

"Mia, why the hell didn't you answer the phone all day?" I asked her.

"We just kept missing each other, and I eventually had to go to work. I checked my voice mail every hour, so I was getting all the updates from you, but every time I called you on the hallway phone in the hospital . . . you were never around to answer."

She was right. I had been going over the plan with Red.

"I'm sorry," I said. "Thanks for coming through."

It was a long ride back to town. Red quickly fell asleep. Mia and I sat in silence for a while. It felt like a dream. I stared out the window, watching the road signs flash by. I was overcome by a wave of emotion. You know when you go through some shit, but never have the time to process any of it, and when you finally pause for a second, it all rushes up to the surface, letting itself out in a kind of ca-thartic release? That's what this felt like.

"Mia, thank you. I don't know what to say. You are the only thing that got me through the past two years. And now you are helping me get out. I don't know how to repay you."

"Flynn, you don't need to repay me. This is what people do for one another. I know you can do this. Whatever it is you have planned, I support you. I've seen you fight this. I've seen you suffer and struggle. I've watched you grow and transform. I'm proud of you. I love you."

"I love you, Mia."

As the adrenaline wore off the exhaustion set in, and I dozed off to sleep for the rest of the drive.

Snow fell as Red, Mia, and I stood outside the supermarket entrance. I looked at my watch.

"Ten till," I said.

"Almost midnight," Red responded. I took off my costume and looked around.

"How do we get in there?" Red asked. Still looking around, I spotted a brick on the ground.

I picked it up and hurled it.

"No, Flynn!" Mia shouted, but it was too late.

The brick smashed through the glass of the automatic door like the comet that had wiped out the dinosaurs. Mia covered her face as shards went flying.

"Flynn, you idiot! I still work here!"

"So?" I said. Then she reached in her pocket . . . revealing keys to the store.

"So . . . I could have opened the fuckin' door, dude!"

Embarrassed, I walked past her and into the store. "Sorry 'bout that," I said.

The entire store was dimly lit. I could barely see ten feet in front of me.

"What now?" asked Mia, stepping around the glass so as not to slip.

"Frank's here," I said. "I can feel it."

We were walking near the cash registers when . . . I felt something. I stopped, a confused look on my face.

"What's wrong, Flynn?" Red asked.

"Flynn, are you okay?" said Mia, putting her hand on my arm.

"I'm okay, I just . . . listen. I have to go on alone."

"I really don't think this is the time for a Scooby-fuckin'-Doo moment, Flynn. We should stick together," Mia replied.

"She's right, boy," agreed Red.

"Listen, okay?" I said, looking in their direction. "I can't explain it, but I have to go on alone. You guys stay here."

"What?!" said Mia. "Wait, what do you mean, you guys stay—"

"Look, Mia," I said. "Just trust me, okay. I can't explain it. Just stay here and I'll be back in a few, okay?"

She looked worried, but she agreed.

"Okay, but hurry up. I'm . . . I'm scared, okay?"

"Don't worry, son. I've got her," Red said.

"Okay," I said to him.

As I walked down the aisle, I started to feel like I was being guided by an invisible hand, toward some predetermined place.

I felt an energy as I kept walking, like lost memories

trying to return. I hadn't been here in more than two years. It was like visiting your childhood home as an adult.

I passed the produce section, where Frank had taken all his bananas. I passed the bakery, where I fell for Mia. I neared the break room and tried to enter. The door was closed.

To the left, there was a ladder and some maintenance equipment. I grabbed the door handle and began to slowly turn it. Pushing the door open, I expected to hear an ominous creak, but it was actually rather quiet.

The door swung open. The room was completely dark. I flicked the light switch. It took a few seconds for my eyes to adjust, and as they did, I began to walk, making my way to the long row of dark green lockers against the wall. My fingertips glided along their metallic surface, like a surfer reaching out to the wave he was riding. My hand stopped. It was my locker.

I knew there was something inside, and I knew it was something I had forgotten long ago. When I opened the locker, though, it was empty. Or so it appeared.

I realized this wasn't just my locker; it was also Frank's.

In that moment, I knew what he knew. I remembered. At the base of the locker, if pushed at the right angle, it would give. And underneath was another ten inches of space.

I reached my hand into the dark hiding place. My fingers met a freezing object. I lifted it from the darkness, where it had lain dormant for years. It was the snub-nose .357 Magnum revolver Frank had kept inside his locker.

I flashed back. It was the gun he said he would need "the day some disgruntled schizophrenic nutjob employee shows up and stalks the aisles with an AR-15. Pumping rounds into customers and employees. Or even himself."

I pocketed the gun and stuck my hand back inside—to my surprise, there were a few more items. A pack of cigarettes and a silver Zippo lighter with the words *Vanilla Sky* engraved across it. I jumped when I heard a whisper.

"Flynn."

I heard it again, but no one was around. "You can't run," the voice whispered.

It was Frank.

"He's here!" I yelled out, making my way into the main part of the store. "You guys, he's here!" I raced to the front where I had left Red and Mia together, only to find . . . they had gone.

The lights went out. It was pitch-black and completely silent.

"Mia!!" I called out. "Mia, Red?!" I took a few steps, but my shin collided with a wooden table I knew held pies and different baked goods. "Goddamn it!" I cried out. "I can't believe they still haven't fixed these lights! Where the hell is everyone?" I screamed. I couldn't see a fucking thing.

And then I remembered. I had the Zippo in my pocket! I struck the lighter open, revealing a bright and steady flame.

I headed back to the break room, toward the ladder. Using the flame to illuminate my surroundings, I realized the maintenance tools were for the breaker. DayDay must have been working on the lights again due to bad weather. That was probably why only half the aisles were lit when we'd walked in a few minutes earlier.

First, Dr. Cross's husband had an accident on the icy road, and now this. I was starting to hate the winter.

I put my left hand on the ladder, holding the lighter with my right—the ladder was twelve feet high. While nearing the top, I realized I would be able to see the whole store from up there if I could actually fix the lights. It was a perfect vantage point.

My hands reached the breaker. I opened it up and gripped a switch that said *POWER/LIGHTS*. I pushed it down. *CLICK.* I pushed it up to an even louder click and . . . nothing. I tried again, nothing. My arms grew heavy. It felt like I was holding a bag of cement over my head. I decided to get level with the breaker box. I climbed one step, then another, and lastly a third, finally reaching the top of the ladder.

I held the lighter high over my head. I was now able to read another button that said *EMERGENCY BACKUP POWER.* Then suddenly—

"Oh, shit!" Water began spraying everywhere. "You fucking idiot!" I yelled at myself. I had held the flame under the fire sprinklers! My flame immediately went out and I was now in the dark. Drenched in freezing cold water, I reached out my hands to the last thing I had seen before the flame went out—the emergency backup power button. I pushed the button down on the breaker. *Click!* Then I pulled it up as hard as I could. *CLICK!* Instantly, I heard a generator starting, the system booting, and . . . the power came back on! Each aisle began to light up, one by one. I looked at the entire store from atop the ladder. Aisle one, two, three, four . . . all had lights. Then five, six, and before I knew it, the entire store was back in business.

I looked around.

"Mia!" I screamed. Where the hell was she?

"Get out of your fuckin' head, man!"

Frank. It was Frank, yelling.

"Where the hell are you?" I yelled. The call was met by the sound of the sprinklers still raining overhead. I began to descend the ladder. "What have you done with them? Answer me, Frank!" Hopping off the last step onto the floor, I looked around.

"This way!" Frank yelled. I grabbed the gun from my pocket, pulling it out.

"Where the fuck are you?!" I screamed, making my way past the aisles.

It was like a hurricane inside Muldoon's Grocery! I wiped the water from my face, searching for Frank.

Aisle four! I saw him. Wait . . . aisle six! He was running down aisle six . . .

I shot in his direction. A loud blast. "Show yourself, you coward!" I screamed.

"Shoot me already!" Frank said. I turned. He was standing in front of aisle nine, dressed in his supermarket uniform.

The water in my eyes blurred everything around me. He ran up the aisle, and with my gun pointed at him, I ran after him . . . but I couldn't see him! I turned around to face him, and he was running, nearly at the end of the aisle. Gun in hand, I raised my arm, took aim, took a deep breath . . .

This was it, I could feel it.

I exhaled, and a calm I had never felt came over me. I squeezed the trigger slowly. BANG. And then . . .

Frank hit the floor! I wanted to run up and shoot him again and again. But I knew the bullet had been fatal. I could *feel* it. He was gasping, and I walked toward him, gun still pointed at him in case he tried anything. He continued fighting for his breath, facedown, as I approached. Everything was blurry from the water trickling in my eyes, but the blur that was Frank became clearer and clearer the closer I got.

"Where's Mia?!" I screamed. I walked closer and closer, until finally . . . I turned him over.

To my complete shock and horror . . .

It was Red. Red lay there, dying! In the middle of chasing Frank, in the middle of wiping my face, I had shot the only man who had ever been there for me.

"Red!" I yelled. "I'm so sorry!"

He was choking on his own blood. Spitting it up. His body was convulsing.

"No, Red!" I placed my hands over the bullet wound in his sternum. Trying to stop the blood, I pushed down even harder. Red's body went limp.

"No, no, no no, no!" I began to sob. "I . . . I didn't mean to—"

"FLYNN!" Mia shouted from the other end of the aisle. "What are you doing?!"

I grabbed the gun, looking in her direction.

"Yeah, killer, what are you doing?" Frank said with a joker-like grin.

He had a gun to Mia's head, his left hand clenching the back of her neck. He was using her like a shield.

"Let her go!" I yelled, rising to my feet.

"Flynn, what the fuck?! How could you?!" said Mia, sobbing.

"No, Mia, I didn't kill Red. I didn't kill him, I promise!"

The water from the sprinklers intensified.

"What the hell is going on?!" she yelled.

"Frank, let her go!" I said. "Mia, I thought it was Frank, but he was using Red as a diversion! I didn't mean to, I swear!"

Then she said something that fucked up my entire world.

"Flynn!" she shrieked. "Red never came with us! Why are you doing this?"

"What do you mean, Red never came with us?" I said, utterly confused. "Mia, he's right there—"

As I motioned to the body, I saw there was no corpse.

"Hahahaha." Frank laughed, like some evil villain.

"Oh, my god, what the fuck is going on?!" I screamed at Frank. "What are you doing? Where is Red?"

"Red's dead, baby!" Frank said.

"That's impossible!" I said, shaking my head profusely.

"Is it?" Frank replied. "Think about it, man."

"Think about what?!" I said, taken aback.

"I AM RED, you idiot!" Frank yelled.

"No, that's impossible!" I took a step back.

"Let me go!" Mia yelled. Quickly, I tried to process everything going on.

"Think about it, man. You have a dog that doesn't exist and he wears a red collar. I gave you the red ball that you bounce when you're looking for inspiration. The chess pieces were red and white, and let's not forget . . . his name is fucking RED!"

My eyes widened. "What about—about . . . the moment in the garden! Outside, under the tree when he—"

"Split his hand open with a razor blade and healed it in, like, ten seconds? Haha, you're so naive, man. You really think some sixtysomething-year-old dude is gonna give you that bullshit speech about manifestation and then heal himself . . . right in front of you?"

"I don't understand, Frank! Why do it, then?"

"Because, Flynn, I needed you to believe it all. I needed you to make me real in your head, because if you made me real, if you gave me power . . . then I could kill you! You can't kill a man who doesn't physically exist, but a man who exists only in your head? He can kill you if you give him power over your body." He gave a wicked grin. "So I used Red as a way for you to open yourself up. I used him to coach you into making me truly real in your mind, thus . . . taking over your body."

"But . . . why? Why do this? It's not like you can live without me!" I said, slowly moving closer.

"Nuh uh," said Frank, motioning me back with the pistol.

"Let me go!" Mia shouted.

"I don't plan to live without you, Flynn. You're Batman, and I'm your Joker. Without each other, there is . . . nothing. Kinda poetic, if you ask me."

"What the hell are you talking about?!"

"I'm gonna kill us both, fuck!" he said. "Why must I spell everything out for you?"

"Frank, don't do this," I pleaded. "I don't understand! Why end *yourself*?"

"Because," Frank said, then smiled, "it didn't work out this time. Every awakening from the delusion I had created, you grew stronger. It was harder and harder to bring you back . . . here. To the supermarket. So rather than lose you again, I'll just end the game when I want. It's really a power thing, hahahaha!"

"Flynn!" Mia shouted.

"Mia?" I yelled down the aisle.

"Flynn! Let me go!"

I didn't understand. "What?!"

"Flynn, please," she begged, her crying intensifying. "Please let me go!"

"Think about it, you fucking idiot," Frank expelled. "Who do you think is holding the gun right now?!"

And in that moment, my world collapsed. In that instant, it was like I was sucked into Frank's body—I could see everything from his point of view. The hand gripping Mia's neck and the gun pointed at her head, and down the aisle, like an out-of-body experience, I could see . . . myself.

I was standing there, holding a gun pointed directly at . . . *me*. Or, rather, Frank.

I was Frank. I was holding Mia and yet . . . I couldn't do anything about it. I wasn't in control, Frank was.

And with that, I snapped back into the body at the other end of the aisle—only now I knew I wasn't in my body at all. I was a physical projection. There was only really one gun, and it wasn't in my hand now. It was in Frank's, and it was pointed at Mia's head.

There was only really one person holding her, and it was the man ten yards in front of me.

And it was me.

"Mia, I know this is hard to understand, but it will be okay!" I said to her.

"No, it won't," Frank said.

"Shut the hell up, man!" I said, desperately looking around. Trying to think of something, anything . . .

And then I realized what aisle we were in. The cereal aisle.

"Well, it looks like it's about time to die, little lady," Frank said, cocking the hammer of the gun. "Though technically, this will be a murder-suicide." He laughed.

"Mia! Do you see which aisle we're in?" I screamed.

"What the hell are you talking about?!" she asked, looking so scared and confused. I couldn't see the tears because water was everywhere, but I knew they were there.

"Mia . . . we're surrounded by cereal!"

She looked around and then at me. I motioned to the pile of boxes on the floor beside her. They were Cap'n Crunch. She looked back at me, shaking her head slightly. As if she understood.

"Allllright! Enough of this shit. Say good-bye, honey," Frank told her. Just as he squeezed the trigger, Mia yelled . . .

"Crunch time!" she screamed, raising her right knee high to her chest.

"What the hell?" said Frank, just as the heel of her combat boot came slamming down, breaking his toes.

I knew his toes were broken, because my toes were broken.

"Aaaahrrgghh. What the fuck!" Frank screamed. Furious, he pistol-whipped Mia—she fell to the floor, hand covering the cut above her right eye. I took that second to quickly run toward him.

"You son of a bitch!" I screamed, ready to destroy him. I leaped and tackled him.

We both fell to the ground, the gun skidding across the supermarket floor.

My tooth chipped on the tile floor. In that moment, the water stopped pouring. Frank and I looked at each other for a millisecond before dashing for the gun on our hands and knees.

It was a battle of strength, the two of us pulling and clawing at each other to reach the gun. Frank pulled my hair, exposing my face. He punched me over and over, breaking my nose and splitting my lip from the force of knuckles colliding, forcing the tissue to rip on my jagged tooth. Frank tried to make his way to the gun, but I grabbed his ankle at the last minute and tripped him.

We were both on the ground yet again.

"Motherfucker!" he yelled. I was on my stomach, trying to get to my feet, when he kicked me in the face. The blow forced me back to the ground. Quickly, Frank got on top of me, sitting on my back with all his weight. He picked up my head and slammed it into the solid floor over and over and over again. Tissue from my left eyebrow was completely exposed, spewing violent amounts of blood onto the floor.

"Don't!" said Frank, then slammed my head again. "Fuck!" He slammed it again, and my consciousness started fading. "With!" I began to black out. "Me!"

Frank laid the final blow. Barely hanging on, I could

make out Frank walking over to the gun and picking it up. "It didn't have to be this way, you know!" he said, wielding the firearm carelessly, almost with a laziness. "We had something special, man! And you had to go and ruin it all by wanting your—" Frank made air quotes with his fingers—"'Sanity back!' Hahaha, fuck outta here, man."

I tried to get up, but I slipped on my own blood.

"This place is amazing, man," Frank continued. "I pretend like I hated it, but I loved it here. I mean, I was born here."

Frank turned from me, taking in the supermarket for what seemed to be the last time. This was my opportunity, but . . . *how do you kill a man who doesn't exist?*

Before fully rising to my feet, I was already dashing toward him. Just as he turned in my direction, I landed a fierce blow to the temple.

"Ah, shit!" he yelled. I punched him in the stomach. He keeled over in pain. That's when I drove my knee deep into his nose, breaking it immediately. I grabbed the hand holding the gun and slammed it into the shelf, slicing his wrist on the exposed metal edge. The gun dropped. Frank grabbed me by the neck, punching me in my left ear.

I could only imagine how this fight must have looked on the security cameras—one man beating himself to a bloody pulp. Must have looked like some twisted Buster Keaton bit.

Frank grabbed the gun, turned back, and fired. The burning sensation radiated through my arm. I looked down. Blood started to trickle out of my shoulder.

"You shot me?"

"Yeah, I guess I did, haha," Frank replied.

I always imagined what it would feel like to be shot, and the feeling was . . . like nothing I had ever felt. It felt like someone had cut me open and stuck a fiery piece of coal deep inside me.

"Well, old friend," said Frank, raising the gun to my head. "Looks like this is the end of the line."

I looked down the barrel of the gun. Just as Frank pulled the trigger, Mia came from behind him, pushing the gun from his grip and sending it skidding under the aisle's shelving units. With my good arm, I grabbed Frank by his shirt. We struggled and struggled.

How do I kill a man who doesn't exist? A man who lives only in my head?

He threw punches but couldn't land a swing from the angle I had him at, so he stopped swinging and quickly did something I wish I had seen coming. He stuck his middle finger in front of my face.

"Fuck yoooouuuuuuuu!" he yelled. He pressed his middle finger deep inside the wound.

The pain was agonizing. If the initial feeling of being shot was the worst pain I'd ever experienced, this was even worse because the shock had worn off. I was experiencing Every. Single. Moment.

And even worse than the pain Frank had inflicted? *Knowing there was no Frank.* Not really, anyway. And it was just me, gutting myself all alone there in aisle nine, while poor Mia watched the man she loved fall apart.

I was losing. After all this, I couldn't believe the main character of a fictional book I wrote . . . *was in the middle of brutally murdering me.* He pulled his finger from the wound and grabbed my brown coat by the zipper, pulling me closer, ready to punch me in my already broken nose. I could see his hand, stained in my blood, coming in.

This was it, I could feel it. This next blow would end it. I had to do something! As he cocked his arm back for the final blow, I screamed and . . . punched him back with everything I had. The punch would have knocked him down, but he was still holding on to my jacket.

As he began to fall, he pulled on the jacket, flinging it upward. The upward inertia projected the contents of my right pocket into the air.

It was like slow motion, watching them fall to the ground. Frank leaning to the left, trying to regain his balance, trying to find his footing.

It was the pills. Hundreds of them.

For those of you who don't know, sanity is really just a state of mind . . . quite literally. You see, depression, anxiety, bipolar disorder, and schizophrenia are rooted in a chemical imbalance in the brain. Doctors often prescribe medication to correct the chemical equilibrium. Thus, in turn, they have a positive effect on the body. Take, for example, the term self-medication. With drugs and alcohol, people self-medicate to live in a state of euphoria, abusing the chemicals that force endorphins and serotonin to the brain. However, we aren't supposed to be in this mental state all the time. And when the high is over, we come down and crash. This is why withdrawal plays a huge part in addicts never getting clean—they are running from the problems in their lives that make them sad or depressed. They are finding solace in substances. But the truth is, if they just dealt with their issues in the first place, then they wouldn't need to self-medicate. Now, this is more applicable to anxiety and depression. When we get into more severe mental health issues such as bipolar disorder and schizophrenia, this is where doctors' prescriptions really can help a patient. Due to my paranoia and disgust for ingesting pills, I never took the ones I should have. That not only kept Frank alive, but fueled the delusion I was living in.

How do you kill a man who only exists in your head? How do you kill a chemical deficiency in the brain?

Hundreds of Xanax, lithium, Seroquel, Lexapro, and Risperdal hit the floor. They bounced like Skittles some child dropped by mistake. All the afternoons at Mayberry, when Ann would hand me my pills, all those days, came pouring out onto the floor. And with that, in the blink of an eye, everything went from slow-motion to real time.

"Oh, shit!" Frank yelled as he began to slip, doing everything he could to catch his balance. The full force of the left side of his forehead smacked against the ground, making a noise I could only describe as slamming a raw piece of steak on a marble floor.

As he rolled over, pieces of his skull were exposed, crumbling into his mouth. I could see a small amount of brain matter coming out of his head. Then suddenly . . .

I was where he lay. I saw what he saw, I felt what he felt. Fading, he backed himself up against the shelf, propping his back against it like a pillow. Seeing from his eyes, from his point of view, I felt myself separating from his body. I began to stand, and as I did, I felt myself split in two.

Much like the night in my apartment, when I made Frank real to finish my book by any means necessary, I was splitting in two.

As I rose to my feet, I felt numb. I turned around and there was Frank on the floor. Gasping for air.

How do you kill a man who doesn't exist?

It was the pills. The same pills I'd been stowing away in my pocket for the last two years. The pills that were meant to rid my brain of the chemical imbalance did just that, only from the outside. When Frank slipped and hit his head, I slipped and hit my head. The fall ended in extreme blunt trauma. It was such an enormous blow that the chemicals in my brain balanced out in real time. My whole perspective shifted. My vision crackled, shook, trembled. It then tunneled and finally locked into focus. I was then lifted up from out of my body. From high above I peered down onto my dying self. Suspended in time. At that moment, out of my body, I felt like I could see everything. Not just the entire store below me, but my entire life. The past, the present, the future. I felt embraced by a kind of tranquil serenity. Was this what death felt like? As soon as the moment came, it went, and I was shot back into my corporeal self. My entire frame was reanimated. I groggily lifted my head from the ground. I felt sublime, lucid, crystal clear. I felt terrified and torn. Happy and ecstatic. All at once.

A calm washed over me like I'd never felt before. A calm that made me feel whole again.

The pills did just what they were supposed to. Just not how they were supposed to.

Flicking the lid of the Zippo, I struck the wick to light a cigarette to no avail. "Flynn, you were doing so well," Frank said, bubbles forming from the blood covering his lips, popping as he spoke. He began to evanesce, flickering in and out of sight.

"Mmmm-hmmm," I muttered as I struck it again, this time igniting a cherry at the end of the cigarette. I noticed the words *Vanilla Sky* engraved across the top of the lighter. This immediately made me think of the Paul McCartney song.

"I think the moment calls for it," I said, smoke exiting my nostrils as I brought the lit cigarette to Frank's lips. He reached for it.

"There you go," I said. "Now puff."

I heard sirens approaching in the distance.

Police cars and fire engines pulled up in front of the store.

The blood from his lips stained the butt of the cigarette, like a single mother driving an Astro van in the early 1990s, picking up her fifth-grade son from soccer practice with that poufy hair and shoulder-pad look, you know the one.

"This is all Lola's fault, you know," he said.

"I know," I replied. We both laughed until the jolt in his chest from doing so enhanced the pain, reminding us of the whole dying thing going on.

"Flynn, what's—what's my—my . . . last na—"

"I don't know," I said. "I told you that already."

"Flynn, did we have fun?" he asked.

"You ruined my life."

Frank exhaled a large cloud of smoke. Another breath never followed.

Frank was dead, and I was sane. In the supermarket.

EPILOGUE

Flynn read the last page of his memoir, *Supermarket*. It was about the mental breakdown he had endured while writing *Muldoon's*, his first novel. He turned the page and slammed the book shut.

"The end," he said.

"Well, I think it's a great story, baby!" Mia said. She was sitting across from Flynn, her hand resting on a stack of law books she was using for a case she was working on.

They were in the booth of a diner. But not just any diner, in fact. It was *the* diner, the diner where it all started.

It was their last stop before they caught a flight to New York City, to start their new life together.

It was the diner where Lola had broken up with him years ago, the diner where a waiter by the name of Frank worked. It was the same diner Dr. Olivia Cross told Flynn to visit in order to get closure. That was if he ever made it out of his delusion.

Now he could speak with the waiter who he had based the character of Frank on. The same waiter who had just arrived with a pot of coffee. He began to pour.

The creamer hit the bottom of the cup, marbling the black coffee like two universes colliding.

"Hey, uh . . . Frank, is it?" Flynn asked.

"Yeah?" said the waiter.

"What's your last name?"

The man paused, looked at the ground for a moment, and then looked back up at Flynn, puzzled.

ACKNOWLEDGMENTS

First and foremost I'd like to thank my best friend, Christian. After a week of binge-reading novels for the first time in my life in my midtwenties, I sat up and said, "I'm gonna write a book," to which Christian replied, "You can't write a fuckin' book just because you've been reading them." It was all the motivation I needed.

I want to thank every single fan for joining me on this experience and next chapter of my creative outlet. I'm excited for everything else to come.

I also want to thank Stuart Roberts and the fine people at Simon & Schuster for giving a kid who didn't graduate high school a book deal. Stuart, my editor, has challenged me and helped me grow as a writer, and I look forward to the many years ahead of creating entire universes together.

Thank you to Henry Abrams for reading the first pass

of my book and just genuinely enjoying it. That gave me the confidence to continue.

A huge thank-you to my literary agent, Cait Hoyt, at CAA. Because of you this book found a home.

Chris Zarou. Thank you for believing in my vision and giving me the courage to venture out into another avenue of entertainment. And Harrison Remler for all his late nights in the Visionary office making my wild ideas of how to get things like this in the hands of our fans possible.

Mikey, my partner and producer at Bobby Boy, to whom this book is dedicated. I would like to thank my best friend, Frank, for being the first person ever to read the manuscript, along with Juan and his beautiful girlfriend, Miranda! Thank you both for truly diving into the world I created.

I cannot forget to thank my favorite living author, Ernest Cline. Not only for his work, which has inspired me vastly, but for his friendship. Ernest, Ernie: Thank you for the love and kind words from one author to another. You are the Jedi master—I love and appreciate you.

I'd like to thank Mia, the fictional character I wrote and created from my mind. The sweetest, coolest, kindest, nicest, most understanding, and completely unrealistic woman I ever thought up in my head. At least until I meet a woman greater than even you.

And lastly I would like to thank my fans. Part One of this manuscript was written in my darkest of times, filled and riddled with anxiety and depression. This book is a work of fiction but the undertow is based utterly and completely from my life, both mentally and emotionally. I had written the first half in the depths of my darkest days, and waited two years (as did Flynn) before awakening and writing the second half, Part Two, and overcoming my own loop. I love music wholeheartedly, but I have never coped through written language the way I have in this form of expression. There is more to come. Novels, stories of outer space and galaxies, as well as small towns and family struggles. Movies and filmmaking. Music and messages. And just plain-old fun and connecting with my fans.

Much more, the greatest thing I am excited for is, after a life of hardship, struggle, pain, and suffering, is to now, as I finally venture into my thirties, enjoy the fruits of my labor. There will be ups and downs, happy times and hard. But I say to you, dear reader, dear lover of literature, film, music, or just plain-old fans of Bobby Boy—this is me at my happiest, and I plan to continue to create from the purest part of my heart. Always. Just as I have in this art form.

I have used words and creative freedom to better myself. Whoever may be reading these words, I hope you have the courage to do the same through any form of creative expression. It has been a long road, but I too, finally . . . have escaped the supermarket.

ABOUT THE AUTHOR

BOBBY HALL, a.k.a. Logic, the Grammy-nominated, platinum-selling recording artist, quickly established himself as one of the most original young stars in music. Through a streak of hit records, Bobby Hall has cemented his status as one of the greatest MCs at work, being hailed for his lyricism, cinematic storytelling, and inspiring messages of peace, love, and positivity. His music touches on societal issues that affect us all, including anxiety, depression, and race. *SUPERMARKET* is his debut novel.